Storm Clouds Over Paradise

HARVEST HOUSE PUBLISHERS
Eugene, Oregon 97402

STORM CLOUDS OVER PARADISE

Copyright © 1986 by Carole Gift Page and
  Doris Elaine Fell
Published by Harvest House Publishers
Eugene, Oregon 97402

ISBN 0-89081-545-3

Printed in the United States of America.

*With loving gratitude
to our brothers and sisters
for their love and friendship:
Howard and Elsie Fell,
Susan and Dan Porter, and Steve and June Gift*

CAST OF CHARACTERS

MICHELLE MERRILL: A spirited, aspiring novelist with a deadly fascination for a mystery.

DAVID BALLARD: Michelle's fiance, a rich and successful computer magnate, whose perilous government assignment thrusts them into danger and intrigue on the Caribbean island of Solidad.

JACKIE TURMAN: Michelle's best friend and former college roommate, who gives up wealth and position to follow her husband to the ends of the earth.

STEVE TURMAN: Jackie's husband, the government's key witness in the Morro Bay cocaine trial—#1 on the syndicate's hit list.

JOSHUA KENDRICK: The cool, hard-edged DEA agent who will stop at nothing to win his war against the international cocaine syndicate.

RICARDO CORBRANZA: The Columbian multimillionaire owner of Solidad reportedly leaped to his death from the balcony of Windy Reef's bridal suite.

ALEJANDRA COBRANZA: Ricardo Cobranza's once beautiful wife whose haunting bridal portrait dominates the lobby of Windy Reef Hotel.

ESTEBAN MEDINA: The Executive Administrator of Windy Reef, ensnared in the Cobranza legend and plagued by a staggering secret borne since his youth.

LUCIA MEDINA: Esteban Medina's beautiful Columbian spitfire wife.

SILAS WINTERS: The handsome, elusive concierge of Windy Reef whom Michelle mistrusts from their first grating encounter.

ORVILLE GLOCKE: A boisterous, overbearing hotel guest whose simpering complaints hide a deadly inferiority complex.

RUTH GLOCKE: Orville's plain German wife, a cold, iron-willed woman.

JAVIER: The shriveled, senile gardener whose long guarded secrets are lost in forgetfulness.

DOOLEY EDINGTON: Solidad's only physician, a cynical, widower lost in melancholy memories of his long-dead wife.

PAM MERRILL: Michelle's perky, impulsive kid sister.

NORA KENDRICK: Joshua's bitter former wife.

CARLOS COBRANZA: The Cobranzas' only son.

ISLAND OF SOLIDAD

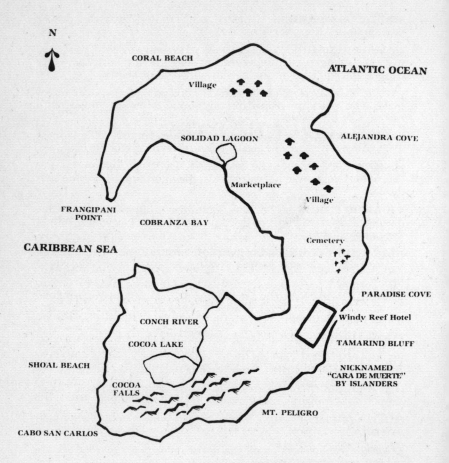

N

CORAL BEACH

ATLANTIC OCEAN

Village

SOLIDAD LAGOON

ALEJANDRA COVE

Marketplace

Village

FRANGIPANI
POINT

COBRANZA BAY

CARIBBEAN SEA

Cemetery

PARADISE COVE

CONCH RIVER

Windy Reef Hotel

COCOA LAKE

TAMARIND BLUFF

SHOAL BEACH

NICKNAMED
"CARA DE MUERTE"
BY ISLANDERS

COCOA
FALLS

CABO SAN CARLOS

MT. PELIGRO

CHAPTER ONE

Late... late... late!

The United flight from San Francisco was an hour overdue. I had left my wedding preparations unfinished on this sultry July afternoon to dash off to Chicago's O'Hare International Airport to pick up my best friend, Jackie Turman, and her young son, Stevie. Jackie, my former college roommate, would be the matron of honor in my wedding on Saturday to the handsome, successful computer magnate, David Ballard.

With effort I made my way through the throngs of hurried, harried travelers to the United check-in counter. "Is something wrong with Flight 506?" I asked the tall, toothy young man whose sparse blond hair was combed charitably over his forehead.

"No," he answered pleasantly, his lean, freckled face all rabbit grin.

"But the plane's late."

He gave a hassled tug at his right earlobe as he scanned the monitor. His tenor voice was singsong. "Planes are late sometimes, even in the friendly skies of United."

I nodded absently, pushing from my mind the ominous thought of a plane crash or terrorist bombing. "You're certain nothing's wrong?" I asked.

"Positive." He met my gaze with a reassuring twinkle. "A

pretty lady like you with such wistful green eyes and golden, tawny hair...you shouldn't have a worry in the world."

I felt my cheeks grow warm.

"Ah," he teased, "the blush looks charming as a rose on such a lovely face."

I gave a jaunty toss of my head. He was such a curious, whimsical fellow, I couldn't help relaxing a little, matching his smile. "You sound like a poet," I said.

"Don't I wish. Ah, to be a Tennyson or a Rod McKuen. Then I wouldn't have to stand here in my official blues apologizing for tardy pilots and congested skies."

I smiled sympathetically. "Or deal with impatient customers?"

"That too," he agreed. "But I promise you, ma'am, your husband's plane will be here before you know it."

"I'm not married," I replied, "at least not yet."

"Oh, really?" he asked, his nose twitching inquisitively.

"I'm getting married on Saturday."

His big bunny grin wilted before my eyes. He glanced at the monitor again and said professionally, "You're in luck, miss. The plane will be touching down any minute...."

"Wonderful!"

"They'll be deplaning through that door over there." He hesitated, then said with a mischievous wink, "Well, miss, if things don't work out on Saturday..."

I laughed merrily as I sashayed away, musing, *You're out of your mind if you think I'm going to let David Ballard get away...after all we've been through together!*

As the passengers emerged from the airliner and entered the sprawling concourse, I stood on my tiptoes scanning the crowd for Jackie. I knew she would stand out as always—a gorgeous, model-thin blonde, stunning and flawless in the latest Paris fashions. But only a straggly line of weary, blank-faced travelers filed past me, dragging their carry-on luggage, their scowls bursting into smiles as they spotted relatives and friends.

My anxiety grew as the throng dwindled. I waited, my palms growing moist. Then, as the pilot and crew strode briskly by, I called out, "Excuse me, please. My friend Jackie was on this flight. She has a little boy with her."

The stewardess nearest me shook her head. "Sorry. The passengers have all deplaned."

"But that's impossible—"

"Check at the desk, miss," she suggested, running on.

I turned away, disappointed, puzzled. Had I made an error—got the date or flight number wrong? I checked my pocket notebook. No mistake! Purposefully, I strode back to my toothsome rabbit friend at the check-in desk. He was shuffling papers, ready to leave the boarding area. He brightened when he spotted me. "Well, miss, have you changed your mind about Saturday?"

"Never!" I smiled, "But I am concerned—"

He sobered at once. "How can I help you?"

"My friends—they weren't on board."

"You're certain? Perhaps they missed their flight."

"No, Jackie would have called...the minute she knew."

"Don't worry, miss." The involuntary twitch of his nose turned the crinkle lines around his mouth into a Bugs Bunny grin. "There are plenty of other flights your friends can catch before your wedding on Saturday."

"Please, sir, you must have a passenger list. Please see if Jackie Turman's name is there."

He paused, his grimace frozen in place.

"You do have that information, don't you?" I gestured impatiently toward the computer in front of him.

"We're computerized, all right, but that's privileged information. I really can't tell you a thing."

I glanced at his name tag. "Mr. Hollins, I assure you, it's very important."

He relented slightly. "There's a white courtesy phone over there. Perhaps the supervisor can help you." He whipped around the counter in a quick darting stride, more like a hop. "Don't fret. Passengers have missed planes before. Your friends will probably be on the next flight."

I wanted to say, *You don't understand. Jackie's husband Steve is the government's key witness in a lengthy cocaine trial. Since Steve turned state's evidence against his fellow drug traffickers, he and Jackie have been threatened. Their lives are constantly in danger!*

But how could I even begin to explain to this stranger the

chaos that had become Jackie's life? I was beginning to fear
that this wasn't a simple case of a missed flight. It could well
be a life or death matter for Jackie and Stevie Jr.

Finally, I mumbled a half-hearted, "Thank you, Mr. Hollins."
The lean, affable gate agent walked me over to the wall
phone, then was gone with a bobbing, courteous nod.

My hand trembled as I picked up the receiver. I reflected
fleetingly that I hadn't known until the last minute that Jackie
could even be in my wedding. She had been so pressured lately
with all that had happened to her husband—his arrest, the
controversial trial, the devastating publicity. Steve had one
thing going for him, though. Jackie was standing faithfully
by his side.

When the United representative answered, my words
tumbled out. "I was expecting friends on Flight 506. They
didn't arrive. Please check your passenger list . . ."

"The names on the manifest are privileged information."

"I know that, sir." There was a gnawing, knotted sensation
in my stomach. "But I'm afraid something's wrong," I pressed,
fighting panic. "My friend wouldn't miss her flight. She's so
fastidious, a stickler for promptness."

"I'm sorry, miss. The rules—"

"This is an emergency," I cut in anxiously.

"An emergency?" he echoed.

I grasped at straws. I couldn't tell him my real fears for
Jackie. "My friend isn't well," I explained. "And her little
boy—they both have chronic asthma."

His silence seemed to shout, *I've heard it all before. Make it
good.*

"I know you have a list—a manifest," I persisted. "If you
could just tell me if Jackie Turman's name is on it."

"Have you tried calling Mrs. Turman's home?"

"She won't be there. She was scheduled to drive from Morro
Bay to San Francisco yesterday—to catch this morning's flight."

There was a moment of hesitation, then the supervisor
conceded, "A Mrs. J. Turman and child checked in at the
United desk in San Francisco."

"But they never arrived here in Chicago!"

"People check in, miss," he said firmly, "but we have no
way of knowing whether they board the plane. There are

always standbys when someone doesn't show."

With my anxieties mounting, I thanked him and put the receiver back in place. What next? I wondered. Should I call David? Would he be back from his tuxedo fitting yet? Should I drive back to my parents' home in Lake Forest and wait for Jackie to call?

As I mused over the possibilities, I sensed someone behind me waiting to use the phone. Then there was a sudden tap on my shoulder. I whirled around and gasped, "Josh! Joshua Kendrick!"

"Hello, Michelle." For a moment I thought he would sweep me up in his arms. He was darkly handsome, his ruddy face rugged and weathered, his frame virile and imposing. A thick shock of chestnut hair curved low over his forehead.

"I didn't expect to see you until the wedding," I exclaimed.

"I know, but I'm here temporarily with the Drug Enforcement Administration."

"Here in Chicago?"

"Yes. I have Jon, my older boy, for the summer so I'm doing desk work for the agency."

"And chomping at the bit, I'll bet."

"You know me. I'm not a desk man, Michelle. I belong out in the field." His expression changed subtly. "We still haven't closed the DEA file on Steve Turman and Morro Bay."

"I'm sure you haven't."

"And you, Michelle? You're looking as gorgeous as ever. How are you?"

"I'm fine."

"When did you and David arrive from California?"

"A week ago. I wanted David to have plenty of time to get acquainted with my parents before the wedding."

"So how's that going?"

"Mother thinks David's a jewel. They hit it off right away. And Dad—well, he's coming around at his own methodical pace. But I think he feels a little intimidated by David's wealth and position."

"Well, it's not easy for fathers to lose their little girls," Josh noted. With a catch in his voice, he added, "If I were in his shoes, I think I'd have a hard time giving you up myself, Michelle."

I laughed uneasily, remembering the spark that could have ignited between Josh and me last year had I not just fallen in love with David and had Josh not been a divorced man yearning to reconcile with his former wife.

"It's just such a coincidence running into you here at the airport," I rushed on. *Should I tell Josh why I was here? Push an alarm button for him?* Finally I blurted, "I was expecting Jackie Turman and her son, Stevie, in on the United flight, but they never arrived—"

"I know." Josh's nod was barely perceptible. He took both my hands in his strong, sturdy grip, his raw umber eyes squinting with a mixture of sympathy and concern. "Keep smiling, Michelle. Whatever I say, keep that expression."

"Something's wrong," I uttered, my heart hammering suddenly. "Jackie...Stevie...you know something, don't you, Josh?"

"Come on, smile, Michelle. You can do better than that." He flashed me a crooked grin of his own. "That's better."

"Josh, I know Jackie checked in at the airport in San Francisco. Where is she?"

He drew in a deep breath, then led me over to the waiting area where we sat down. Turning to face me, he said, "Someone else took Jackie's place on the plane."

"Someone else? I don't understand—"

"Keep smiling, Michelle," Joshua urged.

"But who took her place? Why? Jackie's supposed to be my matron of honor on Saturday."

"She won't make the wedding." I could read regret in his eyes. Gently he touched my hand. "The smile, please, Michelle."

"Something's happened—!"

"The Turmans are all right—for now. But the DEA couldn't risk letting them come to Chicago at this time."

I squeezed out the words. "What's going on, Joshua?"

"I'll explain to both you and David shortly. Trust me."

"I want to, but—"

"You told me once that you'd do anything for the Turmans. They need your help now. It's absolutely essential that, for all outward appearances, Jackie Turman participates in your wedding as planned."

"But how—if she can't be here—?"

"We have it all worked out—"

"You mean, you and the DEA? Don't forget, this is my wedding, Joshua!"

His gaze was unflinching. "But it could be the Turmans' funeral."

The light fuzz on my arms stood straight up as icicles formed inside me. "Go on," I whispered.

Josh's eyes narrowed. "In a minute I want you to look behind me. There's a young blonde woman across the lobby with a small boy."

I glanced over hastily. Indeed, they were standing by the wall, the woman gazing around nervously, the child on tiptoe, fidgeting with the water fountain. "What about them?" I asked.

"That's my former wife Nora and my younger son, Juddy."

"You're back together?"

"No—I wish." His words drifted. "We've talked reconciliation. She was scheduled to fly here next week. Then, when we needed someone to take Jackie's place on the plane, I called Nora and urged her to fly out a few days early."

"You mean, your wife checked in at United as Jackie?"

"Nora was innocent, Michelle. A friend from the agency took Nora and Juddy to the airport. He didn't give them the tickets until the last minute. Nora never would have done it otherwise."

"That's deceptive, Josh."

"No—necessary, Michelle." He looked away momentarily. "Nora is furious with me. It may cost me that reconciliation."

"Just what do you expect—Nora to go right on playing Jackie?"

There was a hint of tension in Joshua's usual cool reserve. "When the plane landed, I met Nora and told her you need her in the wedding. She resembles Jackie. They're about the same size."

"Nora doesn't even know me. Are you saying she agreed to take Jackie's place, just like that, without question?"

"Nora long ago stopped asking questions."

"And you actually expect Nora and me to go through with this charade?"

"She won't, unless you ask her."

My anger moved in like a storm cloud, gray and threatening. *Never*, I thought. *You're not rearranging my wedding, Joshua Kendrick.* Aloud, I said, "This is ridiculous, Josh. Why should I ask Nora to do such a thing?"

Joshua stood up and offered me his hand. "Because we're buying time for the Turmans' safety, Michelle. Even 24 hours will help. Five days would be better."

"I still don't understand—"

Joshua ignored my protest. His voice low and controlled, he said, "Nora will be down at the baggage claim area . . ."

I looked quickly past Joshua. Nora and Juddy no longer stood beside the fountain.

"Our agent in San Francisco switched Nora's luggage," continued Josh. "In fact, he put Nora's cases inside Jackie's. If you agree to my plan and decide to drive Nora and Juddy to your house, then go pick up Jackie's luggage at the claim area. That'll be Nora's signal to approach you and apologize for missing you when she deplaned."

"You thought of everything, didn't you, Josh? But how do you expect me to recognze Jackie's luggage?"

"Jackie sent her bright plaid cases with the large Hopewell College stickers on them. She said you'd know them."

With that, Joshua gave me a good-bye embrace, turned, and briskly strode down the corridor.

I stood watching him helplessly, feeling suddenly alone and distraught. The joyous anticipation of my wedding had been smothered in a single encounter with Joshua Kendrick. Fighting bitter tears of frustration, I wondered, *What would David do?* One thing was certain: David wouldn't leave a lady waiting, forsaken at the baggage claim area. And he wouldn't stop until he knew the whole story.

Joshua was completely out of sight before I made my decision. I squared my shoulders and headed toward the escalator. Fortunately, I had missed the usual crowds, chaos, and confusion at the luggage turnstiles. Just a few impatient passengers were still pushing and shoving, lunging for their suitcases, boxes, and golf bags. I wedged in, wondering how in the world I would ever recognize Jackie's cases. At last I spotted two oversized blue plaid bags moving toward me, the yellow and purple Hopewell colors blazing across their sides.

Promptly after I dragged the cases off the conveyer belt and signaled a nearby skycap, Nora Kendrick made her way toward me, her reluctant youngster in tow. "Michelle, Michelle," she called out woodenly. "I've been looking all over for you."

I reached out, gave her an awkward hug and cried, loudly enough for the milling throng to hear, "Jackie! Jackie Turman!"

CHAPTER TWO

As I headed my Dad's Chevy toward Lake Forest, I stole a glance at Nora sitting stiffly beside me. Nora was a petite, intense woman with striking Norwegian features and a brittle edge in her voice. Her silver-blonde hair was swept back with an elegant twist, accentuating the graceful angle of her slim neck.

"You're not what I expected, Michelle," she announced crisply.

"I'm not? What kind of picture did Josh paint?"

"I could tell by what he *didn't* say that he was taken with you. He talked about meeting you in Morro Bay when he broke open the Turman case. He didn't tell me you were going with David Ballard."

"But I thought you and Josh were divorced quite some time ago."

"Two years...but not because I didn't love him."

I sensed Nora's pain but was reticent to tell her that Joshua's feelings were mutual. He loved her, too.

I glanced in the rearview mirror, then looked again sharply. Joshua was following us in a blue sedan. "We're being followed, Nora."

"Joshua?" she said knowingly.

I met Nora's gaze and nodded. Her eyes were ice-water blue

and darted about with a self-protective wariness.

"Then it is drug-related—this whole charade?" Nora sounded wounded, her tone scathing.

"Yes. Joshua said the Turmans' lives are at stake."

Nora's words were clipped. "I flew here using Mrs. Turman's ticket, and I told Josh I'd attend your wedding as Mrs. Turman, but I must confess I have misgivings about this entire deception."

"So do I, Nora," I admitted. "But Joshua promised to explain everything at the house."

"Oh, sure. Mr. Evasive himself. More of his cloak and dagger games. And I was foolish enough to think we could reconcile."

I chose my words carefully. "I'm just beginning to learn that sometimes love must take risks."

"That's easy for you to say, Michelle. Your fiance doesn't have a life-threatening job. Joshua lives with danger. I never know where his assignments will take him. I can't cope with the constant fears. What would I ever tell the boys if something happened to Joshua—your daddy's a hero—a dead one?"

Juddy piped up from the backseat, "My daddy is a hero!"

At a stoplight just outside of Lake Forest, Joshua pulled up beside us. He didn't give even a flicker of recognition. When I finally turned into my parents' driveway, he swerved over to the curb and parked.

"What a lovely old home," said Nora wistfully. "The kind I've always dreamed of sharing with Joshua."

"I was born here." I looked up at the rambling English Colonial two-story with its wide bay windows and sprawling, gable-lined front porch. "I think I spent half my childhood on that old oak porch swing, reading Nancy Drew mysteries and writing in my diary."

"Sounds wonderful."

"Wait'll you see inside." I opened my door and stepped out.

My heart leaped as I spotted David striding from the house with the quick, smooth agility he had learned on the tennis courts. There was an energy about him, an efficient, take-charge manner that melded appealingly with his coppery, sun-and-surf good looks. Only the pale white scar that zig-zagged across his jaw to his cleft chin hinted at the painful, dark side of his life—his plane crash in Vietnam and the years he had mistakenly blamed himself for his best friend's death. Now, in his casual slacks and open sports shirt, no one would take him for a former Vietnam veteran wounded in action or a prosperous, conservative business tycoon. He was just David—my dear, adoring David.

He waved, grinning expectantly. I ran to meet him. Something electric happened whenever our eyes met.

"Darling, I missed you," he said, gathering me into his arms.

I laughed self-consciously. "I've only been gone a couple of hours."

"But you're late. I was worried. I had this uneasy feeling—" He glanced toward the car. "Was Jackie's plane delayed?"

"Yes, but that's not why—"

He strode over to the automobile and opened the door before I could stop him. "Hey, Stevie—Tiger, how've you—?" His smile froze, then crumbled as he looked inside. A frown creased his forehead. He drew back and stared at me, a blend of bafflement and shock etched in his expression. "Michelle, where's my little buddy?"

"They didn't come."

"I see that. Then who—?"

"We'll explain everything. Just give us a chance."

"Us? Who on earth—?" He glanced back into the vehicle at Nora and extended his hand. His tone was kind, apologetic. "I believe introductions are in order. I'm David Ballard."

"Nora Kendrick." She accepted his hand with restrained politeness.

"Kendrick?" David's voice arched with curiosity. "Any relation to Joshua Kendrick?"

Nora uttered the words with a precise coolness. "He's my former husband."

"And this young fellow?" David inquired, reaching back and tousling the blond boy's hair.

"My son, Juddy."

"I'm six," declared the apple-cheeked boy proudly. "That's my daddy over there. He's got a gun. He catches bad guys." He triggered his chubby forefinger. "Gotcha, mister!"

"That's enough, Juddy," scolded Nora.

I took David's arm. "That's Joshua's car out at the curb. He wants to talk to us."

David's gaze took in the blue sedan, then darted back to me in alarm. "Something's happened to the Turmans?"

"No, David. Not yet. That's what Joshua wants to prevent." Joshua stepped out of his car and waved us over. I glanced uncertainly at Nora.

"Go on," she urged. "Juddy and I will wait here."

David and I walked over to the sedan. He and Joshua greeted each other politely, shaking hands and making the usual small talk.

"Come on inside," I suggested, nodding toward the house. "I'd like you and Nora to meet my folks."

Joshua's eyes narrowed. "We can't, Michelle. You, David, and I need to talk privately."

"Where?" asked David. "Your car?"

"Right." Joshua opened the door for us and we slipped into the front seat.

He walked around and climbed into the driver's side. "Enough room?" he quizzed, eyeing us with a certain wry amusement.

David nodded, smiling. "Michelle and I don't mind sitting close. It gets us in the mood for Saturday."

Josh cleared his throat—a guarded, perfunctory sound. His expression clouded. I could tell he was ready to talk business.

David sensed it too. "What's up, Kendrick?" he queried. "Just how bad is it for the Turmans?"

Joshua pulled no punches. "It's critical. We've had to take extravagant measures."

"What measures?"

Joshua thumped his fingers on the steering wheel. "Perhaps I'd better start at the beginning." He drew in a deep breath and expelled it slowly. "Have you noticed newspaper accounts lately about the brutal murders of several DEA agents?"

I thought a moment. "Yes, I have. There was an agent in Mexico awhile back and, of course, your friend Paul Mangano—"

Joshua broke in. "Several agents here and in foreign countries have been killed, Michelle. Mexico, Guatemala, Colombia, the United States—"

"I'm so sorry, Josh."

"There's more, Michelle. Our undercover sources have

learned that the international cocaine syndicate has broken the DEA's secret code and seized confidential information on agents and informants around the world."

"Then what you're saying," David interjected, "is that these haven't been random killings."

"Exactly, David. One by one, our agents and those involved in the government's witness protection program are being gunned down, their families kidnapped and terrorized."

"What does this have to do with Steve and Jackie?" I asked warily.

Joshua's brow furrowed, shadowing his russet eyes. "Two days ago our undercover contact in Mexico City learned that Steve Turman is next on the syndicate's hit list."

"Oh, Josh, no!"

"Jackie's flight to Chicago for your wedding was already scheduled for this morning," Joshua continued. "We couldn't let even the slightest change in plans tip off the underworld that we were wise to them. Yet we had to take immediate action to spirit the Turmans out of the country. That's why I asked Nora to take Jackie's ticket and fly here a few days earlier than she'd planned. We're buying time, Michelle. I want the syndicate to believe the Turmans are going on with their usual activities, suspecting nothing."

"But you said the Turmans have already left the country—?"

"Yes, Michelle. For their own protection they are being secretly relocated with new names and identities."

"Does that mean—are you saying I'll never see Jackie again?"

David's hand tightened on mine. "I'm afraid that's exactly what he's saying, Michelle."

Hot tears burned in my eyes and spilled down my cheeks. "I—I can't believe—my best friend—how can I go on with my wedding as if nothing's happened?"

"You must, Michelle. Everything must go as planned, except that Nora and Juddy will be standing in for Jackie and Stevie."

"But people will know! What if someone who knows Jackie attends my wedding—our friends from college?"

"By the time the truth comes out, the Turmans will be safely relocated and already living under their new identities."

I dabbed at my tears. "But they'll be dead to all of us—their friends, their families—"

Joshua's expression softened. "I'm sorry, Michelle. Extreme measures must be taken in crisis situations."

"I—I'm beginning to understand what Nora meant..."

"What's that, Michelle?" asked Joshua.

"Nothing, Josh." Glancing in the car mirror, I wiped the smeared mascara from under my eyes. "We should all go in, David. My folks will start wondering—"

"No, Michelle," said Josh. "You and David go in. I'll take Nora and Juddy with me now."

"But what will I tell my parents?"

"Just tell them there's been a problem and that Jackie and Stevie must be kept under DEA surveillance until the wedding."

"I won't lie, Josh—"

"I'm just asking you and David to say as little as possible for now. The fewer people aware of what's happening, the better."

I nodded reluctantly.

David opened the car door, stepped out, and helped me out. "You'll be in touch with us soon, Joshua?"

He nodded. "I'll see you before the wedding. We still have important things to talk about."

"You know where to find us." David shook Joshua's hand with a brisk formality. We watched as Josh strode over to the Chevy, helped Nora and Juddy out, and walked them to his sedan.

With a final wave, David and I turned and went inside.

Mother was waiting for us in the living room, her small, crinkly dark eyes snapping with curiosity. "Michelle, why in the world were you standing out in that heat for so long? Where are Jackie and Stevie? I thought your friends were staying with us."

"There's been a change in plans, Mom," I began haltingly.

Mother anxiously touched the white cloud of hair framing her wide, tanned face. "I stood here watching at the window, wondering where your manners were, Michelle—leaving your best friend out there in that hot car. I was ready to march out there myself and bring her in, but Dad said I should mind my own business."

"That's right, Laura, my dear," said Dad, lumbering out from the kitchen. He put a casual arm around Mom's shoulder and squeezed her close, making her short, stout frame look small and cuddly against his barrel chest. His steely blue-gray eyes gazed bemusedly at me through large, rimless glasses. Dad was a straight, proud man with sun-toughened skin and mottled age spots on his full, fleshy face. He had an unruly shock of coarse, reddish-gray hair and fuzzy, snow-white sideburns that he tugged whenever he was irritated. "Well, Michelle," he continued in his great, booming voice, "I'm curious, too. What happened to your friends?"

"They—well, I mean—" I looked helplessly at David.

David cleared his throat. "Well, Mr. Merrill—Andrew—the DEA has decided that Jackie and Stevie should stay elsewhere."

"A problem?" queried Dad, scowling.

"Yes, sir. It's serious, and I'm afraid we're not at liberty to divulge any further information."

"Not that we know all that much anyway, Mom," I added. "Joshua asked us to trust him. We have no other choice."

Dad turned away, the permanent wrinkle lines in his forehead becoming hard, angry ridges. "These young people that get caught up in drugs sure make a mess of their lives— and, Michelle, you want people like that in your wedding!"

"Daddy, you're talking about my best friend, and she never took drugs. You wouldn't want me to forsake her just because she's in trouble—"

"Of course not, Michelle," exclaimed Mom. "Andrew, she's just doing what you've always taught her—being loyal to her friends."

David stepped forward. "Mr.—uh, Andrew—I can assure you that Steve Turman is no longer involved in the drug scene. In fact, he has been one of the state's most valuable witnesses. His testimony resulted in the breakup of one of the West Coast's largest cocaine rings. Over a dozen drug runners have been imprisoned since Steve turned state's evidence."

Dad gave a quick wave of his hand. "You've told me all that before. So now the guy's a hero. But what's going to happen to his wife and kid while he's rotting in jail?"

"He won't go to jail," I began, then stopped abruptly, knowing I'd said too much.

David came to my rescue. "Let's just say the whole Turman

family faces a long, hard journey," he interjected.

Mother raised her hands placatingly. "Enough of this talk about drug rings and jail and other people's problems. We have a wedding on Saturday and only a few days left to get everything done. Let's concentrate on that—all right, Andrew?"

"Suits me," he grunted and ambled over to his favorite chair.

Mom patted my arm reassuringly with her graceful, work-worn fingers. "Don't you worry, darling. Jackie will still be your matron of honor, no matter what your dad says."

"Oh, Mom, you're such a sweethcart! I love you for being you." I cupped her golden, grainy face in my palms and kissed her forehead.

Mother broke away and clasped her hands excitedly. "Oh, dear, I almost forgot. Your sister Pam called while you were out. She and the Thorntons are flying in tomorrow. I just hope there's enough time to finish Pam's gown before Saturday."

"Oh, you'll do it, Mom. You're an expert seamstress."

"I should be after making dresses for you and your sister all these years—"

"To say nothing of all the curtains, sofa covers, and Christmas gifts you've made." I smiled up at David. "Mom's wonderfully frugal and competent, but don't get too hopeful. I didn't inherit all her homemaking skills."

"Michelle was too busy reading mysteries and writing poems and stories on every scrap of paper she could get her hands on," Dad mumbled from behind his newspaper.

"Mysteries?" echoed David. "Then when did you develop such an interest in Shakespeare, Michelle?"

I laughed. "It was long after Nancy Drew and the Hardy Boys. Actually, I started reading the Bard at Hopewell. I had some terrific lit professors."

"Back to the wedding," declared Mom. "Dad will pick up Pam and the Thorntons tomorrow. David, you can see that your friend Rob Thornton gets to his tuxedo fitting, and I'll put his mother Eva to work in the kitchen helping me with the hors d'oeuvres. Michelle tells me Eva's quite a gourmet cook."

"That she is," agreed David, slipping his arm around Mother and me. He kissed us each on the cheek. "It's going to be great being part of a family at last. Of course, I've had Eva Thornton as a stand-in mother for years, but now, to have a wife and a mom and a—" David paused, glancing over tentatively at my dad.

Dad peered over the top of his paper with a shrewd, knowing gleam in his eyes. "And a stubborn, crotchety father?" he finished wryly. "You ready for that, David?"

Grinning, David shot back, "I'm game if you are . . . *Dad.*"

CHAPTER
THREE

On Thursday afternoon, two days before my wedding, Joshua Kendrick paid David and me a visit at my parents' home. He greeted me cheerfully, but his smile was thin and tight and his cleft chin was thrust forward, almost defensively. I detected an undercurrent of tension in his deep, reserved voice. "Is there some place we can talk privately?" he asked.

"My dad's den," I suggested. "David's there on the phone, conducting some long-distance business. You know him, he can't keep his mind off computers and software programs for very long."

"Good. I've been wanting to chat with him about some computer ideas of my own."

"You're not thinking of leaving the DEA, are you?"

"Not by a long shot, although Nora is still pushing for that."

As we walked toward the den, I asked cautiously, "How's the reconciliation going?"

"Let's just say things are at a standstill, but I haven't given up. And it's been great spending time with my sons, Juddy and Jon."

"Well, I'm pulling for the four of you," I told him. I opened the door to the den and motioned Josh inside.

"Are you sure we won't be interrupted?" he asked quietly.

"Positive," I answered. "Dad and David's friend, Rob

Thornton, are giving the backyard some final touches for our garden wedding, and Mom has Eva and my kid sister Pam in the kitchen making wedding favors."

As we entered the den, David was just hanging up the phone. Joshua shut the door behind him, then strode over and shook David's hand vigorously.

David and I sat down on the tufted Colonial sofa while Joshua took Dad's leather rocker. Josh sat balanced on the edge as if he might jump up at any moment. I sensed he had something urgent in mind to discuss with us. We spent a few minutes in small talk before he brought up Jackie and Steve Turman.

"I just wanted to assure you that everything went as planned. The Turmans are safely out of the country."

I sighed deeply, feeling a mixture of relief and regret. "I—I can't believe I'll never see Jackie again."

David slipped his arm around my shoulder. "It's been hard on Michelle, Josh, losing her best friend like this. It's cast a shadow over the entire wedding."

"I even tried telephoning Jackie at her home in Morro Bay," I admitted. "It was the same day Nora arrived in her place. I kept thinking Jackie would answer. But the phone kept ringing unanswered. That's when the terrible realty began to sink in. I realized I had to accept the fact that she's gone. But it isn't easy."

David massaged my shoulder comfortingly. "Joshua, are you certain such extreme measures are necessary? I mean, once things blow over..."

"Josh," I interrupted, "isn't there some way you can tell us where they've gone—not now perhaps, but when we return from our honeymoon?"

Joshua stood up and walked over to the window. "You don't understand, Michelle. We're in a war here—nothing less than war. There are countries pushing cocaine into our nation who consider drug trafficking part of their battle plan, their strategy for destroying America without firing a shot. The international drug syndicate is extremely well-organized—and lethal. They won't stop at anything to accomplish their purposes."

"I—I can't comprehend the enormity of it all," I confessed. "All I know is that ever since Morro Bay David and I have done everything we can to keep in touch with Steve and Jackie, to encourage them spiritually. We just want them to be at peace with God. But now, if our paths never cross again. . ."

Joshua turned from the window and gave me a wry half-smile. "Isn't that God of yours big enough to span time and place?"

I winced, feeling properly reprimanded, then shot back with, "You're right, Josh—just as He's big enough to heal the breach between you and Nora."

Joshua ambled back over to his chair and sat down, his expression clouded, doubtful. "Listen, what I really came here for is to discuss a business proposition with you, David."

"Business?" echoed David with a hint of humor in his voice. "If it's like Morro Bay and our deadly encounter with Clarence Harvey and his drug smugglers, forget it!"

"But don't forget, David," I interjected silkily, "that's where we fell in love."

He laughed. "And to think it all started with an innocent little business trip to sign a computer contract."

"That's what I want to talk about," said Joshua seriously, "—a computer contract."

David's interest sparked at once. He leaned forward, his eyes intent, his strong jaw jutting forward. "You've got my attention, Josh."

"Fine. You'll have to forgive me, David, but we've run a check on you—your character, your background, your abilities, the works."

"Apparently I've passed the test," David remarked dryly.

"It was necessary, David, since this is a programming assignment for the Drug Enforcement Administration."

"I gathered that."

"The project will help the Turmans," Josh added meaningfully.

I slipped my hand into David's. "Oh, if only we could help them somehow—!"

David sounded guarded. "Tell me about it, Josh."

Joshua drew in a careful breath. "Well, like I told you the other day, the underworld has broken our secret code and confiscated crucial information about our witness protection program."

"What's that got to do with me?" David asked.

"We need someone with your skills to come up with a fail-safe computer program to keep track of our relocated government witnesses."

"Just what would such a program involve? I'm not sure just how much time I could give it."

"We need a coded system with full information about the international network of government witnesses. It would include both their true and assumed identities, their families, and their whereabouts."

"Then what you're saying, Joshua, is that this isn't just your idea, or the DEA's. You're talking about a government assignment."

"You got it, David. You have an excellent record, not only scholastically but as a Navy pilot. You served your country well in Vietnam, won the Medal of Honor, and went on to establish yourself as a distinguished leader, a trailblazer in the computer programming field."

"And you think I'm the man to handle this job?"

"I'm convinced of it, David. I don't need to tell you that the documents involved will be top secret and that your participation in the project, if you accept it, will be kept in strictest confidence."

"How much time do I have to decide?"

"Let's just say I'm counting on you."

David looked at me. "What do you think, honey?"

"I think you've already decided. You're not one to turn down a challenge, especially when it comes to helping your country."

David smiled knowingly. "See, Joshua, this lady reads me like a book."

"Great!" exclaimed Joshua. The tense lines in his face were already softening. "Listen, you two, I'll fill you in on the details after your honeymoon."

We all stood up and started toward the door. "Then we'll see you at the wedding on Saturday," David told Josh.

"Yes, and I want to thank you for letting Nora stand in for Jackie as your matron of honor."

"I still feel uncomfortable about it, Josh," I admitted. "What should we say if someone asks why Jackie isn't there?"

"Just play it cool. Change the subject, if necessary."

"You're asking a lot, Josh."

"I'm going to ask even more, Michelle. We plan to run a wedding announcement on the society page of both the *Chicago Tribune* and *Chicago Sun-Times*, listing Jacqueline Turman of Morro Bay, California, as the matron of honor."

"That's crazy, Josh."

"No, Michelle. Essential." He reached over and patted my arm reassuringly. "Someday you'll understand."

"I know your old refrain, Josh," I answered skeptically. *"Trust me, Michelle. Trust me."*

But my irritation with Josh and his schemes faded as another, more pressing mystery unfolded. Just before dinner, there was a persistent ring of the doorbell. Like old times, I raced my kid sister Pam for the front door. I was only steps behind her lean, agile form when she swung open the screen door to the mailman. She turned back to me with an impish, tantalizing grin. "Special delivery," she purred, her velvety blue-grey eyes meeting mine.

"For me?"

"Well, you might say that." She studied the envelope again, deliberately dawdling. "It says the David Ballards."

I reached for the letter but she pulled back. "Think I'll just hold this until Saturday," she teased. "Then you'll really be Mrs. Ballard."

I grabbed again, but she yanked the letter back triumphantly. My patience thinned. "Pamela Merrill, you give that to me now!"

With a quick twist of her head, she flipped back her long, burnished ringlets. "No way, sis!"

From the living room Dad called out, "Laura, dear, they're at it again. Why don't you tend to those two girls of yours!"

Grinning relentlingly, Pam tossed the letter my way. "Cool it, Michelle. It's just a letter."

"*My* letter, thank you," I snapped. I knew my nerves were frayed, easily ruffled. They had been ever since my disappointment over Jackie. Somehow not having Jackie here—not even a wedding present from her—had left a heavy shadow. Now as I took the letter in my hand, I felt a flicker of hope. Perhaps Jackie had written.

I looked up at Pam. She was watching me with a curious,

provocative expression on her childlike face. "Michelle," she drawled, "it's easier to read the letter if you open it."

"I will when I find David."

"He's not hard to find. He's on the telephone again." Pam pointed toward Dad's study.

As I made my way toward the den, Pam declared, "You better make sure David doesn't take a phone on your honeymoon." I slammed the door behind me, but I couldn't shut out Pam's hearty, husky chuckle.

David sprang from his chair at once and met me halfway across the room. "Michelle, if I didn't know differently, I'd think that was Pam's pouty smile on your pretty face. What's the matter, darling? Wedding jitters?"

"No. I just don't feel up to Pam's teasing right now." I brightened as I held up the letter. "Look what just arrived."

David took it and read, "To the David Ballards. That sounds great to me." He tore open the envelope and pulled out the contents. As he examined the thick packet of papers, his smile faded to a perplexed frown. "Honey, look at this. Airline tickets...hotel reservations."

"For Honolulu?" I asked expectantly.

"No. Martinique."

"Where's that?"

"The Caribbean."

"But I thought we were going to Hawaii for our honeymoon."

Ridges furrowed David's brow. "So did I. That's where I had Eva make our reservations. I have the airline tickets to prove it."

"Then who sent these?" I pressed close to David as he unfolded a small note on the travel agent's stationery. "Congratulations, Mr. and Mrs. Ballard," David read aloud. "Friends of yours who wish to remain anonymous have sent you the enclosed wedding present—a one-month, all-expenses-paid honeymoon vacation in the Caribbean. Your itinerary is included, along with a pamphlet on the Windy Reef Hotel, located on the private, sparsely populated island of Solidad. The Windy Reef is a luxury hotel that caters exclusively to the rich and famous."

"Rich? Famous?" I laughed. "David, is this some sort of joke?"

"I don't think so, Michelle. These tickets—they're genuine."
Silently we scanned the itinerary.

> Chicago to Miami, American Airlines, Sunday, July 20
> Overnight at Fountainebleau Hilton, Miami, Florida
> Miami to Martinique, Eastern Airlines, Monday, July 21
> Martinique to Solidad by motor launch, Tuesday, July 22
> Bridal suite, Windy Reef, Solidad, July 22-August 19

"David, is this your surprise? Tell me the truth. You arranged all this."

"I wish I could say I did. But honest, hon, I never even heard of Solidad until now."

"Then who would pay our way to a luxury hotel in the Caribbean?"

"I haven't the faintest idea. But I do know—although it's a generous, incredible gift—we can't possibly accept it, Michelle." David's tone was firm.

I felt a stab of disappointment. "But, David, how can we refuse? We'll offend someone."

"Perhaps. But whom? It's just too bizarre, Michelle." He slipped his arm around me. "We can't simply fly off to some strange island and have a lavish honeymoon at someone else's expense."

"But, darling," I argued back, waving the Windy Reef folder like a banner, "think of it! We'd have a whole island to ourselves and nothing to do all day but . . ." I let my words drift off provocatively, then added with a lilt in my voice, "Besides, a tropical island would make a grand setting for that romantic novel I want to write."

David shook his head in mock retreat. "My impetuous little wonder! How I love you. If only you were a little more practical!"

"And less creative?" I countered, momentarily wounded. But I rallied quickly. "David, maybe Eva Thornton planned this."

"It's not like Eva. She's up front. She'd sign her name."

"And if she did, you wouldn't accept it. So if it wasn't Eva, who else . . . ?"

Resolving something in his mind, David suddenly broke

away from me and strode to the phone. "I'm calling Joshua
Kendrick."

"Joshua Kendrick? What in the world for?"

David thumped the special delivery envelope against the telephone cord. "About this letter."

"No way," I protested. "It's none of Joshua's business."

"It may well be."

I was at David's side now. He was dialing slowly, deliberately. I put my hand on his. "Please, David. Joshua has already
put a damper on our wedding. Let's not give him a chance
to plan our honeymoon too."

"This may be important, Michelle."

"More important than our privacy? It's our wedding,
David—our honeymoon. Not Joshua's!"

He put the receiver down and drew me to him. "It's also our
lives, Michelle, perhaps our very safety." I felt his chin nuz-
zle my hair, his warm breath against my ear. "Doesn't it seem
strange, Michelle? First, Jackie doesn't arrive on her flight.
Then we find out someone else flew here in her place. No one
seems to have any answers except the DEA, and they're not
talking. Now we're caught up in this whole charade with Nora
and even pending news clippings falsifying our wedding—"

"The wedding won't be false," I said through tears. "Just
Jackie's name as matron of honor."

David held me tighter. "And now, Michelle. Tickets. Legiti-
mate ones, obviously. A month's honeymoon. No gift card
enclosed." He sighed heavily. "I really have to call Joshua."

Two hours later, as David and I rocked on my parents' porch
swing, savoring the first cool breeze of the evening, Joshua
Kendrick drove up. Nora was with him. Though he offered
her his hand as she stepped from the car, Nora ignored it. They
walked up the porch steps together, but I noted sadly that they
were obviously miles apart in spirit.

"Well, let's see this letter that has you so concerned," said
Josh as they joined us, taking the nearby lounge chairs. He took
the envelope David handed him and looked it over. "Can't
make out the postmark," he said as he casually removed the
contents.

Nora peered over his shoulder. "It looks like Chicago to me."

"It's local then," said David. "Must be a friend of yours,

Michelle. Or a rich uncle?"

"No such luck," I said thickly.

Josh flipped through the pamphlet on the Windy Reef Hotel, then read the note. A smile played at the corner of his mouth. Then he looked up, threw his head back and laughed uproariously. "Come on, David, you've got to be kidding. This isn't a problem. It's an invitation—to Paradise!" He scratched his head thoughtfully. "You two didn't really believe I'd have something to do with this, did you?"

"He's right, you know," Nora interjected. Her tone was cold, cutting, bitter. "He'd hardly have time to concern himself with your honeymoon plans when he never had time for his own."

Josh ignored her. "I don't see any cause for alarm, David," he went on. "It looks to me like a wedding gift. Simple as that."

"A very expensive gift," I noted.

"The groom usually pays for the honeymoon," David added.

Josh arched one brow. "A tycoon like you . . . you've got business associates, friends—this probably wouldn't even put a dent in their wallet." He stuffed the tickets back into the envelope and handed it to David. "Don't worry about your mysterious donor, you two. Just take the tickets and fly away. After all, a tropical isle sounds like a great spot for a honeymoon. Doesn't it, hon?" he said, turning to Nora.

"Does it, Josh?" she asked plaintively. "Then why didn't you think of it 12 years ago?"

Josh pivoted slightly and shrugged, but his irritation with Nora was evident. "We'll wait and see how David and Michelle like Solidad. If they give us a good report, maybe I'll take you there on a second honeymoon."

"Don't bother," she snapped. "Camping from here to Atlanta would be cheaper."

Josh winced. In answer to our quizzical glances, he explained, "That's what Nora and I did for our honeymoon. I thought we were having a great time—camp-outs in the woods, fresh trout over an open fire, just the two of us under the stars. . ." There was a hint of yearning in Josh's voice, partially masked by a sardonic smile as he glared at Nora.

"David and I would love taking a trip like that," I offered.

"I did love it," Nora answered quickly. "Insects, sleeping bags, and all—until we got to Atlanta and I found out that all along Joshua was on his way to a new assignment in the DEA's regional office. Once we got to Georgia, I spent days alone in a cheap hotel room waiting for him to come back, wondering if he would come back or get his fool head blown off." Her voice grew small and hard. "It does something to you, living with terror like that for 12 long years."

Our conversation had cooled like the evening air. The only sound now was the creaking of the old porch swing as it swayed slowly back and forth. I wondered how the Kendricks would ever patch up their wounds. For a fleeting second I thought, *Without Christ they never will. . . but for their sons' sakes, they must.*

My thoughts were interrupted as the screen door squeaked open and Mother said, "Why don't you bring your friends inside, Michelle? I have an apple pie cooling."

"We really need to be going," Joshua answered politely.

There was enough hesitation in his voice that Mom came back with, "Nonsense, you really should come inside and have some pie." She opened the screen door wider. "You must be Joshua Kendrick. I've heard a great deal about you. And you, my dear," she said, turning to Nora, "must be Michelle's matron of honor." Mom gave a knowing chuckle as we filed into the house.

Inside, Mom took Nora's hand in hers. "I think we're going to get along splendidly, my dear. I went camping on my honeymoon too. My Andrew couldn't afford anything except Lake Michigan, but I've never forgotten those wonderful days."

For a moment Nora looked self-conscious, uncertain, as if she might tumble into Mother's arms and weep her heart out. "Mrs. Merrill, there's something you should know—"

"I already know, Mrs. Kendrick," replied Mom kindly as she hustled us into her cozy kitchen. "Or am I supposed to call you Jackie?"

"Nora would be fine."

As we finished our pie, David looked over at Mom and said, "How would you and Andrew like to take a trip to Hawaii—compliments of Michelle and me?"

Mom looked aghast. "You—you're inviting us to go with you

on your honeymoon?"

"Not exactly. Michelle and I have had a change of plans."

I stared at David in joyous surprise. "You mean, we're accepting our anonymous gift—we're going to Solidad?"

His eyes danced with a mischievous merriment. "Why not? We only live once. And I can't think of a better setting for your romance novel."

I flew out of my chair and nestled on his lap, nearly toppling his chair backward. "It'll be wonderful, darling. I'll write our own love story."

David embraced me tenderly. "Sounds good to me. I'll do my best to give you plenty of romantic ideas."

I looked at Mom. "How about it? Will you and Dad accept our gift?"

"Go to Hawaii? Your father would never hear of it."

"I think he will, Mrs. Merrill," replied David confidently, "after I tell him it's my way of thanking the two of you for raising such a wonderful daughter—the woman of my dreams."

Suddenly everyone was talking at once, caught up in the excitement and intrigue of the moment, contemplating fanciful excursions to exotic islands filled with moonlight and romance. David was outshining us all, painting outrageous imaginary pictures of swashbuckling adventures with hidden treasures and Spanish galleons, the two of us surrounded by crystal-clear lagoons, coral reefs, and secluded beaches.

I was catching a rare glimpse of another side of David—a rhapsodic, impractical, castle-building dreamer. Or was I just seeing myself reflected in his eyes?

But even as we fantasized over how glorious our honeymoon would be, I silently wondered what strange new twists and turns our lives would take on the faraway island of Solidad.

CHAPTER FOUR

On Saturday, dawn burst upon me like a morning glory—full of sun and warmth and the sweet, heady fragrance of freshly cut flowers on my bureau. A lush summer bouquet—pink and purple phlox, red poppies, yellow irises, and white peonies. Sweet David! He must have gathered them for me from the garden. *My wedding day!* I realized in joyous disbelief. *This afternoon I will become Mrs. David Ballard!*

I lay in bed, wafting in a rosy twilight between slumber and wakefulness, luxuriating in a cozy cocoon of warmth, reflecting that this would be my last morning to wake up alone. From now on I would be able to reach out at night and find my beloved David beside me. Oh, the joy of sleeping in his warm, protective arms!

At last I rose and took my time bathing and dressing, moving leisurely, feeling somehow detached from the rest of the world. I wanted to trace every minute, every lovely detail of this day on my heart, knowing I would cherish today for the rest of my life.

But the morning passed like the crystal mist evaporating on the roses. The house sang with activity—everyone scurrying about, the air charged with excitement. Eva insisted we all sit down and eat a hot breakfast. Mom anxiously followed the caterers around, giving them countless instructions. Dad groomed the garden with a final loving touch, while Rob and Pam decorated the trellises with white satin ribbons and garlands of daisies and pink rosebuds.

David had left the house early this morning to pick up the tuxedos and run other last-minute errands. We had both agreed that we wouldn't see each other today until I walked down the silk-lined garden path to become his wife.

Before I knew it—even as I touched my cheeks with blush and fluffed my tawny hair around my face, the hour of my wedding arrived. In the chintz-curtained bedroom of my childhood, Mom and Eva helped Pam, Nora, and me slip into our gowns. Pam and Nora looked stunning in their dusky rose gowns with matching seed pearl headpieces.

Nora, who had arrived only minutes before it was time to dress, remained subdued and unsmiling. I felt a pang of regret that it wasn't Jackie in the matron of honor's gown, but I forced a cheery smile and told Nora, "You look beautiful. Wait'll Josh sees you!"

"It won't matter," she said curtly. Then, her expression softening, she added, "All eyes will be on you."

I glanced automatically toward the full-length mirror and caught my breath. Was it really I in ivory-white with yards of lustrous satin lavished in lace? I moved gingerly, getting accustomed to my bouffant flounce slip, until I glimpsed with a thrill of excitement my flowing cathedral train of heirloom lace.

"You could be a model in *Modern Bride* magazine!" Mom exclaimed proudly. While I held up my hooped petticoats, she stooped down and slipped my beaded satin pumps on my feet.

"I—I think I'm ready," I said, laughing nervously, "but is it normal to feel so light-headed and dizzy?"

"All brides feel that way, hon. There's just one more thing."

I looked around. "You mean I've forgotten something?"

Mom removed her own antique gold locket and fastened it around my neck. "You need something old and borrowed, darling. This belonged to your great-grandmother. Someday it will be yours."

I fingered the locket appreciatively, then kissed Mom's cheek. "Thank you, Mom. I'll love wearing it."

"And here is a lacy blue garter—something new...and blue."

"David will love this," I exclaimed, pleased, as Mom bent again and slipped the garter over my ankle.

"I know he will," she agreed, choking back a sob. "Your dad still has the one I wore 26 years ago."

Mom and I exchanged knowing, tearful smiles. For the first time I felt like her equal; we were no longer just mother and daughter but two women sharing treasured bits of trivia about the men we loved.

From the garden below, I could hear violinists playing, accompanied by the sweet, lilting strings of a harp. Mom quickly adjusted my elbow-length veil. I clasped her hands urgently. "It's begun already? My wedding? Are the guests all here?"

"Yes, dear. The garden is brimming with people. Standing room only, as they say." She looked over at Pam. "Oh, my two beautiful daughters—a bridesmaid and a bride. I'm so proud of you both!"

We embraced stiffly, careful not to muss our full, ruffled gowns—Mom and I, Pam and I, then Mom and Pam. Mom thoughtfully drew a reluctant Nora into our circle as well. We were all about to weep when Pam exclaimed, "Come on, you guys. Enough of this mush. My mascara will smear. So will yours, big sis. David won't want to say 'I do' to a lady with plum eye shadow all over her face."

We all laughed, breaking the tension.

As strains of the wedding march filtered up from the garden, Eva called from the doorway, "Michelle, dear, the menfolk are ready to escort you all downstairs."

As I moved, my gown swished and swirled, floating around me like a sequined cloud. "I feel like Cinderella," I said breathlessly.

Eva nodded, winking. "Prince Charming is waiting downstairs."

As we reached the yard, my father stepped forward and kissed me. "You're beautiful," he said, a catch in his gravelly voice. I took his arm. The next few minutes became a lovely, pastel blur—a sea of smiling faces looking my way, the garden a blaze of magnificent colors—apricot roses and bright red tulips, golden zinnias and flaming dahlias. And there, near the trellis, stood David straight and tall waiting for me, his eyes drinking me in, adoring me. He looked imposingly handsome in his silver-gray tuxedo with its cutaway coat and striped trousers. Seeing David, I saw no one else.

Finally, seemingly from a distant isle, I heard Pastor Rawlings ask, "Who gives this woman to be married to this man?"

Dad spoke up, his deep voice erupting with a mixture of love, pride, and pain. "Her mother and I, with all our love."

Moments later, David and I faced each other to exchange the wedding vows we had written. His eyes glistened as he pressed my hands securely in his. His baritone voice rang out bell-clear. "I, David, take you, Michelle, to be my wife, my helpmate, my lover, and friend. I promise to honor and care for you, believing that God has called us to be one, trusting that we can serve Christ better together than apart. I will seek always to love you as Christ loved His bride, the church, and sacrificed Himself for her. In sickness or health, in poverty or wealth, whatever our circumstances, I will protect you, cherish you, encourage you, and hold you in highest esteem."

He paused as our eyes locked in love. Then he continued, his lips forming the slightest arc of a smile. "Michelle, since marriage is an illustration of the relationship between Christ and His church, I accept responsibility as head of our home for your spiritual welfare—and for the spiritual growth of our children, if God chooses to bless us with them. In turn, God calls me to complete obedience to Him and to godly, sacrificial love for you. With the Holy Spirit's help, I promise to pray for you, be available to you, and walk with you in obedience to the Scriptures."

David and I were both smiling now. His voice was warm, husky. "Michelle, I desire to give you not just casual affection or fleeting physical and emotional responses, but *agape* love—deep, abiding, godly love measured by sacrifice. I recognize that the ultimate purpose of our love, like the purpose of our individual lives, is to glorify God and to bring others to a personal walk with Christ. Therefore, Michelle, before these witnesses, I dedicate my life to you and to our Lord Jesus, with the prayer that God will fulfill His will in us all the days of our lives."

Now it was my turn. I looked up into David's eyes, but my voice wouldn't come. The words I had written with such care seemed just out of reach. I stared at David in desperation. His warm gaze enfolded me, caressed me. I breathed deeply. My words spilled from an overflow of love. "I, Michelle, take you, David, to be my husband, my helpmate, my lover, and friend. Recognizing you as my spiritual head, I freely agree to submit myself to you as unto the Lord, not from compulsion or fear, but voluntarily, in response to your love, as the church, Christ's bride, responds voluntarily to His love."

I paused, drew in a breath. The summer air was still, as if the entire earth had grown hushed around us. "David, because Christ loved me and gave Himself for me, I have opened my heart to God. Even so, because you love me and have committed yourself to me, I pledge you my love and allegiance for as long as we both shall live.

"I know that the spiritual authority you exercise over me—and over our children someday, if God chooses to bless us with them—is not your own authority, but an authority vested in you by God, and that by obeying you I demonstrate my obedience to Christ. As we accept the God-ordained roles in our marriage, we do not surrender our own individualities, or diminish our separate personhoods, or minimize the uniqueness we each contribute to this union.

"Rather, in the sanctity and security of our marriage, we are each free to flourish, to grow, and to spread our wings and soar with joy, just as the fragile chrysalis bursts forth as the bright and wondrous butterfly. So our marriage is cause for celebration. We are more together, David, than either of us could have been apart.

"I love you, David, with all my heart and soul. I cherish you all the more because I feel God's pleasure in our love."

Minutes later, at the close of our ceremony, David carefully lifted my veil and kissed me soundly while Pastor Rawlings declared, "Ladies and gentlemen, I present to you Mr. and Mrs. David Ballard!"

We were greeted by a hearty round of applause. Then, as we stood in our reception line at the opposite end of the garden, old friends and new, neighbors and relatives filed by, lavishing us with kisses, congratulations, and good wishes. A couple of old college friends—Hopewell graduates—inquired about Jackie, but I dismissed their questions with a casual, "She couldn't make it after all." To my relief, no one pursued the matter.

After David and I had greeted everyone, the photographers insisted we pose for pictures. First, I drew David aside and handed him a small wrapped package. He looked surprised. "What's this?"

I smiled with anticipation. "My wedding gift to you."

David carefully removed the paper and opened the velour case. Grinning appreciatively, he lifted out a gleaming gold pocket watch. "How did you know I've always wanted one of these?"

"I didn't, but you look like a man who should own a pocket watch—distinguished, successful." I hesitated. "There's an inscription engraved inside."

He flipped open the lid and read, "To David with love—more than yesterday, less than tomorrow. Michelle." He clipped the chain on and tucked the watch into his breast pocket, then gathered me into his arms and kissed me. "I'll carry this with me always, darling, just as I'll carry you always in my heart."

We were about to kiss again when Eva touched my arm lightly. "I'm afraid the photographers are growing restless, Michelle."

I glanced in their direction, but someone else a dozen feet away caught my eye—a gray-haired woman in a plain black dress. Her wide-brimmed hat partially shaded a stern, tight-lipped expression. When the woman's gaze met mine, I found myself staring into icy blue-gray eyes that glared through thick, magnifying, wire-rimmed glasses. A chill shot up my spine. I nudged David. "Who's that woman in black?"

He raised one eyebrow. "I thought she was your old maid aunt."

"I've never seen her before in my life."

"You're sure?"

"You think I'd forget someone like that?"

Eva stepped closer and asked confidentially, "Are you talking about that older lady over there?"

"Yes," I said quickly. "Do you know her?"

"No, but she's a curious sort. She was asking me questions. Very persistent, intense."

"Questions? What questions?"

"About your friend, Jackie Turman."

David and I exchanged stunned glances. "Oh, David, no!" I uttered. Impulsively I broke away from Eva, lifting my hooped petticoats and lace train as I proceeded awkwardly across the manicured lawn. David passed me with his long, determined stride. But the woman slipped away in the crowd. She was nowhere in sight.

"Stay here," David told me. "I'll find her."

Minutes later he made his way back through the milling guests, looking baffled, frustrated. "She's gone, Michelle."

"Gone? But how, David? We just saw her."

"I don't know. It's like she just . . . disappeared."

I gripped his arm. "Who was she? Why did she ask about Jackie?"

"She's nobody, Michelle. Just a harmless, eccentric old lady. Come on, honey. We're letting ourselves get paranoid."

"Is that what you think?"

He pulled me against him. "I'm thinking this is our wedding day, Michelle, and I'd like us to enjoy it."

"Oh, David, darling, I want that too!" But even as we embraced, I realized I'd never forget the cold, steely glint—ominous and searing—in that strange woman's eyes.

CHAPTER
FIVE

David and I spent our wedding night in a private beach house
on the shore of Lake Michigan. When we arrived, we found
a cozy table for two brimming with gourmet delicacies—
caviar, fresh fruit and cheese, king crab on ice, Chateaubri-
and with bearnaise sauce, and chocolate mousse. We ate
leisurely beside a huge stone fireplace in the posh, but rustic
bungalow, then took a moonlit stroll along the vast, star-
spangled beach. The breeze coming in off the lake was cool
and moist, but the sand was still pleasantly warm from the
fierce midday sun.

In a moment of sweet abandon we stripped down to our
swimsuits and ran in the foamy surf, splashing each other,
frolicking like children. Finally, laughing and shivering, we
raced each other back to the beach house.

We bathed with a giddy freedom in the luxurious pool-size
tub. Then, while I slipped into my white silk spaghetti-strap
nightgown, David stoked the embers in the fireplace, more for
atmosphere than warmth, and turned the stereo on low.

When I entered the room, David turned and gazed at me
with a slow, appraising smile. "You look beautiful, Michelle."
As we melted into each other's arms, he whispered huskily,
"I've waited all my life for tonight, my darling."

"Me, too, David," I murmured. As I pressed my head against

his chest, I could hear his heart thumping wildly, echoing my own quickening heartbeat. "Always before, when we were close like this, we had to pull away—"

"And I had to go home and leave you behind. But tonight, dear Michelle, tonight . . . I stay!" He gathered me tenderly in his strong arms and carried me over to the king-size bed. We cuddled together under the fluffy comforter, watching the hungry flames devour the dry timber. Gradually, inevitably, we forgot the crackling fire and the wistfully melodic ballads. The entire world seemed to ebb away as David's lips moved with a soft, warm urgency over my mouth and my neck to my bare shoulder. Our joy crescendoed as we lost ourselves rapturously, consummately in each other.

• • •

Early Sunday afternoon David and I tossed our clothes into our luggage and left our honeymoon cottage for a frantic, hurried trip to O'Hare International for our mid-afternoon flight from Chicago to Miami. We laughed all the way to the airport, wondering if we would miss our plane. "Even if we have to reschedule, Michelle, it was worth it." His dark eyes were alive and dancing as they met mine. "Right now I don't care about Solidad. I'd just as soon go back to Lake Michigan and spend a lifetime there with you."

I blushed and nestled contentedly against him as our taxi careened through the crowded streets toward O'Hare.

But by nine Tuesday morning, as David locked our suitcases once again, we were beginning to think our honeymoon would be a never-ending series of packing and unpacking. In three short days, we had already travel-hopped from the shores of Lake Michigan to the balmy, bejeweled Caribbean, stopping overnight at the Fountainbleau Hilton in Miami. Making another mad airport dash, we had flown from Miami over a string of stepping-stone islands to tropical Martinique. In spite of our tiny, quaint, unbearably hot hotel quarters, we found Martinique to be a colorful island of exotic flowers, lush green valleys, and blinding blue skies. Pastel aquamarine waters bathed Martinique's irregular coastline, cutting dramatically into picturesque bays and coves.

We had spent most of Monday strolling over Martinique's tiny, winding streets, our steps echoing the rhythmic beat of calypso tunes. Savoring the windborne scent of bougainvillea and hibiscus, we mingled with Martinique's lovely brown-skinned people and browsed in her curio shops and straw markets. But now we were eager to keep our appointment at the dock and board the motor launch for Solidad.

In the musky lobby, David asked a barefoot bellboy to carry our luggage to the dock. The young man gave him an indifferent shrug until he saw the shiny coins in David's hand. He grinned, his smile broadening until he was mostly white teeth and crinkly eyes. Then, mumbling something in his native Creole, he balanced our suitcases on his head and led the way through the doorway along the narrow streets to the sea. The dock was little more than a dilapidated fishing pier extending a few yards over the Caribbean. David shaded his eyes and stared out over the glistening water, then along the shoreline. He took my hand and led us past a few rustic, red-roofed homes and tilting palm trees, stopping finally a hundred yards from an antique stone church.

"This must be the place," said David, gazing at several fishing vessels beached along the lava-encrusted shore, "but there's not a motor launch in sight." He paced impatiently back and forth.

"What's wrong, David?" I asked.

"I don't like it," he answered, glancing at his pocket watch. "The launch is overdue." He squeezed my hand protectively. "It's rather unnerving not knowing exactly what we're looking for. After going first-class these past couple of days ...I thought..." The jagged scar along his jawline paled. "Michelle, I hope I haven't taken you on a wild-goose chase."

"Maybe we could swim to Solidad," I said, making a weak stab at humor.

David managed only a flicker of a smile as he turned to the boy with our luggage. "When does the motor launch arrive for Solidad?" he asked, enunciating each word carefully.

The youth swayed slightly, beads of perspiration gleaming on his golden face. "No motor launch to Solidad—just fishing boat—few times a week."

David's eyes flashed with irritation. "You know, Michelle,

I'm beginning to think our benevolent benefactor is playing one enormous joke on us."

"But why, David? Why would someone bring us all the way to Martinique and then leave us stranded?"

"That's what I intend to find out," he replied stoutly.

"Maybe we're worrying for nothing," I suggested. "Perhaps we need to get used to the unhurried time schedule of the islands."

But after a tedious half hour of waiting, we dismissed the bellboy and ducked under a palm tree to escape the baking sun. Idly we watched schooners and trading sloops bob on the horizon—some just setting sail, one or two moving steadily inland.

Just as David and I were debating whether to head back to our humid, airless hotel room, a deep male voice called out, "You two must be the Ballards!"

We whirled around to see a tall, tanned, rough-hewn man— blond and ruggedly good-looking—sauntering toward us, his thumbs linked on the pockets of his tennis slacks. He had the sturdy, broad shoulders and narrow hips of a surfer. His sport shirt was open at the neck, revealing a muscular, hairy chest.

"Yes, we're the Ballards—David and Michelle," said David.

The man grinned slyly. "I figured you were. Not many Americans with a mountain of luggage hanging around these parts."

"Not many Americans get left high and dry when their ship's supposed to come in," I quipped dryly, irritation stealing in.

"Make that a fishing vessel," said the stranger, scooping up two suitcases. "The motor launch is out of whack."

As our gaze locked, I felt compellingly drawn to the man's shrewd dark eyes, magnetic and disconcerting at once. He had a rectangular, square-jawed face with thick arched brows, aquiline nose, and a trim brown mustache. His windblown, sun-bleached hair had a flaxen cast.

"Are you ready to go?" he said.

"Where?" I exclaimed.

"Who are you?" demanded David.

The swarthy young man paused and grinned cockily at us.

"I'm Silas Winters, the concierge from the Windy Reef Hotel on Solidad."

"Concierge?" echoed David skeptically.

I looked up at David and whispered, "He doesn't look like the genteel type to roll out the red carpet for hotel guests."

"Actually they call us distinguished purveyors of service," Silas Winters intoned mockingly. "Not exactly the European variety that caters to a guest's every whim, but we do our best. That's why we'll be substituting a fishing schooner for the stalled motor launch. Come with me, please, Mr. and Mrs. Ballard."

Wordlessly we gathered our remaining suitcases and followed the arrogant, athletic Silas Winters along the beach to a modest white fishing schooner bobbing at the weatherworn dock. We boarded and sat on a narrow, chipped bench beside a pile of brown hemp fishing nets. The pungent, salty smells of mackerel and crayfish turned my stomach. I clasped David's hand for support.

An old black fisherman with coarse, sun-baked skin, a flat, flaring nose and thick, leathery lips signaled to another Creole seaman. Skillfully the two pulled in the ropes and eased the primitive vessel away from the pier.

As the narrow, orange-trimmed boat rolled out to sea, Silas leaned nonchalantly against the mast, his brawny frame silhouetted against a periwinkle sky. "Great day for sailing," he remarked.

"How—how long will it take to get to Solidad?" I uttered weakly.

"Not long. Maybe an hour." He gave me a half-amused glance. "You look a bit squeamish, ma'am. But hang in there. Moses has been handling this rig for years. It's his livelihood."

I reeled at the stench of raw, rotting fish, thinking that there must be an easier way to make a living. "David," I moaned, "I'm not sure I can—"

Silas spoke up. "If you feel sick, Mrs. Ballard, just put your head over the side of the vessel. But lean way over," he added.

"Thanks," I muttered sarcastically, "but I thought a good concierge might carry a gold-trimmed emesis bucket."

"Most of our guests are experienced sailors, not novices," Silas countered. "But leaning over really will serve the purpose."

I noticed Moses watching me intently from the stern of the boat, his large, coarse hand steady on the rudder. There was something warm and compassionate about his gentle, sun-wrinkled face, his solemn eyes that gazed out intently under puffy lids. The whites of his eyes were yellowed, red-rimmed, but spoke of immense patience and a quiet acceptance of his toilsome, slow-paced existence. He reached over and picked up his battered straw hat and waved it toward the horizon. "Solidad," he said in a heavy accent. "Solidad...over there."

Silas made a sweeping gesture from east to west. "On clear days like this you can see a whole string of islands between Martinique and St. Vincent."

"Are they all inhabited?" I asked, forcing my mind off my queasy stomach. "Some of them look so barren, so lifeless."

"That's because they were once active volcanoes." I could tell he was warming to the subject as he continued buoyantly, "Some are still remnant volcanic spikes jutting up from the ocean bed—dry, charred masses. Others are anonymous little islands with just a handful of people."

"Isn't St. Lucia near here?" asked David.

"To the south."

"And what about Grenada?" I questioned.

Silas squinted out over the wide expanse of water as if he alone owned the lush, tropical wonderland around us. For a moment his thoughts seemed caught in time, as though Grenada had stirred some elusive memory. While our vessel swayed and dipped, tilting with the waves as the breeze billowed the ragged sails, Silas held his position, balancing effortlessly, precariously against the mast. "Grenada?" he mused. "It's one of the Windward Islands, but it's just 90 miles off the Venezuelan coast. Great sailing waters."

"Then you've been there?"

He hesitated. "On business."

"Oh, you were a concierge there?" I asked. "At what hotel?"

Silas appeared not to hear me. Brusquely he said, "There's Solidad—over there—just southeast of us."

"What can you tell us about the island, Mr. Winters?" queried David. When Silas didn't respond immediately, David went on, "Actually, it's a fluke that we're even vacationing on Solidad—"

"I assure you, it will meet your expectations, Mr. Ballard. Solidad is a very special place."

"Mostly for vacations, they tell us," I said.

"That, too," Silas answered. "But it wasn't always a vacationer's paradise, not in the beginning."

Moses leaned forward eagerly and said, "You tell them about the legend, Mr. Silas?"

Silas laughed. "They don't want to hear the whole history of Solidad, Moses."

"Sure we do!" I insisted, my nausea already abating.

Silas shrugged relentingly. "It's a long, complicated story, Mrs. Ballard, but I must admit, a fascinating one."

"Oh, please, go on. I love a good story," I cried.

David leaned over and whispered, "I thought you were concentrating on *our* story."

"Of course, David, but if we're going to live on Solidad for a month, I want to know all about it."

Silas folded his arms across his chest. "The island belonged to a Colombian multimillionaire named Ricardo Cobranza—a political outcast from his own country. He had a stunningly beautiful wife named Alejandra. Rumor has it that she was severely disfigured in a fire during a political uprising in Colombia that left a price on her husband's head."

"Oh, how tragic!" I exclaimed. "What happened to them?"

"After they fled their homeland, Cobranza purchased this island and built a huge, castle-like mansion for his wife. Legend has it that Alejandra remained in seclusion there for the rest of her life. Only a few trusted servants ever saw her face."

"How sad. Then are both the Cobranzas gone now?"

"Right," said Silas. "The old man couldn't take losing his wife. The natives say he leaped to his death, diving into the ocean from the east wing of the hotel, but they never found his body."

"The hotel, you say?" questioned David.

"Yeah. The Cobranzas' son Carlos turned the old mansion into a luxury hotel after his parents' death and opened the island to limited tourism." Silas paused. "Enough of the history for now. That's the island just ahead. The tip of land on our left is called Frangipani Point. Moses will take the boat around the natural sandbar into Cobranza Bay."

I felt my heart hammering with excitement as the island of Solidad loomed ahead—a dazzling, picturesque fantasy isle. I could see the crystal-clear waters of Cobranza Bay, the powdery white beaches, the bushy-crowned palm trees swaying along the shore. As we pulled along the dock, we could see the marketplace and hear the happy, lilting voices of the Creoles accented by the rhythmic drumbeat of a steel band. "Oh, David, it's absolutely enchanting. I love it already!"

He slipped his arm around me and chuckled, "Maybe this will be a honeymoon paradise after all."

"Well, you'll be living near Paradise Cove," offered Silas. "At least, that's the name the Cobranzas gave it." He pointed toward the jagged cliffs on the far side of the island. "You can see the Windy Reef from here—that palatial chateau sitting in all its splendor on Tamarind Bluff." There was a hint of contempt in Silas Winters' voice, as if splendor and glamour had no place in his life.

"You don't like luxury hotels?" I asked. "You—a concierge?"

He ignored my question and said instead, "We'll be docking in a moment. I've made arrangements for a surrey to take us to Tamarind Bluff."

"Cara de Muerte," Moses muttered as he secured the lines and glanced up at the cliffs. He walked barefoot over the fishing nets and leaped onto the pier. "Cara de Muerte," he repeated ominously.

"What's he saying?" I asked Silas.

"It's Spanish."

"But what does it mean?"

"It's a nickname the natives gave Tamarind Bluff. It means 'the face of death.' "

I shivered involuntarily. "What a strange name for such a lovely place."

"The bluff is a sheer drop-off on the Atlantic side of the island," Silas explained dryly. "It's so treacherous that only the foolhardy approach Solidad from the ocean side."

"So, it's an appropriate name," remarked David practically.

Silas frowned. "There's more. The islanders believe you can see the face of death—an ominous skull—in the rock formation. I figure it's probably just some cave or grotto washed out by the surf. But you know these people," he said, nodding toward Moses. "They're too superstitious for their own good."

Moses turned and glared hard at Silas. His voice was hushed, raspy. "The face of death—it kill Sr. Cobranza—many years ago."

"See what I mean about their superstitions?" said Silas irritably. "Just because that's the spot where Ricardo Cobranza perished, the islanders fear a death sentence for anyone who ventures near the cliffs of Tamarind Bluff."

CHAPTER
SIX

Silas escorted David and me over to a bright red-and-yellow surrey—a quaint one-horse carriage with large, spindly wagon wheels and a fringed awning. David boosted me up onto the wooden bench with its flat, worn pad. The harnessed dappled gray mare tossed her mane to ward off swarming flies and pawed nervously at the dirt, sending up swirling clouds of dust. The horse wore blinders and an old straw fisherman's hat with a tattered sign that read, "The name of this horse is Sweet Hibiscus."

Silas settled up front with the golden-skinned Creole driver—a sturdy, smooth-faced young man with warm, wistful brown eyes. "Okay, Kikko," Silas ordered, "head for the Windy Reef."

The horse shambled along at a slow, lumbering gait past the marketplace. A string of crowded, open-air booths spilled over with fresh fruits and vegetables, handwoven straw goods, and burlap sacks bursting with black beans and dried red peppers. The hot, humid air was heavy with the pungent smell of raw fish lining countertops and brimming from huge metal buckets.

Kikko flicked the reins against the nag's sweaty hide. Sweet Hibiscus broke into a jaunty trot over the narrow, dusty road. As we jounced along, David asked, "Are there any automobiles on Solidad?"

"A couple of the hotel people own jeeps, although I have the only four-wheel-drive van on the island," said Silas. "Mainly we depend on bikes and surreys for transportation. They'll always be available at the hotel if you want to go visit Shoal Beach or Cocoa Falls." As we reached a fork in the road, he pointed to the left and said, "That's the scenic route that takes you around the island to Coral Beach or Frangipani Point. It's a must while you're here."

"You can get there by surrey?" I asked, already feeling numb from the bumps in the uneven road.

"That's right. Just make arrangements at the desk with Esteban Medina, the hotel manager. Or with me, for that matter."

Kikko nudged Silas and declared with a grin, "Sweet Hibiscus and me—we take missus and her man for trips."

Silas turned around and announced, "Looks like you already have yourself a driver. Kikko's a good man. He'll take you anywhere on the island—for a price, of course. You can take the whole day and he'll just sit dozing in his surrey, waiting for you."

"Sounds good," said David. "How do we get in touch with Kikko?"

"Now that he knows you want him, he'll make a daily appearance!"

I clasped David's arm happily. "This is so exciting. It's like being in a whole new world."

"You can get a better view of the hotel now," said Silas, nodding toward the stark, white cliffs ahead. "Windy Reef occupies the entire bluff. Your bridal suite in the east wing juts out over the ocean. There's no other view like it in the world."

"And to think the hotel was once someone's home!" I marveled.

"Actually, the east wing is the original Cobranza estate," continued Silas. "The west wing, with its 50 luxury suites, was built later. Our select clientele comes from all over the world—corporate heads and celebrities seeking the privacy and solitude we offer. They give the hotel a unique international flavor."

Kikko sat forward intently, urging Sweet Hibiscus up the

slanting cobblestone road. I stared ahead, spellbound. There stood the sprawling, two-story Windy Reef Hotel, looming like a refurbished Georgian plantation, its pillars glistening white in the sunlight. The glittering mansion, looking as if it were carved into the limestone hillside, was surrounded by a profusion of riotous colors—full-blooming scarlet bougainvillea, exotic lavender orchids, and sweet-scented frangipani. The lush gardens and manicured grounds abounded with ruby-red African tulips, feather-shaped ferns, banana and breadfruit trees, and coconut palms.

Our horse and surrey wended around the hotel's oval driveway in a quick clippety-clop, coming to a halt beside the immense front porch. David helped me out of the wagon. As we climbed the steps, I noticed a frail old man trimming the hedge that hugged the porch.

Silas paused and greeted the shriveled gardener with a polite, "Good afternoon, Javier."

The feeble man lifted a snowy-white head and peered at us through glazed, vacant black eyes. I stared at him, intrigued. He had a gentle face with thin, mottled skin stretching over fine, angular bones. His rimless bifocals slipped low on his nose as he raised his shaggy brows in a quizzical frown. He spoke through pursed lips, a slight quiver in his voice as he asked anxiously, "What day is this? What day?"

"Tuesday," said Silas tolerantly. "We have some guests, Javier," he added, nodding toward David and me.

The elderly fellow gazed blankly at us, then turned away, his shoulders stooped, and shuffled back to his hedge.

"What a sad old man," I said. "He looks too weak to be working."

"Javier has been around here for years," explained Silas. "He was the original gardener and caretaker of the Cobranza estate, but now he's just a harmless, senile old man."

"Does he live here at the hotel?"

"Right. Esteban Medina, the hotel manager, insists on keeping him on because of his years of loyal service to the Cobranzas. He gets free room and board in the gardener's cottage out back."

"Then he doesn't have to work?" I asked with concern.

"No, ma'am. He just putters around in the garden for hours

every day. Seems to get some pleasure out of it."

David and I matched Silas' energetic stride, passing through the open double doors of Windy Reef into an enormous, ornately decorated lobby. The walls were wainscoted in oak with crown moldings. A wide spiral staircase graced the left side of the lobby while an open, nineteenth century gold elevator occupied the opposite corner. Lacquered bamboo ceiling fans revolved slowly overhead, stirring the sluggish air. Casual groupings of rattan sofas and chairs created a cool, homey aura—cushioned mandarin love seats, oval swing chairs, hand-crafted wicker rockers, and squat cocktail tables. The breezy furnishings were accented by dozens of natural rattan hanging planters and bamboo wind chimes.

Finally my eyes riveted on a huge, antique-framed oil portrait that consumed an entire wall—the fragile, haunting image of a beautiful young bride. I lingered, transfixed, as the painting flamed my imagination. Because I, too, was a new bride, I felt as if I knew this woman, shared a common bond with her. She sat regally in a mahogany chair, dressed in a floor-length wedding gown with a ruffled bodice and flowing lace sleeves. She was a small, full-figured woman with a long, graceful neck. A bejeweled, heart-shaped locket nestled against her breastbone. Her shiny black hair was swept back, fan-shaped, and fastened with a gold, jeweled conch shell. Her face possessed the smooth, untouched innocence of a child, her skin creamy and flawless. But her eyes revealed the budding passion of a woman in love.

"Michelle, are you coming?" David's voice echoed hollowly across the spacious lobby.

I turned reluctantly, feeling somehow dazed by the captivating face in the portrait. I joined David and Silas at the registration desk. "That woman in the picture—who is she?"

"The woman I told you about—Ricardo Cobranza's wife Alejandra."

"You mean, the Colombian woman who was disfigured in the fire?"

"One and the same. A shame, isn't it? She was one good-looking dame," mused Silas. But he was all business again as he introduced David and me to the brawny, swarthy-faced man behind the desk. "This is Esteban Medina, Windy Reef's executive administrator."

At first glance, Medina's face seemed alarmingly distorted, his features blunt and exaggerated—a large head capped with thick, ebony hair and bushy brows sprawled across a knobby forehead. His enormous nose meandered down his face, stopped only by the black swath of his bristly mustache. His chin was lost in a short, cropped beard. "Welcome to Solidad, Mr. and Mrs. Ballard," he boomed.

I gingerly extended my hand. "We're delighted to be here."

"The bridal suite is ready for you," Medina replied, crushing my fingers in his powerful hand. As he gazed at me, I noticed that his heavy eyelids drooped jarringly over his wideset, olive-black eyes. One eye, distinctively larger than the other, seemed to bore into me with mystical scrutiny. "You'll find much happiness here in Solidad," he assured me in a deep, gravelly voice. "If you have any problems, my door is always open. Feel free to drop by anytime."

His spontaneous smile softened his ill-favored features. I relaxed a little. "Thank you, Mr. Medina," I replied as David signed our names in the guest registry.

Silas scooped up two of our suitcases. "I'll take them up," he told Medina.

"No need, Winters," Esteban answered. "I'd like you to stay here until the desk clerk gets back."

"I usually don't take the desk, Medina," Silas said caustically. There was a glint of contempt as their eyes met. "If you don't want me to see our guests to their room, I have other work to do."

Except for a barely perceptible twitch of Medina's mustache, he remained professionally polite. "Yes, of course," he acknowledged coolly. "Yes, please feel free to attend to your other assignments."

Silas Winters replaced our luggage abruptly on the polished mahogany floor, gave us a curt nod, and stalked out the lobby door. I watched him take two porch steps at a time, then halt beside the hedge to talk with Javier, the gardener.

"Mrs. Ballard," Medina's voice drew me back. "Don't worry about Winters. He's a volatile fellow—independent and stubborn—"

"If he's so insolent, why do you. . .?"

"Why do I keep him? He's a good worker. . . and a charmer with the ladies. Our guests like that." Esteban picked up a key. "I'll show you to your suite."

"But the desk clerk—" I began.

"No matter. Winters won't be far out of sight. If there's a problem, he'll tend to it. He doesn't miss much."

Medina snapped his fingers at a barefoot bellhop with kinky black hair. The youngster, in an embroidered shirt and Bermuda shorts, came at once and loaded our luggage on a cart. Medina dropped our room key in the boy's hand and said, "The bridal suite in the east wing."

"Sir?" the lad hesitated, a flicker of apprehension on his face.

"The east wing," Medina repeated.

The bellhop stood his ground, his eyes wide as saucers.

"Something wrong?" David inquired.

"Nothing you can change," Esteban confided. "Superstition is nebulous, hard to deal with. Send these boys anywhere in the hotel but the bridal suite."

The young bellhop shuddered. "Cara de Muerte," he mumbled, pushing the cart reluctantly toward the elevator.

"Is he talking about the Cobranza legend?" I ventured.

Medina fell into step beside us as we followed the boy toward the elevator. "There's no legend," Medina snapped. "A rich man built this mansion for the woman he loved. Nothing more."

"You sound so certain, Mr. Medina."

"I am. I grew up on the island."

"Then you knew the Cobranzas?" I asked excitedly.

"Yes. Ricardo Cobranza and my father, Juan Medina, were friends. They came to Solidad together when they were young. My father managed the Windy Reef Hotel until his death three years ago."

I hesitated, mulling over something Silas Winters had said earlier. Haltingly I said, "Your Mr. Winters mentioned—he said Ricardo Cobranza jumped to his death from the east wing of the mansion. He didn't mean the bridal suite, did he?"

"The bridal suite is only part of the east wing, Mrs. Ballard."

"But the bridal suite," I persisted. "Mr. Winters says it juts out over the ocean—"

"And you're wondering if Sr. Cobranza leaped from its balcony?"

I nodded, feeling suddenly foolish as the elevator door opened.

"No one knows for sure. They never found his body."

I shuddered as Esteban ushered us into the quaint antique enclosure, then squeezed in with us, his taut, muscular frame towering above me. The embossed metal doors clanged shut, then the elevator lurched and quivered as we began the slow ascent to the second floor. We were standing inside a gold gilded cage with a full, dizzying view of the hotel lobby.

I cowered against David. "I'll take the stairs from now on."

"Mrs. Ballard," offered Medina, "the elevator is the only way to the sun deck over the east wing. The deck is private and the view splendid. From one side you can see our calm and beautiful Cobranza Bay, and from the other side, the swift and violent Atlantic Ocean."

I nodded perfunctorily, but my mind wasn't on the view from the sun deck. Through the open grill of the elevator I caught a fleeting glimpse of Silas Winters in the lobby below. He was standing by the beveled glass entryway to the dining room, staring up at us with a dark, disquieting intensity.

CHAPTER
SEVEN

After showing us the east wing, Esteban Medina left David and me in front of the bridal suite, the gold key to the room conveniently in the latch. We lingered, watching Esteban disappear down the long corridor in quick, easy strides, his back erect, his raven hair clipped evenly at the neck. He turned at the end of the hall, gave us a spontaneous wave, then stepped back into the elevator and was gone.

"At last, Michelle, we have the world to ourselves!" David exclaimed, embracing me.

"Not exactly," I smiled, pointing across the hall. "Mr. Medina told us he's expecting guests in both of those rooms."

"Not until Thursday morning. David removed the key from the door and turned the knob with a flourish. "So, forget the neighbors, my darling."

"Even the family at the end of the hall?" I teased.

"The Marshalls?" David repeated, his eyes twinkling mischievously. "Esteban said they're part of the staff, Michelle. They'll respect our privacy."

"I certainly hope so, David," I whispered.

Impulsively, David scooped me up in his arms and crushed me against him. I nestled happily against his chest as he pushed open the door and carried me over the threshold into the bridal suite. He whirled me around and set me on my feet, exclaiming, "Take a look at this layout, Michelle!"

I gazed around in astonishment past the three-panel decorative rattan screen that separated the half-circle entryway from the spacious living room. "It's an entire apartment, David. I was expecting a—a bedroom!"

"I'm sure it's got that too," David said in his most seductive voice.

"But this is incredible—so huge and luxurious!" The whole room was charming and informal, richly understated, the furnishings of natural rattan done in a warm, butternut-stain finish. I flitted around the room like an exuberant child, running my fingers over the bronze-colored plate glass coffee table, testing the thickness and comfort of the camel-cushioned sofa and love seat, fingering the soft, shiny foliage of a palm plant in its stand-up brass tub in one corner of the room.

A breakfast nook table with wicker armchairs stood near a window that looked out on a balcony with a panoramic view of the ocean. A large glazed vase full of freshly cut flowers—wild orchids, fire-red African tulips, and star-shaped frangipani blossoms—sat in the middle of the table.

I was looking for a way out to the balcony when David's deep chuckle stopped me. He was surveying our surroundings from an armchair, his legs stretched out comfortably on the matching ottoman. "Apparently you like it here," he remarked, amused.

"Oh, David, I love it."

He pulled himself leisurely to his feet, strolled over and enveloped me in his arms. "Shall we check out the bedroom now?"

David released me and pushed open the swinging bamboo doors to the master suite—a gargantuan room with an imposing king-size canopy bed of stunning brass and rattan. A bright Gauguin painting of Tahitian natives graced one wall. Louvered white shutters were folded back from the sliding glass door to give an unobstructed view of the Atlantic. David and I crossed the polished hardwood floor and entered an immense bath and dressing room. The bath area sported a sunken heart-shaped marble tub and jacuzzi, double sinks with antique gold fixtures, and wall-to-wall mirrors.

Back in the bedroom, David slid open the door that led to

the open veranda. We stepped outside and looked over the white pillared railing onto rows of glistening villas that dotted the hillside like a terraced garden of gardenias. In the distance beyond was Cobranza Bay, fishing vessels and schooners bobbing in her tranquil waters. Directly below our bedroom, lush, tropical gardens surrounded the hotel's oval swimming pool where hotel guests swam or relaxed in umbrella-shaped lounge chairs. Some distance from the pool, almost hidden by palm trees, was a stone walkway winding around the flower beds to a quaint, vine-covered cottage.

"David, do you think that's the gardener's cottage?" I asked.

"Michelle, I'm new around here too," he said with a twinkle. "But it could be Javier's little hideaway. I'm sure you'll find out soon enough."

We explored to the corner of the building and found to our delight that our balcony extended along the back wall of our bridal suite. David and I leaned gingerly over the railing where our private veranda jutted out precariously over the blue, windswept Atlantic. Tamarind Bluff was both awesome and terrifying. The cliffs stretched out as far as we could see— gigantic limestone masses with deep, muted shades of brown and purple along the coast where the late afternoon sun carved its shadows. Toward the horizon, the ocean seemed almost still, at peace with the luminous sky and placid Solidad. But as those gentle distant waves dipped and rolled toward shore, they gained momentum, hitting the ragged rocks with a ferocious intensity, crashing, erupting against eroded cliffs, clawing out grottoes, the remnant spray showering us even as we stood on the balcony.

"No wonder they didn't find his body," I breathed, staring down into the dark, swirling waters.

"What?" David scrutinized me with a half-amused frown.

I shivered. "You know. Sr. Cobranza."

"That again? Can't we let the poor old man rest?"

I stepped back from the railing. "David, I want to go inside."

"Wait, Michelle, look over there."

I shaded my eyes as I scanned the coastline. Far to the left lay a large inlet sheltered by volcanic rocks where a small stretch of sandy-white beach and untroubled waters formed a picturesque cove.

"I bet that's Paradise Cove," said David.

"Maybe tomorrow we can get into our bathing suits and hike over with a picnic lunch."

"A picnic maybe. But no swimming."

"Why not, David?"

"The undertow. The tides. It's deceptively calm."

"Why isn't there a stretch of beach all along the cliffs?"

"There probably is—when the tide's out."

"But the Atlantic doesn't disturb Paradise Cove?"

"Apparently not. There's probably a natural barrier reef out there taking the ocean's fury."

"Leaving the cove just for us?"

"I think you can say that."

As we returned to the bridal suite, I said, "We'd better unpack and get dressed for dinner."

"No need," David answered. "I asked Mr. Medina to send dinner up. Candles, lobster on the half shell and all. Tonight is ours."

I eased into David's arms and assumed my most provocative tone. "Shall I slip into something comfortable?"

He nuzzled my neck. "Please do, darling."

● ● ●

With no telephones or wake-up calls, David and I slept almost until noon the next day. We rose, dressed leisurely, and went downstairs to the dining room for a late brunch. We were seated at a table for two near the window. We were eating sliced bananas with coconut cream when, suddenly, a small boy came scampering across the room and flung himself into David's arms.

"Whoa, what's this?" David exclaimed as the chubby arms clutched his neck.

"Uncle David, Uncle David!" the child trilled.

"Hey, Tiger, you rascal!" cried David. "Where in the world did you come from?"

I stared in speechless disbelief. Little Stevie Turman—Jackie's son! Was it possible? "David," I uttered. "What—how?"

The flaxen-haired four-year-old turned and pointed across the dining room. His dark eyes danced. "Mommy—Daddy—there."

I looked to my right and blinked, stunned. There sat Jackie and Steve Turman, looking our way. My eyes locked with Jackie's. I moved, began to spring up, but David seized my hand.

"Wait, Michelle. Don't blow their cover."

"But it's Jackie—!"

"No, don't say a word. Let them make the first move."

I stiffened, forcing my gaze back to David. "What are they doing here?"

"That's exactly what I'd like to ask Joshua Kendrick right now," replied David quietly.

"He must know they're here."

"Of course he knew. And now I'm beginning to . . ."

"What, David? What's going on?"

Stevie squirmed around and wiggled out of David's arms. He clasped my hand. "Come see Mommy."

I looked helplessly in Jackie's direction. She and Steve were already walking our way. Jackie's delicate oval face was serious and unsmiling, her sinuous frame moving gracefully around the tables. She was as elegant and flawless as ever in a wishbone-slim halter dress. Steve, tall and slender in tennis shirt and slacks, touched her elbow protectively. A sober, sandy-haired man, Steve still possessed the dark, haunted eyes I so vividly remembered from our days in Morro Bay. Now, however, he boasted a healthy golden-brown tan and a more confident gait than I expected after his exhausting months of testimony in the West Coast cocaine trial.

Before I could utter a word to Jackie, Steve hoisted his son into his arms and announced in a booming voice, "I'm sorry if my little boy bothered you." He extended his free hand to David. "I'm Steve Marshall and this is my wife, Jackie."

Jackie gazed at me, her eyes urgent, entreating, registering more than either of us could say. "My son—he loves meeting new people."

"No problem," David assured her. "We're getting along just fine, aren't we, Tiger?"

"I show you my toys?" Stevie shook the blond curls from his eyes. "We play with my yellow goose."

David's eyes moistened suddenly. "Yeah, kiddo, I'd like

that." He gazed up at Steve and Jackie. "Maybe we can get together sometime—swimming, a picnic? We're in the bridal suite upstairs."

"We—we'd like that, wouldn't we, Steve?" urged Jackie.

He nodded uncertainly. "The staff doesn't usually mix with the guests—"

"Then you work here?" I asked.

"Yes. I'm assistant to the concierge."

"Not Silas Winters," I blurted.

"One and the same," said Steve. "You've met him?"

"He brought us to the island."

"I see." Steve glanced around stealthily. "We can't talk here."

"Then, our room, Mr. Marshall?" suggested David. "A half hour?"

"We'll be there."

CHAPTER EIGHT

We had been back in the bridal suite for over an hour when I turned to David and asked anxiously, "What time is it? The Turmans are late."

"The *Marshalls*, Michelle." He glanced at his shiny new pocket watch. "It's five minutes later than the last time you asked."

I stopped pacing the living room. "David, I can't believe Jackie is actually here—on Solidad. It's wonderful, incredible!"

"It's too perfect, Michelle."

"You sound almost angry, suspicious," I said accusingly. "Aren't you glad to see them?"

"You know I am."

"Then why don't we go look for them? Mr. Medina said the Turmans—I mean the *Marshalls*—live on this floor."

"Convenient, isn't it?" David was obviously agitated. "It's all too pat, Michelle. Like it was prearranged."

"David, I don't understand you. A week ago I thought I'd never see Jackie again. And now she's here in the same hotel with us."

David studied me from across the room, his gaze deliberate, critical. "Michelle, I am glad to see them, but not under these circumstances."

"Please, David, don't begrudge me my happiness," I pleaded,

my lower lip trembling. "Jackie's my best friend."

"Michelle, Michelle." David strolled over to me and tipped my chin toward him. "Don't be upset with me, honey." I started to pull away, but he held me firm and urged, "Stop a minute and think. Forget the excitement of seeing Jackie again. . ."

"But I can't," I fretted.

"Reason it out, Michelle. Do you think it's coincidental that we're on this island with the Turmans? Of all the places in the world where the DEA could have relocated them. . ." He pursed his lips and blew out angrily. "How I allowed us to get into this, I'll never know. We shouldn't even be here. We should be sunning ourselves on the beach of Waikiki!"

"Then you're not just angry," I said with growing comprehension. "You're really worried."

David's expression was so intense, his tone so brittle, I felt alarmed. "Someone wanted us here on Solidad badly enough to pay our way, wanted us here with the Turmans."

"But who?" I whispered.

"I was thinking about that all through breakfast."

"That's why you deliberately stalled in the dining room after Steve and Jackie left?"

A funny little perplexed scowl cut deeply between David's brows, sending waves of wrinkles across his sunburnt forehead. The jagged battle scar along his chin pulsated. "If anyone was watching, I wanted them to know the Ballards were in no hurry, that we had plenty of time on our hands."

"Then that's why we took a leisurely stroll around the lobby after breakfast?"

"You're catching on."

"And here I thought you had taken a sudden interest in Alejandra Cobranza's portrait."

His eyes twinkled. "Well, she is a beautiful woman."

"*Was*, David. She's dead, remember?"

"Well, I figured if we lingered in the lobby awhile, we'd look harmless enough, just in case. . ."

"I know Mr. Medina saw us. He waved. But with all the guests there, who would really care what we were doing?"

"Perhaps no one. Or perhaps our honeymoon benefactor." David was serious again. He pressed my head against his chest. "I don't want to alarm you, Michelle, but I'm convinced Solidad wasn't just a friendly little wedding present."

I looked up at him. "But Josh Kendrick saw no problem with our accepting the gift. Surely if he had thought there were questionable motives behind it—"

"My mind keeps going back to Morro Bay," said David. "We got involved in something sinister there. Unwittingly, I know. But if we hadn't gone to visit your friend Jackie, Clarence Harvey and his cocaine syndicate would still be operating freely on the West Coast."

"But, David—"

"Wait, Michelle. Hear me out. Ever since Morro Bay, we've taken satisfaction in knowing that Clarence Harvey, Royce Adams, and the others are behind bars where they belong. They killed Josh's friend Paul Mangano, and exploited thousands with their illegal drug trafficking. They've ruined many families, the Turmans included."

"But Steve wanted out. He turned state's evidence against Harvey—"

"We both know that. But I never stopped to realize that as far as Clarence Harvey is concerned, you and I are partly responsible for him being in prison."

I shuddered. "Then you suspect retaliation from the syndicate?"

David gripped me tighter. "I wondered about that at first, but Kendrick wouldn't have taken that chance and allowed us to come here, unless. . ."

"Unless what?"

"Unless Kendrick himself was involved."

"Then you're saying—?"

"I don't know exactly how, but I think Kendrick, the government, or the DEA sent us here for a purpose. Perhaps it even has something to do with the computer project Joshua mentioned."

"That's crazy, David. Besides, Josh denied having anything to do with our trip to Solidad."

"Kendrick has a job to do, Michelle. He'd do—or say—whatever he felt was necessary to accomplish his purposes."

"But what right would he have to interfere with our honeymoon?"

"None whatever. But Kendrick doesn't walk with a conscience. If he didn't care about his own honeymoon, he certainly wouldn't have qualms about rearranging ours."

The minutes ticked on. Five. Ten. Fifteen. David tugged at his pocket watch. "An hour and a half late already," he remarked.

"Oh, David, do you suppose something's happened to them?"

"No, Michelle. There's no reason to suspect—"

Suddenly, there was the gentlest tap at the door. David answered promptly and ushered Steve and Jackie into the room with a briskness born of wariness and concern. While Steve and David shook hands with a polite formality, Jackie and I flew into each other's arms, laughing and weeping at once. "Oh, Jackie," I cried, "when you were relocated, I was afraid I'd never see you again!"

"Me too!" she exclaimed. "This is a dream come true." She stepped back and faced me squarely, her fragile china features about to break, etched with pain and remorse. "I'm so sorry about missing your wedding, Michelle. I never meant to disappoint you—" She swallowed, choking back the rest of her apology.

"I know, I know. Joshua explained everything."

"He wouldn't let me call—he said it wasn't wise."

"He was right," I agreed. "Come sit down." I led Jackie over to the sofa where we collapsed together, still holding hands.

Steve pulled over a chair from the breakfast nook and sat beside Jackie. He appeared awkward, uneasy. The confidence he had exuded in the dining room was gone now.

David took the lounge chair, kicking the ottoman out of the way. He leaned forward, listening intently. "Where's Tiger?" he asked.

"Down for a nap," said Jackie. "We had to find a sitter. That's why we're late."

"You found someone reliable?" I asked.

"Yes. Esteban Medina's wife, Lucia. She's watched Stevie before. She loves children. She doesn't have any of her own."

I looked closely at Jackie. "Tell me how you are—how you really are."

Jackie shook her head wearily. In spite of her impeccable good looks, there was a strain in her face I'd never seen before. Her usual vibrant eyes were shadowed with—what? Worry? Exhaustion? Frustration? "You just don't know, Michelle," she sighed distractedly. "This whole experience has been so devastating. Can you imagine? To be told that you must suddenly wipe out your past, forget your entire identity, and pretend to be someone else—how can the DEA expect a person to just step into some role they've concocted, to pretend things—everything—not just occasionally before a few people, but forever, before everyone, living a lie—"

I squeezed Jackie's hand consolingly. "Oh, Jackie, I've lived through the whole harrowing experience with you in my heart. You don't have to pretend now, not for David and me—"

"But don't you see? Now you'll have to pretend, too—pretend you don't know us, pretend—" Jackie's shoulders shook involuntarily. "Oh, it's hardest on little Stevie. He doesn't know what's happening. He doesn't understand why we've whisked him away from everything familiar. He's only four. We have to hold our breath that he doesn't say something, do something to blow our cover—"

"But surely you're safe here," I soothed. "From what I've seen so far, people on the island seem to live such anonymous lives. It's like being at the end of the world, or in a fantasy land—"

"But Michelle, I've been so lonely, so miserable here." Jackie looked over at Steve with apology in her eyes. "It's not Steve's fault. We've both been so—oh, how can I tell you?—the way we were uprooted, sent here without time for proper good-byes, literally fleeing for our lives—Michelle, you wouldn't believe—"

Steve nodded soberly. "It hasn't been easy for Jackie living with a man marked for execution."

David looked at Steve. "Are you at liberty to tell us what happened? Was there a breach in security? Why did the DEA consider the witness protection program your only way out?"

"Because they learned my name was high on the syndicate's hit list. Through all my months as a professional witness in the cocaine trial, Clarence Harvey vowed he'd get even with me somehow. Even though he's in a high-security prison, he must have found a way."

Steve glanced at Jackie. "I suggested to the DEA that Jackie and Stevie go live with her parents in Switzerland. They'd be safer that way." His voice caught. "But Jackie wouldn't go for it—"

"Did you choose Solidad?" I asked.

"Choose it?" Steve retorted. "We never even heard of it. We just got in the car and headed for the airport for Jackie's flight to Chicago. We were taken to the far end of the field and whisked away on a helicopter while armed DEA agents stood guard."

"We left everything behind except for the clothes on our back and a couple of suitcases," continued Jackie tremulously. "They wouldn't even let us take Stevie's baby book or our wedding album."

Steve picked up the story. "We transferred to a private plane at some honky-tonk airstrip in Arizona. On board they gave us our new identifications—the *Marshall* family. New birth certificates. New social security numbers. High school diplomas from somewhere we never even heard of." He rubbed the back of his neck and stretched stiffly. "That night at a hotel in Florida they grilled us on our background, our new personal histories. They installed a panic button in our room and placed agents outside our door. I never slept. I kept my finger an inch from that button all night."

Steve twisted his wide wedding band in mindless agitation. "They rolled us out of bed before sunup, put bullet-proof vests on us, and sped us to another airport for the final flight here."

"We knew before the wedding that you were safely out of the country," David told him.

"Yeah," Steve muttered. "In just a couple of days the Turmans ceased to exist and we became the Marshalls. I stepped into the position of assistant concierge here at Windy Reef, working under Silas Winters—his little errand boy. But there's just one thing that bothers me, David."

"What's that, Steve?"

"Joshua told us we'd never see anyone we knew again. *Ever*. And then you two appear. I don't like it."

"We don't either," David answered. "I keep thinking, if the four of us are actually here together on this anonymous little island in the middle of the Caribbean, then anything's possible."

"So how did it happen?" asked Jackie. "What brought you two here? What incredible circumstances?"

"I think it was *someone*," replied David, sounding more than a little perturbed. "Joshua Kendrick, to be exact."

Steve broke in, an undercurrent of anxiety in his voice. "It has something to do with the cocaine trial, doesn't it?

Something to do with the government witnesses being picked off like flies."

"You may be right," said David. "Before the wedding, Joshua approached me about a computer assignment. I agreed to take a stab at it after our honeymoon, but there was certainly no mention of our being spirited off to some tropical island." He hesitated. For a minute I thought he would tell them about our anonymous wedding present. Instead, he said calmly, "It looks like we were intended to see one another again, Steve."

A bewildered, guarded expression crossed Steve's face, momentarily giving his skin a dusky color. "You mean, you think your God arranged this?"

David's gaze never flickered. "Steve, you already know that we pray for you and Jackie. More than ever now that all of this has happened to you. The government can relocate you, Steve. They can build up a wall of security as solid as Tamarind Bluff. But in the end, only God can be your stronghold."

"Yeah, you could be right," Steve said, his eyes downcast.

"I've been doing what you suggested, Michelle," Jackie said tentatively, "reading my Bible and praying. Maybe while you're here, we can talk, pray together."

"I'd love that," I told her.

"We could take in church together on Sunday," said David. "You too, Steve."

"No way," replied Steve. "There's no church on Solidad."

Jackie spoke up. "That's one of the things that bothers me about the island, Michelle. No churches, no hospitals, no post office, no contact with the outside world. Steve and I—we feel as if we're suspended in time, cut off from reality. You'll notice it too. There's an eerie unreality about this place. Oh, sure, it's beautiful and sumptuous and glamorous, but there's something disconcerting about this entire island—the hotel itself—it gives me the creeps. And the people—some of them—well, you've already met Silas Winters. He's so impertinent, elusive, remote—an egotistic bachelor who fancies himself a real ladies' man. I don't trust him."

"That's how I felt about him, Jackie—anything but charmed."

"And then there's the doctor—"

"Doctor?" I echoed.

"Dooley Edington. He's a retired American doctor, the island's only physician. Just don't ever get ill, Michelle. Doc's a lush, plain and simple. Every night he drinks himself under the table—it's tragic, a real waste."

"He's friendly enough, and knowledgeable," said Steve. "He claims to have been an emergency room doctor in the States. Why he ever came here—who knows? Maybe he wanted to escape the rat race—"

"What Steve's really worried about is Stevie's asthma—and mine. And then there's . . ." She looked questioningly at Steve. "Can I tell them?"

"Tell us what?" I asked.

Steve nodded. "Go on. They'll find out soon enough."

Jackie beamed. "I'm three months pregnant."

"Oh, Jackie—a baby? How wonderful!" I reached over and embraced her. We clasped hands like sentimental schoolgirls. "No wonder you're concerned about medical facilities on the island!"

Jackie gazed tearfully at me. "Oh, Michelle, it'll be all right now with you here. I'll make it after all."

"But I'm no midwife!" We hugged again and reached for tissues to wipe our eyes.

I realized then that David had drawn Steve over to the window. The two were looking out and talking quietly, with serious undertones. I knew David had no intention of my hearing, but I got up anyway and walked over and heard Steve say, "What do you make of it all, David? Why are we here like this—the four of us?"

"I don't know," replied David. "I just know it's no accident."

The severity of David's expression made me shiver inside. For an instant I thought of saying, *Let's go home—tonight, tomorrow!* But then I glanced back at Jackie—so fragile, a baby on the way, her eyes filled with such gratitude to have us here. I was convinced we'd have to see this through to the end— whatever we'd gotten ourselves into, or whatever *someone else—unknown*—had lured us into.

Steve pivoted and walked over to Jackie. "We really need to go now, Jacqueline. Stevie will be frightened if he wakes up and we're not there."

As we walked them to the door, I asked Jackie, "What about

your parents? Do they know where you are?"

"Only that we had to leave the States."

I gave Jackie a quick hug. "We'll talk later."

She nodded, her eyes tearing again. "But don't forget, we're the Marshalls now. In public we can never talk about Hopewell College or Morro Bay..."

"Or about our popcorn escapade in college, when we popped a whole jar and blanketed the laundry room with crunchy white kernels?"

Jackie stifled a laugh. "That too."

Steve motioned for silence as David opened the door. The Marshalls stepped out into the hallway. "It was nice to meet you both, Mr. and Mrs. Ballard," Steve said formally, shaking David's hand. He raised his voice and added, "Please let us know if there's anything we can do to make your stay more comfortable."

"We appreciate your hospitality," David answered congenially.

Was I mistaken or had David raised his voice too, so that the stranger who had just stepped out of the room across the hall could hear him?

The man—tall, barrel-chested and fortyish—balanced a bottle under one arm. He locked his door, then turned and gazed briefly our way. He had a long, coppery, hangdog face, a high, shiny forehead and gray-streaked brown hair slicked neatly to one side. Ragged brows hugged his small, intense, ball-bearing eyes. He gave us a passive, benevolent nod, then headed for the elevator. As he ambled by us in an almost tipsy gait, I caught the pungent smells of Old Spice and rum. Close up, the man's features were angular and pronounced—an elongated, slightly bulbous nose, high, deep-set cheekbones and an after-five shadow on his cleft chin.

"Good afternoon, Dr. Edington," Steve greeted pleasantly.

I looked quizzically at Jackie and mouthed the words, "That's your doctor?"

She grimaced mildly and quipped, "That's him—the illustrious, inebriated Dooley Edington himself."

CHAPTER NINE

When I awoke on Thursday morning, David was sitting at the desk going through his briefcase, his expression sober, preoccupied. I slipped out of bed and tossed my silk robe over my shoulders. Barefoot, I pattered over to his chair and wrapped my arms enticingly around his neck. "I should have known you couldn't stay away from business for long," I purred, "but maybe I can distract you for a little...monkey business?"

David glanced up, his expression troubled. "I'm sorry, Michelle. Not now, please."

I drew back, wounded. David as quickly reached out and pulled me onto his lap. He kissed me on the cheek and brushed my sleep-tangled hair back from my face. "Michelle, darling, a few minutes ago I would gladly have taken you up on your offer, but now...I just found this in my briefcase." He picked up a tissue-thin letter and handed it to me.

"What is it? Problems at your office?"

"No. The letter's from Joshua Kendrick."

"How did it get in your briefcase?"

"Joshua obviously has his ways. He was in my room when I was getting ready for the wedding. He even carried my luggage down to the car for me."

"So what earthshaking message does he have for us?" I quipped.

"Read it for yourself."

It took me a moment to adjust to Joshua's slanted scrawl. "Dear David," I read aloud. "As we discussed recently, the underworld has broken the government's code and seized information aiding them in tracking down and murdering many witnesses worldwide. It's my hope that you can originate a sophisticated software program that will safeguard the international network of governmental witnesses and agents. Because of the urgency of the situation, I arranged for your honeymoon on Solidad where you can work in safety and secrecy. As I am sure you realize, island-hopping in Hawaii would not have provided optimum conditions for completing this high-priority project.

"When you reach Solidad, you will find that the computer equipment has already been set up for you, with full instructions for how to proceed." I silently scanned two pages of technical information, then read aloud the last paragraph, where Joshua had started a sentence and crossed it out. He wrote instead, "I don't mean to paint you into a corner, David, but everything is ready to roll at Windy Reef. You'll find your way behind the white sands of Tahiti. Good luck! I'll be in touch. Sincerely, Josh."

I stared up in astonishment at David. "Why in the world did Josh send a letter like this all the way to Solidad? What if someone else had found it?"

"I don't think he intended for it to come this far. Joshua no doubt expected us to find the letter when we reached Lake Michigan."

"What are you going to do about this, David?" I asked warily.

He shrugged. "I already accepted the assignment—back at your place. If Joshua really expected us to find this letter at Lake Michigan, he was offering us a chance to back out. Our coming to Solidad no doubt implied our approval."

"Approval nothing!" I scoffed. "I bet you anything he was banking on our not finding the letter until we arrived here."

"I don't know, Michelle. That makes it pretty risky."

"It sure does," I sighed irritably. I glanced around. "So just where is the computer equipment?"

"It has to be here in the hotel. As far as I know, Windy Reef has the only electricity on Solidad."

"What's Josh think we're on—a scavenger hunt? Are we supposed to ask Esteban Medina where the computer is?"

"No way," said David.

"How about Silas Winters, the charmer?" I teased.

"Be serious, Michelle. The answer must be in the letter." David drew in a breath and shook his head. "Strange. Josh mentioned Tahiti, but Tahiti's not in the Caribbean."

"You're right, David." I opened the letter and read again, "You'll find your way behind the white sands of Tahiti."

"He could at least have said the white sands of Solidad."

I scanned the room again, baffled, then slipped off David's lap and walked to the opposite wall. "I've got it, David! Josh meant what he said. Look—Gauguin's painting. It's a beach scene."

"What's that got to do with anything?"

"Plenty, I bet. Most of Gauguin's paintings are of Tahiti." David's dark eyes flashed with interest. He jumped up, nearly tripping over the desk chair, and shoved it out of the way. He strode over and ran his hands around the frame, then lifted the painting from the wall and leaned it against the bed. "Man, nothing behind it but a picture hook," he said in disgust. "Why can't Kendrick just be straightforward, down to earth?" He slammed his fist against the wall, then grabbed up the painting to rehang it.

"Don't wreck Gauguin," I warned. "His works are priceless."

"And my patience is limited." David reached up to stabilize the brass hook. As he turned it slightly, we heard a low, creaking sound in the wall beside the wardrobe. We stared in astonishment as one of the teakwood panels slid back, revealing a room beyond.

I clutched David's arm. "Oh, I knew this place was mysterious!"

"Okay, Sherlock, after you," David quipped.

"Let's go in together," I suggested. We stole inside. David felt along the wall for a light switch. Suddenly the room was flooded with fluorescent light, revealing a complex array of computer equipment, simple office furnishings, files, and bookcases. I jumped as the panel closed promptly behind us. "Oh, David, we're trapped!"

"Maybe not." He switched the light off, throwing us into an impalpable darkness. But only for a second. Slowly the panel opened again. "Well, we've discovered the secret—Gauguin, a brass hook, and the light switch," mused David. "How clever."

I nodded. "Joshua Kendrick's ingenuity, no doubt."

"More likely, Ricardo Cobranza's genius," countered David. "I imagine this secret room has been here since the mansion was built. But how Kendrick found out about it—"

"Josh makes it his business to know everything," I noted wryly.

David flipped the switch on again, bathing the room in a garish brightness. Again, the panel shut automatically. He seemed almost pleased. A small, boyish grin crossed his face. He walked over to the computer equipment and began examining it with careful, admiring hands. "This is incredible, Michelle. State of the art, all the way. I've rarely seen a setup like this."

"Then you're going to go for it—create the program Josh wants?"

"I'm going to give it a whale of a try. Do my absolute best."

"You sound...almost excited about it," I murmured.

David didn't hear me. He was inspecting some gadget with all sorts of knobs and keys. I stepped back toward the panel door. "I suppose you'd rather spend the day in here than on the beach?"

David gave me a swift, entreating glance. "Would you mind, Michelle?"

"No, of course not. I—I've got my romance novel to work on."

Perhaps if I'd known that David would indeed spend his entire day working in the secret room, I wouldn't have been so quick to agree. As the hours passed and I drifted aimlessly around our suite, I had visions of spending the rest of my honeymoon alone and bored. Was this what it had come down to—a lush tropical paradise at my fingertips—and my husband holed up in a cramped, windowless room?

I was pleasantly relieved when David finally showed his face at dinnertime and asked, "Are you ready to go down to the dining room?"

"I can be ready in a half hour," I told him.

"Make it 45 minutes. I want to grab a quick shower."

It was after seven when David and I strolled down the spiral staircase in our fanciest clothes—I in my rose crepe de chine gown and David in his charcoal gray tuxedo. "I feel like every eye is on us," I whispered as we crossed the lobby in sweeping strides.

"All eyes are on you," David replied with obvious pride, tucking my hand in the crook of his arm.

Just outside the wide double doors of the dining room, I spotted a striking young woman with ivory skin, red lips, and dark, fiery eyes. Her auburn, upswept hair was gathered loosely on her regal head, with burnished strands falling gracefully around her classic, sculpted face. I couldn't take my eyes off her. Neither, I noticed, could David. "Who is she?" I whispered.

"Never saw her before," David replied, adding meaningfully, "I'd remember if I had."

The woman was apparently waiting for someone. She gazed around the lobby with an irritated frown that only slightly marred her impeccable beauty. I noticed then that she held a cigarette poised between her fingers. She lifted the slender taper to her lips, inhaled deeply, and blew out a perfect ring of smoke. At that moment our eyes met. She raised one finely plucked brow and her glossy lips curled slightly.

"Looks like she recognizes us," whispered David.

"But how—?" I began.

The woman swept toward us in her strapless, black sequined gown and extended a gloved hand to David. "You're Mr. David Ballard, no?" she said in an affected, lilting voice. "Welcome to Windy Reef!"

"Thank you," replied David, obviously flattered. "This is my wife, Michelle. I'm afraid we haven't had the pleasure, Miss—?"

"Mrs. Esteban Medina. But call me Lucia, please." Her gaze passed fleetingly over me and settled again on David. "My husband has told me about you. You are from California, no? I hear so many exciting things about California. Is where they have Hollywood and movie stars—"

David chuckled indulgently. "Well, yes, but I must admit I haven't seen many movie stars—"

"I am actress," Lucia rushed on in her high, silky voice. "Before my marriage, I act in Barcelona and Madrid. I dream of Hollywood. I want to meet—you know—what they call—talent agents?"

"Well, I can't say I've run across any lately," replied David with unmistakable regret as we entered the dining room.

Lucia signaled the maitre d'. "These are my guests for dinner." She turned to David and me, still brandishing her cigarette in her long, graceful fingers. "You will join me, won't you? Esteban—he is so busy—he work too hard—he leaves me to eat alone. But tonight we get acquainted, no?"

"We'd love to, Mrs. Med—I mean, Lucia," I heard myself saying. "Actually, I just remembered where I've heard your name. You took care of Mrs. Tur—uh—Marshall's little boy yesterday."

"Why, yes!" exclaimed Lucia. "Little Stevie. Beautiful little boy! Tell me, you know Mrs. Marshall?"

I felt David's searing gaze on me. "Well, we—we met yesterday, quite by accident," I stammered. "They live just down the hall—"

"Ah, such nice people," trilled Lucia. "Mr. Marshall—he work for my Esteban. He work under Silas Winters. You meet him, no?" She nodded toward a corner table. "Mr. Winters over there . . . with Nicole. She work in hotel gift shop. They very good friends."

I glanced over at the table where Silas Winters sat absorbed in conversation with a pretty brown-skinned mulatto girl in a sensuous red sarong, her silky jet-black hair flowing over shapely bare shoulders. *Typical Silas Winters, charming the ladies*, I mused.

Before I realized it, we had reached the far end of the dining room where we were seated at an elegant, linen-draped table near a window overlooking Tamarind Bluff. While David scanned his menu, I sat in silence, still mulling over my near blunder about Jackie. Meanwhile, Lucia talked on blithely in her heavy Colombian accent. "I meet all the guests—is my only excitement on Solidad—sometimes very famous people—very rich—your vice-president, he come here once—and a man with strange name—he what you call rock-and-roll singer—very interesting fellow with hair like this—like palm leaf—and the makeup very thick on his eyes. He sing in the lounge here, very loud, with the big noise like thunder . . ."

Lucia paused as a waiter arrived to take our order. She ordered for Esteban too.

"Will your husband be here in time?" I asked.

"Perhaps. Perhaps no. If he can break away from Javier."

"You mean Javier, the gardener?"

"Yes, that one—the little old man. Esteban insists on taking his meals to him. My husband—he is very loyal. I tell my Esteban to send the old man away, but he will not hear of it."

"Doesn't Javier come to the dining room to eat?" asked David.

"Oh, no. The crowds—the noise—they confuse him. He—"

Suddenly a gruff male voice broke through the polite, restrained din of conversation around us. "Hey, I can't eat this slop! What is this—seaweed floating in my soup? Someone get me a steak! You Creoles know what a steak looks like?"

I glanced over at a nearby table where a hulking, paunchy man with a puffy face and double chin sat banging his fork on the table. "Where's some service around here?" he demanded. "I thought this was a classy joint!"

Across from the blustery, boorish man sat a plain, middle-aged woman in an expensive dress that looked somehow dowdy on her lumpish frame. Her egg-shaped face revealed thin, penciled, hairless brows and marble-cold eyes magnified by thick bifocals. Loose, drooping pouches of fat obliterated her receding jawline, as if she had recently dieted and lost a great deal of weight, leaving useless, flabby skin no longer elastic with youth. In a bizarre contradiction of images, she wore what could only be described as a bouffant, flaming apricot-orange wig that gave her the appearance of being slightly top-heavy. The woman kept patting the bulky man's hand in a futile, nervous gesture. "Orville, please, remember your heart," she hissed. "Where are your pills? Take one of your pills."

Lucia was aware of the disruptive couple now too. She paused in her rapid-fire monologue, lit up another cigarette, and looked around the dining room with a slow, appraising gaze.

Then she leaned toward me and said confidentially, "You see over there—the couple at that table? The loud man and his peculiar wife? They are our new guests. They arrive this morning. Mr. and Mrs. Glocke. How you say, little bit crazy. But very rich."

"Then he could afford a few lessons in manners," I remarked, loud enough for him to hear. I glanced back at Mr. Glocke just as he looked my way. I flinched when our eyes met. He had a florid complexion and small, disconcerting eyes buried under fleshy, drooping lids. His shaggy brows were knit in a gesture of perpetual puzzlement. Most noticeable was his immense, crazy-putty nose and cauliflower ears. Instead of the anger I expected to feel toward him, I felt a sudden stab of pity. Immediately I regretted my cutting words. Somehow I managed a half-smile in his direction. He looked away abruptly, before I could read his expression, but at least for the rest of the evening he never raised his voice to its earlier high-decibel level.

As our dinner was served, Lucia regaled us with fascinating tales of the island—hearsay and rumors about people we would never meet, bits of local color, and chilling accounts of native legends and superstitions. "Solidad is beautiful, I know," she went on earnestly, "but I would leave it all today—go home to Colombia or travel to United States. I tell my Esteban, 'Let Carlos Cobranza have his island, run his father's hotel.' But Esteban—his ties to the Cobranzas are too strong."

While Lucia talked on tirelessly, David and I consumed a sumptuous meal of fresh, exotic fruits, seafood salad stuffed with crabmeat, yams baked in cream, and curried goat stew, which we picked at rather gingerly.

At last, when I was positive I couldn't eat another bite, a waiter brought us the dessert menu. I waved him off at first, then relented and opened the menu to an insert marked SPECIAL OF THE DAY. As my eyes fell on the scrawled message under the caption, I felt the blood drain dizzyingly from my head. In stark, black letters was the warning: GET OFF THE ISLAND IF YOU WANT A LONG, HEALTHY MARRIAGE!

CHAPTER
TEN

Mornings in Solidad came earlier than they did back home, bursting on us suddenly with an explosion of sunbeams showering the bedroom through the expansive sliding glass doors. Since David insisted on leaving the louvered shutters open at night so that we could enjoy the brilliant starshine, we had awakened to the sun's warmly caressing brightness every morning this week. Now it was Saturday and again I opened my eyes to the slanting yellow rays crossing our canopy bed. I stretched leisurely and reached over for David, but he was already up, no doubt cached away in his secret computer room. Sure enough, the Gauguin painting was slightly askew.

The ominous note I had received in my menu Thursday night had unnerved me completely, but surprisingly it only served to spur David on. He was more determined than ever to remain on the island until he completed his computer project. "I won't let a cruel hoax or someone's idea of a joke intimidate me, Michelle," he insisted. But the strange anonymous note had left a cloud shadowing my feelings—it had, in fact, cast a momentary pall over paradise. I argued with myself, struggled to throw off my apprehension. I was not one to shun a mystery or turn away from an adventure. Why then was I giving in to these wordless anxieties that seized me now?

As if to negate my nebulous fears, I jumped out of bed with forced energy, resolving to pursue some daring ventures on my own. The hotel pool beneath our bedroom balcony was already a buzz of activity—guests enjoying a morning swim before breakfast. I considered joining them but didn't feel like accounting for David's absence. I meandered into the living room and peered out the window, focusing on nothing in particular until I spotted Javier in the distance, bent and alone, shuffling along the sun-washed beach close to the cliffs, his snow-white hair blowing in the wind. "So there is a stretch of beach there after all," I mused. "The tide must be out. But how did that frail man get down those steep steps to the ocean?"

My curiosity aroused, I showered and dressed quickly in shorts and a halter, scribbled a note for David, grabbed an apple from the basket on the buffet, and headed for the door. At the last minute I ran back for my sunglasses and wide-brimmed, floppy straw hat.

I took the elevator down to the lobby and slipped out the back door. A narrow, flower-edged path led to the pool, then forked off toward the cliffs, circling around a row of neatly trimmed hedges. I followed the trail past the gardener's cottage nestled among sheltering palm trees. A few feet from the cottage I found the stone steps that I had seen from our veranda. I shivered as a cool ocean breeze wafted over me. Or did I feel a ripple of fear? I glanced nervously over my shoulder. Was someone watching me? Then, feeling foolish, I began my cautious descent down the craggy steps.

As I neared the bottom stepping-stone, I flipped up the brim of my sun hat and scanned the beach. Javier was nowhere in sight. There was no one—nothing at all except an isolated strip of powdery white sand. Ocean waves, bubbling and foaming, collapsed in a final burst of energy against the shoreline, then rippled back to sea, merging with the next onslaught of waves. I felt unexpected disappointment. Why hadn't I passed Javier making his stumbling way back up the steps? As I looked up and down the beach again, my feet slipped on the sea-washed rocks at the foot of the cliff. I caught my balance just as a woman's husky voice called out, "Be careful, young lady!"

I whirled around, bracing myself on a jutting lava formation, and spotted a middle-aged woman lumbering down the path behind me in a gray cotton dress and flat, laced shoes. I waved. "Good morning!"

As she drew closer, I recognized the strange woman from the dining room the night before. Sun rays bounced off her garish bouffant hairpiece, giving the bizarre impression of a plump Florida orange perched on her head, the color clashing with her sallow face. Flecks of fine hair had blown free, but she tucked them back quickly under her wig. She was taller than I realized, bony and broad-shouldered with scar-like creases around her tightly drawn mouth. It was the sad, mirthless face of a lonely woman, old beyond her years.

I offered her my hand as she climbed down over the last slippery step, warning her to be careful.

"Thank you," she said in a precise German accent. Her grip was sturdy and powerful, but her peculiar attempt at a smile seemed detached and indifferent. She released my hand and pushed her wide leopard-toned sunglasses to the bridge of her long, prominent nose.

I flexed my fingers until I felt the circulation flow back into my hands. *What a handshake*, I mused. Aloud I said, "I'm Michelle Mer—I mean, Ballard." I laughed self-consciously. "Excuse my blunder. You see, I'm a new bride."

The woman's expression remained stoic. "I suspected as much when I saw you and your husband in the dining room last night."

"Yes, I—I noticed you, too. I understand you just checked in. In fact, I think we're neighbors. David and I are in the bridal suite in the east wing."

"Oh, well, then we are neighbors."

"I didn't catch your name," I said tentatively.

"It's Glocke. Ruth Glocke."

"And you're here on vacation?"

"You could call it that," said Ruth, her tone clipped. "My husband and I are on an extended vacation. Forced, actually. Orville has a severe heart condition and can't work for a while. His doctor told him to get away, relax, or else he may face open-heart surgery."

"I'm so sorry. It must be very difficult for you..."

Ruth's rigid expression softened slightly. "Yes, it's been very hard. Orville's condition is so debilitating he can walk only short distances. I hope he can rest on Solidad, get back his strength."

Ruth and I were strolling silently along the beach now, almost shoulder to shoulder. I wondered what to say. The woman seemed aloof, preoccupied, yet I had the distinct feeling she was studying me, sizing me up from the corner of her eye. I noticed that she walked with the vigor and purposeful stride of a much younger woman. It was a boundless energy, perhaps born of frustration over her husband's illness. She strode with her face down, her eyes scanning the tide-washed sand. She broke her pace often to pick up a shell, examine it, and tuck it into her pocket.

"You must like the beach," I mused. "I see you collect shells."

"I grew up near the beach," replied Ruth tonelessly, "a war-torn one, but a beach nonetheless. When I was growing up we didn't have toys to play with. Just seashells and pebbles."

"Your accent—did you grow up in Germany?"

She gave me a scaring glance and said, "It was during the war."

I felt her coldness, her bitterness, her pain. Groping for words, I asked, "Is that where you met your husband?"

"Yes." She turned her expressionless face my way. "He was an American G.I. stationed in West Germany as part of the peacekeeping force after the war. I was only 15, but Orville promised to take me to America if I married him." She bent down, plucked up another delicate shell, and brushed off the particles of sand.

Ruth struck me as guarded, apathetic. Yet I felt that she was telling me exactly what she wanted me to hear, like a well-rehearsed speech. "Then you've been married a long time," I remarked.

"Over 40 years." Her weary sigh stretched it to 50.

"Then your children must be grown by now."

Ruth stopped and stared me straight in the eye. Stonily she said, "We have no children. I'm barren."

I swallowed hard and looked away. "I'm sorry."

"Don't apologize. I've learned to accept it. It's Orville who's never. . ." Her voice drifted off. She stared out toward the horizon, then abruptly walked to the water's edge and kicked at a slimy string of seaweed. "I really must get back to the hotel," she declared. "Orville never remembers to take his medicine—except for his nitroglycerin tablets. He eats them like candy."

"Well, it was nice meeting you," I offered. "I'm sure we'll see lots of each other—"

"Do you go walking each morning?"

"Not really. Just this morning. I was looking for someone, and my husband—" I stopped, startled that I had almost admitted that David was at his computer.

Ruth Glocke acted as though she hadn't heard me. "Bridegrooms usually have other things in mind, besides walking." With that she turned and hurried back over the vast stretch of beach to the stone steps, her wide, solid hips swaying heavily.

I kicked off my sandals and walked on alone for another half hour, enjoying the solitude, the invigorating ocean breeze, the hot sand on my bare feet. The rhythmic sound of the waves lulled me, lured me on. Finally, reluctantly, I turned to make my way back to Windy Reef. I looked around in surprise. The beach had narrowed; the waves washed closer to my feet. I felt a dark, cloudlike warning inside. Far ahead, on the other side of the stone steps, the waves were already splashing the boulders of Tamarind Bluff.

My throat tightened. The waters were rising around me. Did high tide always come in this quickly? It was a crazy notion, but I wondered if Ruth had known the beach would be flooded shortly? If so, why had she hurried off without warning me?

With growing alarm, I picked up my pace and ran, stumbling blindly over the pocked, uneven beach back toward the hotel. The sand was wet now with castle-building dampness. Minutes later, as I approached the steps, the spumy waves were rolling in swiftly, breaking with a threatening intensity. Drenched and shivering, I tore off my sunglasses and groped frantically along the boulders toward the steps. Just short of the primitive natural rock stairway, I noticed an old tan fishing hat floating in the shallow water, inching out to sea. Javier's? I lunged for the hat, then, clutching it tenuously, scrambled up the first few stone steps on my hands and knees.

Finally I straightened and, balancing precariously, stared back at the raging Atlantic. Rushing streams of water were already covering the sands where I had just stood, bubbling foam filling in my footprints. The ocean was gathering momentum, surging, clawing at the ragged cliffs with a stormy, vengeful ferocity.

I shuddered as I realized how close I had come to being swallowed up by the waves. I stared down at the battered old fishing hat in my hand. Was it Javier's? Had he made it back safely to his cottage? Or had he wandered aimlessly, unwittingly into the water and been caught in a rip current or a sudden undertow?

There was no time to go for David. Panting, I sprinted up the rough-hewn steps and raced to the gardener's cottage. I knocked loudly, impatiently. After a moment, Javier peeked out the window. With a sigh of relief for his safety, I held up his hat and waved.

Slowly the cottage door creaked open. Javier took a halting step toward me. He lifted his timeworn face and gave me a withered, wrinkly smile. It was a sensitive face, sad and childlike. His cheeks were hollow and sunken as if he were sucking in his breath. Bushy salt-and-pepper brows crouched over his olive-black eyes.

I held out his hat to him. "I found this at the beach," I said, carefully enunciating each word.

He took the scruffy hat in his quivering hands and crushed it to him tenderly, like an old friend. Then he beckoned me inside. "Coffee. I have only coffee."

"Yes, that would be fine," I answered eagerly. I stepped inside and gazed in amazement at the tastefully decorated room with its antique cherrywood furnishings—a pedestal table with spindle-back chairs, a vintage tea wagon, brass lamps, upholstered wing chairs, and a Chippendale sofa. A sprawling bookcase covered the eastern wall.

How was it possible, I wondered, that a simple, ill-clad gardener could live in such luxury? It made no sense. "Your home—it's lovely!" I exclaimed.

Javier hung his shabby hat on a hook by the door, almost toppling as he reached up, then crossed the room in a shambling gait to the small round table by the window. I followed him.

The table was already set for two—Queen Anne bone china cups and saucers with the exquisite pattern of white dogwood and deep moss roses. I noticed dregs of dark coffee in the bottom of each cup.

"Sit down," he said, his voice raspy. He lifted the coffeepot to pour me a cup, then looked down startled, puzzled.

"Let me get some clean cups for you," I offered.

He nodded and pointed to a beautifully carved china closet near the tiny kitchenette. As I opened the cabinet doors, jarring the cherrywood shelves, the fragile crystal glasses made a tinkling melody. I breathed in the sweet, heady fragrance of fine, aged wood. Selecting two dainty lavender cups, I felt as if I were intruding on Javier's past—some special, intimate memory gone with the wings of time. I went back to the table and sat down across from Javier.

"Colombian coffee," he said as he filled my cup.

I was afraid the dark, rich brew would be bitter, but the taste was surprisingly mild. I sipped lingeringly, wanting to know this lonely gardener better. If Javier had been the original caretaker at the Cobranza estate as Silas Winters had said, then he would know more about Windy Reef and Solidad than anyone else at the hotel. If I could get beyond his memory lapses, I could learn some of the intriguing history of the island. Why not? It was obvious David intended to spend long hours at the computer, giving me ample time to track down background material for the novel I wanted to write.

"I hear you've lived on the island for a long time," I began, speaking slowly, so that Javier would understand all of my words.

"Many, many years." He clutched his cup in his tissue-thin hands, the bluish veins bulging like road maps. He stared out the window, his view blocked by thick, flowering bougainvillea bushes. "Solidad is my home," he said sadly, with a high, erratic timbre.

I tried again. "Javier, can you tell me about Windy Reef? About the Cobranzas?"

His filmy eyes darted about with a certain puzzlement, taking in the cushioned rocking chair and smoking stand near the bookcase. His eyes scanned the hefty, leather-bound volumes, then moved on to a half-open door revealing a bedroom with a canopy four-post bed. "You see Alejandra? She tell you."

"Alejandra? You mean the woman in the portrait, the bride of Ricardo Cobranza?"

Javier's voice took on a sudden, unmistakable tenderness. "Ah, she was so beautiful, like the flowers in the garden."

"Did you come to the island with the Cobranzas?"

He nodded. "Long time ago. We come from Colombia."

"Then you knew the Cobranzas well?"

Javier swallowed another mouthful of coffee, then awkwardly wiped away a trickle that meandered down his stubbly chin.

"I understand the Cobranzas have a son," I persisted. "Do you know him?"

Javier hoisted himself out of his chair and lumbered across the teakwood floor to the bookcase. He picked up a framed snapshot of three men standing before the Tower of London. "Carlos," he uttered.

I studied the photograph. The faces were blurred, indistinct. Nevertheless, I was sure I recognized the homely, irregular features of Esteban Medina.

Before I could question Javier further, there was a sharp knock on the cottage door. "Javier, open up. I'm here," came a deep, husky voice. Before Javier could respond, the knob turned and the door flew open. I caught the distinct scent of rum and Old Spice.

Dooley Edington, dressed in charcoal gray slacks and a green polo shirt, swaggered through the door, strode into the room without reeling, then stopped in his tracks when he spotted me. Edington scowled, plucking at his thick, pastry-brush mustache. His beady, smoldering eyes took me in with a sweeping glance.

When I met his gaze without flinching, he gave me a curt nod, then turned and led Javier to the Windsor chair by the table. He reached for Javier's wrist, his fingertips firm on the old man's pulse. "Nice and steady," Doc Edington said. He took a bottle from his black satchel. "Here, Javier, I brought your medication." He checked the label and tapped out two pills into Javier's unsteady hand. Then he called over his shoulder, "Perhaps you would be so good as to get us some water." He didn't look at me but I knew the crusty order was mine. When I didn't immediately comply, the physician's broad shoulders stiffened. He was miffed and I knew it, but I was concerned about the brusque way he was dealing with Javier.

Javier's uncertain gaze went from the pills to Edington's face.

"Go on," the doctor urged, thrusting a cup of coffee at him.

Slowly Javier bent his head back. His Adam's apple bobbed in his lean, fleshless neck as he took several gulping swallows.

"Good," Edington told him, placing a firm hand on the old gardener's shoulder. "I'll be back this evening." Dooley glanced scornfully my way. "I suppose your business here with Javier is over. Why don't I see you back to the hotel?"

"No need," I protested. "Javier and I were just having coffee."

"Really?" Edington challenged, turning Javier's cup upside down. "It appears that his coffee is gone. And it seems to me that you're more interested in browsing among Javier's things than in partaking of a friendly coffee klatch."

I felt a rush of anger and resentment toward the pompous, ill-mannered physician. But I was chilled, too, as his cold, calculating eyes bored through me. I realized I was still holding the photograph of the three men standing by the Tower of London. Returning the framed picture to its spot on the bookshelf, I took another hasty glance at the bearded young man who so strongly resembled Esteban Medina. "Well, I guess I should be going," I conceded, turning to Doc Edington. "Besides, David will be wondering where I am."

"Good," Edington answered, his gruff mood brightening slightly. "I want Javier to rest now." He extended his hand toward the door. "You first," he invited.

As we left the cottage, I looked back briefly. Javier was standing in the doorway, a forlorn expression on his sun-wrinkled face. I waved good-bye. He lifted one hand barely to his chest, his fingers managing only a flicker of a wave in return.

I turned and walked on with Dooley Edington the short distance back to the hotel.

"We really do frown on Windy Reef's guests fraternizing with the staff," he said.

"I see no problem," I answered defensively.

"Obviously." His tone was sour, thin-edged. "Every time I see you, you're with one of the staff."

I glanced up at him, my temper flaring. "Do you think it's appropriate for the staff to tell the guests what to do?"

A wry smile twisted at the corner of his mouth. "I'm just a little protective of my patients."

"Protective? Javier wasn't exactly enthusiastic about your visit or about taking his medicine."

"He never is. But you must understand, Mrs. Ballard, that someone in Javier's condition is quite fearful about medication."

"What condition? Is Javier seriously ill?"

"Now you're intruding on patient confidentiality." His guard eased slightly. "Surely you realize the old gentleman is senile—"

"Confused, but not—"

"Not senility?" he retorted as we entered the hotel lobby. "Do you medicate for that?"

Dooley Edington stopped and pushed the elevator button. As we waited, he rubbed his ruddy cheek, brushing against his gray-streaked sideburns. "What would you know about it, Mrs. Ballard? Have you been through a dozen years of medical training?" When the elevator arrived, he started to step in, then changed his mind. "I think I'll see if the bar is open."

I rode up alone and hurried down the corridor of the east wing, anxious to see David. I barely tapped on the door of the bridal suite when David swung the door open. "Remind me, David," I said as he swept me into his arms, "not to get sick on Solidad."

But David didn't hear me. "Michelle, I've been worried about you. Where have you been?" He brushed back my wind-tossed hair and pressed his cheek against my forehead.

"I left you a note."

"I know, I know," he said huskily, not letting me go, "but that was three hours ago."

"Three?"

He tipped up my chin. "Three hours without you, Michelle."

I pushed away. "But David, you were with your computer."

He looked momentarily hurt, rebuffed. "At least I was close by. Besides, I had a surprise for you—"

I went back into his arms. "What surprise?"

"A picnic at Paradise Cove with the Tur—the Marshalls."

"Today?"

"Two hours ago. I've been running down to their room every half hour to tell them we'd go later. Steve's been out looking for you and—" David's dark-brown eyes danced merrily. "Kikko's meter has been running for the last two hours."

"You mean Kikko and Sweet Hibiscus are here for us?"

"Uh-huh."

"I can't go like this, David. I'm a mess." I eased out of his arms again and started for the bedroom.

"You do look a bit ruffled. Where have you been, Michelle?"

"I'll tell you all about it—later."

He followed me through the swinging bamboo doors into the bedroom. I kicked off my sandals, tossed my sun hat and dark glasses on the canopy bed and headed for the dressing room. "Give me a few minutes. I'll wash and slip into something fresh for the picnic."

"I'm not letting you out of my sight again, my darling."

"Oh, really?" I whirled around. He was just behind me, his hands slipping around my waist. I laughed tantalizingly. "I'm heading for the heart-shaped tub and jacuzzi."

"So am I."

"But David, Kikko's meter—"

"He can keep it running for another half hour," David answered, following me into the bathroom and shutting the door behind us.

By 2 P.M. David and I, feeling marvelously refreshed, were on our way to Paradise Cove with Steve and Jackie. Kikko was at the reins of the surrey, nudging Sweet Hibiscus on at her rhythmic, clippety-clop pace. In the driver's seat beside Kikko, Stevie Jr. bounced on David's knee and kicked teasingly at the brimming picnic basket. I was sitting in the back between Jackie and Steve, wondering why Steve was so sullen and uncommunicative. He tried to stretch to a more comfortable

position, but there was no room. Turning my attention to
Jackie, I noticed her graceful, manicured hands resting protectively around a large brown sack.

"What's in your package?" I asked curiously. "I thought
David picked up the picnic lunch."

"He did."

"So! What are you guarding so carefully?"

Stevie Jr. peered over David's shoulder. "A surprise," he
announced. "A surprise for you and David."

"Hush, you," Jackie told him, "or it won't be a surprise."

"Ah, the mystery deepens," I smiled.

"Don't worry. All will be revealed after lunch," said Jackie.

"Just like our college days at Hopewell," I laughed. "You
never could keep a secret for very long!"

I heard Steve mutter under his breath, "Can't keep a secret?
Huh! She'd better learn. The rest of our lives has to be a secret."

"This is a picnic, Steve," admonished Jackie. "Please, let's
just have a good time and forget our problems for a while."

"Yeah, sure, forget. Easy to say, impossible to do."

In the uneasy silence that followed, Jackie asked, "So where
were you earlier today, Michelle? David was frantic. I even
had Steve looking all over for you."

"I'm sorry. I didn't mean to worry anybody. I was just
out on the beach walking—would you believe?—with Ruth
Glocke."

"You're kidding! What a strange companion she must have
made."

"Different," I admitted. "I know she's a little odd, but her
life can't be easy with that sick, complaining husband of hers."

Steve stretched uneasily. "They probably deserve each
other."

"Well, I'm glad you got back for our picnic," said Jackie.

"She almost didn't," David interjected. "She told me she
nearly got washed out to sea when the tide came in."

"Why didn't you read the warning sign, Michelle?" Jackie
scolded gently. "You're usually always so observant."

"Sign? What do you mean? There wasn't any sign, Jackie."

"Michelle, there's a sign at the top of the steps. It warns about
the tide coming in—every six hours, regular as clockwork."

"But I tell you, I didn't see any sign."

"She's right, Jackie," Steve spoke up solemnly. "When I was out looking for her, I noticed that the sign was down—pulled up by some mighty strong hands and tossed behind the hedge. I got a rock and pounded it back in place."

"But who would do that—tamper with a sign?" I asked. "Surely it doesn't mean anything. There's no connection with me—is there?"

No one replied. We slipped into another disquieting silence, watching the exotic scenery as Kikko took the leisurely route through the rustic village, past the fishing nets drying in the sun, and around the quaint little cemetery behind Kikko's house. He prodded Sweet Hibiscus along the steep Atlantic coast with its panoramic view of the ocean to the secluded, sandy white beach at Paradise Cove. The cove was nestled among the rocks, protected from the snarling ravages of the ocean, a spectacular expanse of powdery sands with an odd stretch of stunted palms swaying and bending toward the sea.

We took a boulder-strewn trail down to the beach, David balancing the picnic basket on his shoulder, Steve steadying young Stevie along the slippery rocks. Jackie and I followed, stepping cautiously among the stony crevices until we reached the hot, white sands below.

I turned, looked back up the hill, and waved at Kikko. He was already slouched in the surrey, his wide straw hat tipped forward, shading his eyes from the relentless sun.

David and I exchanged bemused glances, then dug our bare feet into the sifting sand and headed down the beach toward the thatched, fan-shaped pavilion provided by the hotel. The tropical midday sun beat down fiercely on the clear cerulean ocean and reflected on the dazzling ivory beach. Wafting palm fronds caught the only breeze.

"Wow, that sun! I'm baking already," I told Jackie.

"The pavilion will give us some protection," said Steve.

We tossed our blankets under the pavilion, doused ourselves with sunscreen, and sat relaxed, marveling over the unexpected surprises in the picnic basket: several imported cheeses cooled on chips of ice; slices of fresh watermelon, pineapple, papaya, and mangoes; an avocado that David sliced with his penknife, and a large salad bowl of pigeon peas and rice with diced red-hot peppers stirred in. There were strips of coconut

meat for dessert and a banana for Stevie, plus fresh fruit juice
and rolls baked in the Creoles' outdoor ovens.

Stevie picked at his food, finally settling on the banana that
David had peeled for him. "How about some rice, Tiger?"

Stevie approached slowly, his dark-brown eyes wide and
curious. He took the spoonful David held out, but seconds later
his startled expression turned to puckered lips and a wincing
scowl. "Yucky, David," he declared as a mouthful of peppers
and rice pelted the sand. He wiped his sticky fingers on his
clean T-shirt.

"Try him on some tropical fruit," Steve suggested.

"Don't, Steve," said Jackie. "You know he just likes bananas."

"Wouldn't hurt him to try something new."

"Strange foods might stir up his asthma."

Stevie had slipped away from David and was peering into
the picnic basket. "No jelly beans, Mommy?"

"No, darling." She reached out and brushed back his blond
curls with her long, tapered fingers.

Our eyes met, Jackie's and mine. The lobes of her ears and
her small, upturned nose were sunburned. She was dressed
so simply in a cotton sundress, it was hard to believe she had
come from a world of elegance, wealth and luxury, of country clubs and tennis courts, designer clothes and European
vacations.

As if reading my thoughts, she said softly, "Quite a change
over the old days, huh? Being anonymous does that to you."

"No, Jackie, that's not what I was thinking—"

"Sure, you were. I could see it in your eyes—a momentary
flicker. Life will never be the same. I don't mind so much for
myself, but sometimes..." Her small, determined chin
quivered.

Steve glanced over with a scowl, then looked away, his
smoldering gaze fixed on some point beyond the ridge where
the ocean swells ravaged the vulnerable lava reef.

Jackie's eyes teared as she gazed desolately at Steve. "Sometimes," she said fiercely, "I'd give anything to tuck my son
into his own youth bed with his Snoopy sheets, or help him
stuff his toys in his Captain Andy toy chest, or hold him and
read to him in our antique oak rocker..." Her voice trailed.

"It'll work out, Jackie," I said. "God didn't throw you away when you came to Solidad. He just led you in a little different direction for a while."

"Like the Israelite wanderings?" Steve asked bitterly, his eyes following the distant scudding waves. "Forty years or something like that, wasn't it?"

David scanned the beach reflectively. "You know, the Israelites would have traded their desert for this paradise any day." He leaned over and scooped Stevie up in his arms. He swooped him through the air like a Phantom jet, then dive-bombed him into his father's arms. "Steve, your life isn't over yet. Not as long as you have your wife and this young hunk of dynamite."

The pint-size "dynamite," a chubby-cheeked replica of his sandy-haired father, wrapped his arms around his daddy's neck, leaned hard against him, and toppled them both onto the sand. They came up laughing, giggling, spraying gritty sand grains as Steve burrowed his head into Stevie's tummy and growled playfully. Moments later, they were filling Stevie's beach pail with sand and running his race cars over a beach-packed roadway.

"Thanks, David," Jackie whispered. "You knew just what to do."

"My pleasure." David began gathering up the dishes for the picnic basket. "We'd better think about getting back."

"Not to your computer," I groaned.

"No." He glanced bemusedly at Kikko. "I just don't want our driver to wake up and take off without us."

"Wait," Jackie said. "I forgot your surprise." She was on her feet at once, grabbing up the mysterious parcel beside the picnic basket. "I—we—" She looked at David and me. "We're so sorry we missed your wedding. But we have a present for you. Something for you to take home when you—leave Solidad."

Stevie and Steve rolled over in the sand to watch. "Mommy's surprise now!" Stevie said excitedly. "Can I tell them, Mommy?"

"Come help me, honey."

He tumbled through the sand to her and began tugging at the brown sack. Jackie removed a rectangular box wrapped in glittering gold foil and ruffles of satin ribbon.

I opened the card on top and read: "To the David Ballards: Wishing you joy and peace in your marriage—The Marshalls."

"It's so beautifully wrapped—I hate to open it."

Jackie smiled, pleased. "Nicole in the hotel gift shop wrapped it. She's very artistic that way."

Stevie's chubby fingers pulled at the ribbon and tore off the foil. "Be careful, Stevie," Jackie warned.

He eagerly lifted the lid. "See, Michelle, see?" he exclaimed.

Inside the box was a delicate spiral conch shell, rosy-hued with scalloped edges, shimmering like a rare gem. I took it gently from the box and held it up in my palms for David to admire, thinking, *A part of Solidad and a part of the Turmans will go home with us in this fragile shell.*

"Neat," said David.

"It's beautiful, Jackie."

"We couldn't afford—and they didn't have much to choose from at the gift shop. Nicole thought it would make a nice wedding present."

"She's right. It does." I lifted the conch shell to my ear, listening for the roar of the ocean. But it sounded hollow, empty. The only sound I heard was the resounding crash of whitecaps along the Atlantic shoreline. As I reached into the shell and ran my hand along the lacquered smoothness, my fingertips touched something. "Oh, Jackie, this shell is full of surprises." I tugged at the packet and brought out a small cellophane bag packed solidly with what looked like powdered sugar. "What is it?" I asked, puzzled.

Steve went white. "Give me that, Michelle!" He grabbed the packet out of my hands, examined it incredulously, then tore it open. A moment later, as we watched in astonishment, he ran insanely into the ocean, wading knee-deep, and scattered the contents into the water. The white particles caught in the breeze. In one last desperate surge, he crumpled the cellophane bag and heaved it out to sea. Thrashing his fist in the air, he cried out, "Why, God? Why!"

David went to him and placed his hands firmly on Steve's shoulders. We could see the two of them talking earnestly but couldn't distinguish their words. At last David came back, his sturdy jaw clenched, his russet eyes flashing with vexation.

"David, what's wrong? What was in that packet?" I asked.

He closed the picnic basket and placed the conch shell back in its box. "Someone put cocaine in our wedding present." Jackie uttered a sudden, anguished sob.

I whirled around and looked at her. She was clutching her stomach, doubled over in pain. "What's wrong? Is it the baby?"

"Yes. Cramps. Sharp—!"

I took her in my arms and held her close. "Just hold on, Jackie. We'll get you right home."

She looked up imploringly at me. "Don't let me lose my baby, Michelle. Please, don't let God take that too!"

I pressed Jackie's head consolingly against my shoulder. "Oh, Jackie, don't you know? When we hurt, Jesus is the first to weep."

CHAPTER
ELEVEN

On Sunday morning I felt a nagging sense of gloom as I looked at the salmon-pink conch shell on the table—a loving gift that had inadvertently caused all of us such pain. I kept wondering how Jackie was feeling after her temporary cramping at the beach, but I dared not risk going to her room. And David still stubbornly refused to talk about the packet of cocaine Steve had hurled out to sea. Nor would he say what words had passed between the two of them as they stood at the water's edge. Silently I questioned whether David trusted Steve now. In fact, I fought back my own wheedling doubts. After all, who else would have tampered with the wedding gift?

Restless and worried, I walked over to the window and looked out at the horizon, caught up in a sad sort of wistfulness. I thought about our church back home. I missed the people, the fellowship, the lilting choirs, the pastor's inspiring messages. For a half hour I wandered aimlessly around our honeymoon suite, then picked up my Bible and told David, "I'm going to the sun deck to read for a while."

"Wait, I'll join you," he said, grabbing up a beach towel.

"You mean you're not spending the day in your computer room?"

David shrugged. "Not on Sunday. This is the Lord's day."

"And we don't even have a church to worship in!" I lamented.

"A church is people, not a building," David reminded me with a wry little smile.

"I know. And since the Bible says, 'Where two or three are gathered together'. . . shall the two of us go have our own devotions in the sunshine?"

David tossed his towel jauntily around his neck. "Sounds like a plan to me, my darling."

My spirits were already lifting as we gathered our beach gear and headed for the elevator. We found a quiet corner on the Atlantic side of the deck where the sun was already beating down with a fiery, blinding intensity. As we settled onto lounge chairs under a huge beach umbrella, I noticed Jackie sunbathing a short distance away.

"Look, David—it's Jackie over there. I'll ask her to join us." Before he could respond, I was on my way across the sun deck. I returned moments later with Jackie in tow, and declared loudly, "You remember Mrs. Marshall, don't you, David? We met the other day."

David nodded. "Hello, Mrs. Marshall. Where's the rest of the family?"

"Down in the swimming pool." Jackie took the chair beside mine. "I'm so glad to see you two," she whispered.

"Me, too. I was so worried about you, Jackie! How's the cramping?"

"It's gone, finally. But I've felt so lonely and depressed today, especially after what happened yesterday. And this nausea—!"

"I felt the same way this morning, Jackie," I told her. "Depressed, I mean, not nauseated!"

She managed an ironic smile. "Well, one of these days you'll probably experience the nausea too—that is, if you and David plan to have kids."

"Why, yes, of course, someday—"

"What's this?" David perked up, raising his sunglasses to his forehead.

"Nothing. Just woman talk," I said. I looked back at Jackie. "David and I were about to read a few verses. Will you join us?"

STORM CLOUDS OVER PARADISE

"Sure, why not? It'll remind me of our evening quiet times at Hopewell College."

David opened his Bible and read aloud Psalm 56. When he finished, I noticed that Jackie had tears in her eyes. "You know, that's a special message to me, David," she murmured. "To Steve and me. I—I feel it here, in my heart. I just wish I understood the words better."

I took the Bible from David. "Jackie, do you want me to read it again and put it in my own words to fit your situation?"

She nodded, moving closer to me.

"Perhaps you could read the passage this way, Jackie." I scanned the verses, paraphrasing those I felt would especially help her. "Be merciful to Steve and me, O God, because the syndicate would devour us; our enemies pursue us all day. Even now there are many who fight against us. Lord, I am afraid, but I put my trust in You. What can mere flesh do to me? You count our wanderings, Lord, our frightening journey to Solidad. You've seen me cry day after day. Place my tears in Your bottle, Lord. Aren't they already in Your Book? When I cry out to You, Lord, You promise that my enemies will turn back. Lord, You have saved my soul from death. Help me realize that You have delivered my feet from falling so that I may walk before You in the light of the living even here on Solidad."

Jackie dabbed at her eyes with a tissue. "I'm going to read that psalm to Steve. He doesn't like to talk about religious things, but he can't help but see that God is saying something to us in those verses. If only I can remember the way you phrased them, Michelle!"

I reached over and squeezed Jackie's hand. "David and I are praying for you both. You know that, don't you?"

"Yes, Michelle. I feel your prayers. Don't ever stop."

I looked over at David. "You know, we ought to start a Bible study right here on the sun deck. I bet there are other hotel guests who would like to come. What do you think?"

David rubbed his jaw thoughtfully. "Well, we're only going to be here a few more weeks, but I think you've got something there, Michelle. I don't see why there should be any problem—"

"Then we can do it? Maybe I could post a notice on the

bulletin board for next Sunday. Surely a hotel this size has a place for announcements."

"Outside the dining room door," said Jackie. "I'll talk to some people too. Who knows? Maybe I can even persuade Steve to come."

"Speaking of Steve," I said, "did you know Silas Winters assigned him as our instructor when we go snorkeling this afternoon?"

Jackie smiled, surprised. "Really? What fun. Steve's awfully good at skin diving and scuba diving. You'll learn a lot."

"I hope so. I'm not the world's greatest swimmer. David's good, though. You should see him."

"Oh, I'd love to come with you today, Michelle, but I'd really better not." Jackie wearily patted her still-flat abdomen. "I'd better not risk a strenuous jaunt after yesterday."

"I understand. I'll stop by your room this evening and tell you all about our day. No doubt I'll find loads of sunken treasure and gold doubloons—"

David leaned forward and chuckled. "What do we do with this girl, Jackie? She's convinced she's living out some adventure in a storybook with pirates and Spanish galleons and all the rest."

Jackie pressed her lips together in a tight little smile. "You don't know how much I wish I lived in a fantasy world. It's got to be better than the real thing. Sometimes, I can't imagine that Steve and I are bringing another child into our lives when all we're doing is running."

"Oh, Jackie, please don't feel that way," I admonished. "God has something special for you and your family. I know He does."

Jackie stood up and adjusted her sunglasses with a studied casualness. "Maybe so," she said tonelessly, "but sometimes I think He sure has a funny way of showing it."

That afternoon, I was still nursing a burden for Jackie as Kikko and his marvelous surrey transported David and me to Coral Beach on the north end of the island. Steve and several Creole divers were already waiting for us when Kikko brought Sweet Hibiscus to an unceremonious halt along the palm-studded shore.

"Hibiscus and me sit in shade and watch," Kikko promised.

I laughed. "Come on, Kikko. I know you. You'll sit in the shade and sleep, like you always do when you take us somewhere."

"I a growing boy, Missus Ballard. I need little nap."

"That's fine, Kikko," said David as he unloaded our rented diving gear. He looked over at me. "Hey, Michelle, maybe we should take the plunge and try scuba diving instead of snorkeling. We'd be more likely to find that buried treasure you're looking for."

"Forget it, my dear—you with your little play on words. Just saying *plunge* gives me goose bumps, and I haven't even touched the water yet."

"You're not chickening out, are you?"

I swatted him playfully with one of my rubber fins and intoned loftily, "Goose bumps do not a chicken make!"

We raced each other to the water's edge where Steve was attaching a flag to a red buoy, his bronzed muscles flexing powerfully as he worked. "Hi, guys," he said, feigning cheerfulness. "Ready for a great day underwater?"

"That's what we're here for," said David, releasing his gear. I noticed an undercurrent of tension between the two men, not in what they said, but in their guarded tones and expressions. "What are you doing?" I asked Steve, too brightly.

"Putting a 'diver down' flag on this diving marker so people will know we're there under the water." He squinted up at me, shading his deep-set eyes with his hand. "You ever skin dive before?"

"A couple of times. I guess I did okay."

"And you, David?"

"I took a course in scuba diving a while back, but I haven't tried it lately."

Steve straightened up. "That's okay. We're going to take it easy—just a little snorkeling, nothing too deep, nothing too daring. We'll stick together, the buddy system all the way. Got it?"

I reached out for David's hand. "Buddies, darling?"

David circled my waist with his arm and whispered beguilingly, "Michelle, my dear, I won't take my eyes off you in that swimsuit."

I elbowed him playfully, then realized Steve was explaining

how to surface dive. He demonstrated different methods, then talked about water pressure and the danger of hyperventilating. He explained how to clear our ears, paddle with our fins, and resurface safely. "If you have ear pain, go down only about ten feet at first. Don't stay under too long or you could black out. And, remember, underwater everything looks 25 percent larger and closer than it actually is."

Steve picked up his flippers and a J-shaped, open-end breathing tube. "When you use your snorkel, inhale very slowly and exhale sharply to clear the tube of water. Like this, see?"

Then he held up his face mask. "You can defog your mask by spitting on the faceplate and rubbing the saliva around the glass."

I grimaced at David. "Oh, yuck!"

"Don't freak out," laughed Steve, sounding more at ease now. "It really works." He leaned down and pulled on his fins. "One last warning. You probably won't run into any man-eating sharks, but do watch out for the flora and fauna. You can really mess yourself up on coral and barnacles, or get tangled in kelp. And beware of the spiny sea urchins. They have spines as sharp as hypodermic needles."

"Are you sure it's safe to go down there?" I asked warily.

"As long as you follow the rules. In other words, be careful. Use good common sense. Okay, let's go. Let's get into our gear!"

David helped me on with my fins, snorkel, and mask. Adjusting the snorkel, I put my lips over the soft rubber mouthpiece. Only the large, awkward flippers presented a dilemma. I had to step with my feet high off the ground to keep the blade from buckling and tripping me. As I lumbered toward the water, teetering precariously, I felt like an absurd blend of circus clown and Navy frogman.

David got his feet wet in the surf, then donned his fins and together we shambled into the water. The Creole divers made a smooth surface dive head-first into the rippling tide. David followed, gliding down into the aqueous swell with surprising grace.

For a while Steve worked patiently with me, showing me how to swim with my fins and flick them with the positive thrust of a fishtail. Finally he signaled that I could try a surface dive. I stretched out on the water, then went into a rolling dive and shot my legs upward. Holding my arms close to my sides, I propelled myself down into a strange azure world of orange coral, undulating seaweed, silvery, lightning-fast fish, and brilliant red anemones.

Before I knew it, my air was gone and I had to resurface. As I broke through the foamy whitecaps, I blew out on my snorkel, then inhaled sharply, hungry for air. Steve, swimming a few yards away, waved vigorously. "Good work, Michelle. Take several quick breaths, expel them, then take a maximum breath and dive again."

This time I felt more confident, more in control. As my fear abated, I concentrated on the shimmering beauty around me. Already I felt that awesome sensation of being cut off from the rest of the world, alone in a timeless, spellbinding fantasia, surrounded by the outrageous creatures and preposterous plant life of an alien environment. *It's like another planet*, I marveled, *another indescribable domain. No wonder men strive to conquer the sea.*

It was everything I had imagined and more—*Alice in Wonderland* and *The Wizard of Oz* in one transcendent, crystalline sphere. I scoured my memory for bits of biology trivia. Yes, there's a starfish. And that swaying, aquatic, confetti-green pasture must be eel grass. And over there—a jellyfish ensconced on a prickly coral bouquet where sponges and mussels form a colorful, crusty covering.

Impulsively I reached out for a darting angelfish, jarring my mask slightly and causing a powerful inrush of water into my eyes and nose passages. Fighting back panic, I blew through my nose to empty the mask, then swiftly treaded water back up to the surface. My lungs felt as if they were about to burst. I expelled the seawater from my snorkel and gulped great mouthfuls of air.

Then, as I stretched out on the heaving breakers, I felt a hand on my shoulder. Startled, I lifted my head and looked around. It was David, ready for another dive. Together, we dove down into a glimmering, chiaroscuro world of liquid and lights, a primordial realm where everything was larger than life and the colors glowed with a stunning purity.

For a moment we hung motionless, suspended in limbo,

surrounded by the cathedral spires of a luminous coral reef, radiant as a rainbow mirage.

David and I swam side by side in our soundless, primitive kingdom. We watched a school of sequined fish approach in perfect formation and then, encountering us, disperse in a silent, glittering explosion. A moray eel slithered among the barnacled rocks, playing water tag with a giant, bug-eyed barracuda with chain-saw teeth.

Suddenly, David circled around me and pointed upward to the ocean's expansive blue canopy. I knew what he meant. *Time to resurface!* With a knot of alarm, I realized my air was almost gone. I waved David on and thrust my flippers down hard against the miry seabed. Instead of the surge upward I expected, my right fin caught on something and held firm.

I twisted sharply and felt my body suddenly entangled in a clinging web—a coarse, bristly fishing net. As I flailed helplessly, my hand struck a lacy crust of rose coral. I drew back in intense, searing pain. *Oh, God, help me!* I screamed silently. My air was completely gone now. My lungs ached for relief. I writhed and kicked and jabbed at the enshrouding ropes, fighting the unbearable urge to suck for air. *Oh, God, I'm going to give in and breathe, whether water or air—*

I gave one last frantic push, my mind reeling, going blank. Which way was up? Everything was dissolving into blackness, my senses collapsing. My lungs were expanding like a balloon, about to rupture. Excruciating pain pressed against my breastbone and throbbed in my bleeding hand.

I was lost now, utterly disoriented in this deadly, mercurial marine world. I could hold my breath no longer. Opening my mouth to the sea, I sensed from some remnant of my consciousness that I was drowning. Then, from the elusive shores of some whimsical phantom dream, I felt strong arms gather me up and propel me upward.

CHAPTER
TWELVE

I felt pressure deep in my chest, as if my lungs were being squeezed in a vise. I coughed and gasped, sucking hungrily for air. As the numbing darkness receded and my dizzying, kaleidoscopic world stopped spinning, I became aware of muffled voices around me calling out in alarm. Out of the cacophony of sounds, I distinguished David's deep baritone voice, asking anxiously, "Are you okay, darling? Promise me you'll be okay."

I opened my eyes. Gradually David's face came into focus. He was bending over me on the wet sand, concern etched in his angular features. "I—I'm okay," I sputtered. But as I tried to sit up, I felt a throbbing, burning sensation in my right palm. I stared down at the blood-soaked handkerchief wrapped around my hand. "What happened to me, David?"

"You cut yourself on the coral, remember?"

"No, I—the net—the water—"

"Don't move, Michelle. I'll carry you." David swept me up in his powerful arms and carried me to the surrey. He pressed my head against his chest and kissed my wet hair with the aching urgency of a parent comforting a wounded child. I relaxed against him, savoring the secure haven of his warm, sturdy flesh against my chilled skin.

David set me in the backseat of the carriage, climbed in

beside me, and wrapped me in beach towels and the worn blanket that usually padded the front seat of Kikko's surrey. Even with David's arms tightly around me, I couldn't stop shivering.

As Kikko flicked the reins, urging Sweet Hibiscus on, Steve ran alongside us and said, "Wait for me. I'll ride to the hotel with you, if you don't mind."

"Hurry," said David. "I want to get Michelle back to Windy Reef."

Steve leaped into the front seat beside Kikko.

I felt David's muscles tense as he asked Steve, "Hey, man, why didn't you warn us there'd be fishing nets down there?"

"I didn't know, David. It's a mystery to me how it got there. But I'll get to the bottom of it, believe me." Steve turned confidentially to Kikko. I heard him demand in an angry whisper, "Who owns that fishing net, Kikko?"

The Creole boy shrugged helplessly. "No one fish Coral Beach. Sr. Medina like Coral Beach for hotel guests."

"Then someone must have thrown the net in the water while we were swimming. You had to see them do it."

"No. Kikko not see."

"You're certain you saw no one?"

"No, sir. Kikko in surrey whole time."

"Dozing?" Steve accused.

Kikko's lean shoulders sagged. The back of his frayed muslin shirt was damp with sweat. "Kikko see no one."

David stiffened, his face blanching. "Steve, are you suggesting that this wasn't an accident? Do you think someone planted that net where we'd get tangled in it?"

Steve turned and looked at David. "I'm not saying that at all. But that beach is off limits to fishermen. It was a rule when Ricardo Cobranza was alive, and Medina has continued to enforce it."

"Then maybe the fishing net has been lying there for years."

Steve shook his head. "You saw my divers bring it in. Did you see any barnacles or crustaceans on it? It's a relatively new net."

"How are you going to find out who owns it?" demanded David.

"Silas Winters has his ways. He'll check into it."

"Then you'll get back to me with a report?"

Steve nodded noncommittally.

As the surrey bounced along on what seemed an interminable ride back to the hotel, I began to cough uncontrollably. Steve looked around at me, his expression riveted with concern. "I want you to see Doc Edington as soon as we get back, Michelle."

"I'd rather see a veterinarian," I rasped sarcastically.

David held me closer and rocked me. "I know you don't like the crusty fellow, Michelle, but—"

"The man's okay," Steve interjected. "He's good, in fact."

"He makes me think of rum and Old Spice," I mumbled, my cough easing. "Really, Steve, you must have noticed. The guy's an old boozer."

"All right, I admit he may have a drinking problem, but Michelle, he was an emergency room doctor for years."

"You're kidding!"

"No. He's well-qualified, well-trained. The natives love him. Ask Kikko."

We didn't have to ask him. Kikko seemed glad for a new topic of conversation. "Yes, sir. Doc Dooley very good. Save Moses' life. Make babies—"

"*Delivers* babies," Steve corrected.

"Then what in the world is he doing out here in the boondocks?" David asked.

"From affluence to Paradise," I mocked through chattering teeth. I moved my hand inadvertently under the blanket and felt a sharp stinging sensation where the coral had cut into my skin. I winced.

David massaged my forehead in a consoling gesture, but his mind was still on Dooley Edington. "So how did the doc end up here?"

"Circumstances, I guess." Steve was riding sideways now, his eyes steady on us. "Money and possessions don't mean much when you lose your wife."

"What happened to Edington's wife?" I asked, trying to forget my own discomfort.

"She was killed in an accident over ten years ago."

Accident? After the past trauma-filled hour, that word took on ominous proportions. I was still shivering from fright, shock, and cold. David brushed back my wet, straggly hair and blew a kiss in my ear. "You'll be okay, Michelle, my love."

I reached for David's hand under the blanket, but my gaze was still on Steve. "Can you tell us more about Edington's wife?"

"She was killed in a head-on collision in Seattle." Steve's dark eyes were shadowed. "According to the Medinas, Edington was on duty at the hospital emergency room when they brought his wife in."

"How dreadful!"

"I guess he tried everything he could to save her life—but he lost her anyway."

"Is that why he started drinking?"

Steve shrugged. "Who knows? But Dooley walked out of that emergency room that night a broken man. He never went back."

"You mean, he gave up his entire career?"

"That's about it. From what I understand, he did everything he could to forget his grief—squandered his money all over Europe. He's a funny guy. You get him talking and he'll tell you all about his travels and how he took care of sick people everywhere he went. But the fact is, he never resumed his stateside practice."

We were passing through the quaint, colorful village now, past Moses' stone cottage and Kikko's thatched hut. The island's cemetery lay just beyond the hill. "But, Steve, you still haven't explained why Edington came to Solidad," I said.

"He first visited Solidad years ago, during his world wanderings. He met someone in Europe who told him about the island. Old Cobranza's son, maybe. I don't know. Stayed a week or two and fell in love with this lackadaisical life-style."

"Saved Moses' life," Kikko interrupted.

"How?" David asked.

"Moses fall from palm tree." Kikko waved his hands vigorously. "All cut bad. Doc Dooley take care."

"The people here worship him," Steve acknowledged. "When he came back to Solidad a year and a half ago, Medina went all out—hired him on as staff physician, bought him all the lab and medical equipment he wanted. Half the time the people can't pay a thing, but Edington is content to accept their fruit and fresh fish for his services."

"Wow," I exclaimed, "he must be more compassionate than I ever imagined."

Steve chuckled as Sweet Hibiscus lumbered up the cobbled road to the hotel. "Don't worry, Michelle. Edington figures the tourists can pay double or triple for his services. Believe me, Doc Edington isn't hurting financially anymore."

"And you expect me to go to him? You've argued his case well, but still . . . "

"I insist you see him, Michelle. You don't want to risk infection with that open wound," said Steve. "Doc's office is in the west wing. He usually opens the clinic a few hours every afternoon, even on Sunday. Check at the desk. They'll tell you if he's in."

Sweet Hibiscus stopped abruptly beside Windy Reef's main entrance. David stepped out of the surrey and lifted me down, still wrapped in the tattered blanket. "I'll be all right, David, after I rest."

"After you see the doctor." David smiled reassuringly. "Don't worry, hon. I'll be right there with you."

"Put me down, David. I'm not going in wrapped up like this. I'm walking in on my own power."

Even as David set me on my feet, I felt a bit wobbly.

"May I at least hold your hand?" he teased.

"If you rescue me from Kikko's blanket." As the blanket and beach towels dropped free, David took my hand and pulled back the blood-soaked handkerchief from the wound. It was oozing, inflamed, with bright red welts spreading along the wrist.

Inside the hotel, we quickly cut across the lobby and headed for the west wing. A slim woman in a striking, flower-print sheath was unlocking the door of the gift shop. She glanced our way with a fleeting smile. I managed an embarrassed smile in return, realizing what a bedraggled sight I was in my damp swimsuit, my hair a straggly mess, my hand bandaged and bloody.

"We're looking for Dr. Edington's office," David told her. She pointed down the hall. "Two doors."

I could sense her eyes still on us even as we passed by. I turned around abruptly. "You're Nicole, aren't you?" I asked.

"Why, yes," she answered pleasantly.

"I just wanted to thank you—the present from the Marshalls —it was wrapped so beautifully."

She frowned, puzzled. "Your present?"

"Yes. The Steve Marshall family bought us a wedding present from the gift shop."

"A conch shell," David added.

"Oh, yes. Now I remember. But I didn't wrap the present."

"Oh, but Jackie—Mrs. Marshall said you wrap all the gifts."

"Not this time. The concierge came by—"

"Mr. Winters?"

Nicole eyed me coolly. "Yes, we had a date—"

"Come on, Michelle," David urged quietly. "I want you to see the doctor."

I kept my gaze on Nicole. Was that a flush behind her natural coppery complexion? "Thank you anyway," I said. "The present was just lovely."

"And you're crazy," David told me, his voice mildly agitated as he led me toward the doctor's office. "What was that all about?"

We paused outside the door. "I just wanted to see what she'd say."

"Michelle, Michelle." He shook his head with a patient, ironic smile, then reached up and swung the shingle above the doorway. "See, it's official, sweetheart: Dooley Edington, M.D."

"That doesn't prove a thing," I shot back.

Ignoring my protest, David led me into the empty waiting room. Immediately a barefoot Creole girl in a white uniform appeared, a clipboard in hand. She asked David to take a chair and fill in the forms, then ushered me into the clinic, a surprisingly compact, aseptic room with modern equipment, a mobile surgical light, stainless steel sinks, and well-stocked medicine cabinets. Dooley Edington, dressed in his usual casual sport shirt and slacks, a rum bottle in his hip pocket, sat in a swivel chair, his gangly arms resting on the desk top. His shrewd, dark eyes watched intently as his nurse led me to the step stool and helped me onto the exam table. I sat self-consciously on the cold, hard surface, wishing I had on more than a swimsuit. My wounded hand burned intensely, but I tried not to grimace or cower in front of Dooley Edington.

He pushed slowly away from his desk, stood, straightened

his lanky body, then loped toward me. "Well, Mrs. Ballard, we meet again under more congenial circumstances." Taking my injured hand in his, he added, "Obviously not more comfortable, but at least more congenial." He turned my hand gently and scrutinized the wound. "Nasty looking," he said, a diagnostic frown between his craggy, saw-toothed brows, "but not serious. You'll recover."

"Thanks," I mumbled hoarsely. "But it burns like fire. Will I need stitches?"

"No, we'll let the wound heal from the inside out." He raised one shaggy brow. "You sound raspy. What happened?" He reached for his stethoscope.

I didn't answer. He was already listening to my lungs, his gaze intent. "Take a deep breath," he said.

I filled my lungs.

"Again."

As he dropped the stethoscope around his neck, he asked again, "What happened, Mrs. Ballard?"

"We went snorkeling."

"Not alone, I hope."

"No, no. The assistant concierge went along to instruct us."

"Didn't he warn you about clearing the coral reefs?"

Before I could respond, a deep voice replied, "Yes, but he didn't warn us about clearing the fishing nets. Michelle got tangled in one and could have drowned." We both looked up at David standing in the office doorway, the medical forms rolled in his hand. No doubt he had grown too impatient to remain alone in the waiting room.

Dooley acknowledged David with a curt nod. "Yes, those fishing nets can be deadly."

"So we found out," said David. "Fortunately we got to her in time."

"Yes, very fortunate," Edington said coolly. He turned to his young assistant. "Consar, bring some papaya juice, please."

She returned promptly with a large metal basin. Edington took my hand and began to scrub the wound.

"What is that?" I asked, peering at the pale pink liquid.

"Like I said, papaya juice. It burns less than alcohol but serves the same purpose." When I winced, he added, "We want to get all the foreign matter out, Mrs. Ballard, to decrease the threat of infection."

"What can you do for the pain?" I moaned.

"The best thing you can do is keep your arm elevated when you get back to your room."

David hovered by the examining table as Edington dried the wound, applied cortisone cream, and wrapped my hand in a sterile bandage. "I'm going to give your wife some antihistamine to minimize any further reaction to the coral. It may make her sleepy, but she should get some rest anyway."

"That sounds good to me," I sighed, conscious suddenly of how utterly exhausted I really felt.

"I'll check on you later this evening," said Edington.

"Is that necessary?" asked David. "I'll be with her."

"That's fine, Mr. Ballard, but I'll want to listen to her lungs again. Besides, you'll want some relief for dinner. I'll have Esteban Medina send someone up to spell you for an hour or two, say about seven?"

CHAPTER
THIRTEEN

That evening I dozed fitfully for nearly two hours, then woke with a start, aware of someone moving in the shadows of my room. The moon streaming through the open shutters cast a pale glow on the Gauguin painting on the far wall. Beside it stood a silhouetted form with arms outstretched, slender hands reaching toward the picture frame. The pungent aroma of cigarette smoke hung heavy in the humid air.

"Who are you? What are you doing?" I cried, sitting up.

"Oh, Mrs. Ballard," came a woman's surprised reply. "I try very hard not to wake you."

I snapped on the bedside lamp and recognized Lucia Medina at the foot of my bed. "How did you get in? What do you want?"

Lucia seemed genuinely flustered. "Esteban send me to stay with you while your husband go to dinner. You sleep so soundly, I look in to make sure you okay."

"I'm perfectly fine," I insisted, slipping out of bed and pulling on my light silk robe. But my bandaged hand throbbed and my legs buckled under me, so I promptly sat back down.

"I have tray of herb tea and muffins in living room," continued Lucia pleasantly. She took a few steps back over to the painting and casually straightened it. "I cannot bare to see picture hanging crooked."

"It—it's one of my pet peeves, too," I said, the words catching in my throat. I shuddered as I realized how close Lucia had come to activating the sliding door to David's secret computer room.

"Well, is straight now," said Lucia. "Here, I help you. We go have tea. You feel much better."

With a supportive arm, Lucia accompanied me into the living room where I settled weakly onto the sofa. She wrapped her own knit shawl around me, then served the tea and muffins and sat down in the wing chair across from me.

"Thank you, Lucia. I appreciate your kindness. I didn't want David to miss dinner on my account."

"Oh, I very happy come here, help you." Lucia's flawless ceramic complexion flushed slightly. "I like to hear more about California. Someday I visit Hollywood, see place where they write names in—what you call—sidewalk?"

I laughed in spite of myself. "Oh, Lucia, if you ever get to Hollywood, I'd love to show you around."

"Good, good. I come. You be sure. We have nice time. We are close in age, no?"

"I suppose so. You're what—25?"

Lucia leaned over confidentially. "I am 30, but I say I am 28. I do not want to be old."

"You're somewhat younger than your husband," I noted, then wondered if I'd spoken out of turn. "I mention it only because there's an age difference between David and me too."

"Yes, I always like older man," said Lucia, fishing in her handbag for a cigarette. "Esteban is 38. Sometime he act older still. He is very serious man. But he is strong. He has body of much younger man. He swim like fish, so graceful. He never grow tired."

"You sound very proud of him."

"Oh, I am proud. Esteban is—how you say—plain man, but he is good man. He is man of honor. He treat me well."

"It sounds like you have a wonderful marriage."

Lucia's face clouded slightly. She tapped her cigarette on her palm, then placed it between her glossy red lips. A gold lighter glinted in her hand; an orange flame ignited the slender taper. "I am happy sometimes," she said tonelessly, "and I am unhappy too. When I marry Esteban, he a very wealthy businessman, what you call a banker. We live in Colombia many years. Then we move to Europe and go to many parties and travel to Paris and London and Madrid. But three years ago, Esteban's papa—he die and everything change."

"I don't understand. Why did things change?"

Lucia fingered the ruffle on her low-cut red blouse. "Is very long story. And I don't speak the English so well."

"Oh, you do beautifully, Lucia. And I'd really like to hear the story," I said, thinking of the novel I wanted to write someday.

"Very well. Esteban's papa, Juan Medina, run Windy Reef for many years. He very good friends with Ricardo and Alejandra Cobranza. Long ago Juan come with them from Colombia. In fact, my Esteban born on Solidad, grow up here. When the Cobranzas die, they leave part of estate to Esteban's father, Juan. Juan help their son Carlos turn mansion into great hotel. When Carlos go back to Europe, Juan stay on to manage Windy Reef. He stay here all his life."

"Then what you're saying is that after Juan Medina died, Esteban felt obligated to take his father's place here at the hotel?"

"Yes, that is so." Lucia drew in deeply on her cigarette. "The Cobranza ties—they are very strong. Ricardo and Alejandra reach to Esteban from their graves and make him stay here on Solidad. He give up his life—and mine—for them. I do not understand. Sometime it make me very angry inside, but I smile and say nothing."

I nodded sympathetically. "After such a cosmopolitan life-style, you must have found it very difficult to adjust to life on Solidad."

"Yes, it is hard. I keep hoping Esteban will tire of the island and forget his loyalties to his father and the Cobranzas. But he is stubborn. I fear he will never leave. The debt will never be paid."

We lapsed into silence for a minute. Lucia put out the stub of her cigarette and lighted another.

"Did you ever know the Cobranzas personally?" I asked.

"No. It is 20 years ago they die. Long before I meet Esteban. But he tell me much about them. They have very sad and beautiful love story."

"I've heard talk—rumors," I said. "And the portrait of Alejandra in the lobby—it fascinates me. There's something in her face, her eyes, that makes me long to know her. And yet I realize the portrait must have been painted over half a century ago."

"Yes. The portrait—it touch many people," agreed Lucia. "Esteban know Alejandra after terrible fire burn her face. He see her only few times. He say on one side of face beauty remain. On other side, ugly scars. Alejandra hide. Let no one see her. Ricardo Cobranza buy Solidad and build mansion just for Alejandra to hide from world. Is very tragic."

"How was Alejandra burned? What sort of accident—?"

"I do not know whole story." Lucia exhaled a wispy ringlet of smoke. "Long ago political uprisings bring heartache to Colombia. Ricardo Cobranza flee with his family and Juan Medina. They come to Solidad. Before they leave Colombia, Alejandra burned. Ricardo hang her bridal portrait in mansion so everyone admire her beauty. But no one, except Esteban and trusted servants, ever see real Alejandra."

"How did she die?"

"Tropical fever. Twenty years ago."

"I don't mean to pry, Lucia, but—" I phrased my words carefully. "Someone mentioned a suicide..."

"It is true. Ricardo Cobranza heartbroken over Alejandra's death. After funeral he jump from balcony into ocean. Some people see him jump, but no one find his body."

I shivered involuntarily. Falteringly I said, "I heard he—he jumped from the balcony of this very suite."

Lucia glanced around as if she expected to glimpse the specter of Ricardo Cobranza lurking behind some curtain or chair. "Yes. This is the suite. This is the original mansion where Cobranzas live before Windy Reef become hotel." Her fingers trembled as she reached for another cigarette. "I am sorry, Mrs. Ballard—"

"Call me Michelle, please."

"All right. Michelle. I feel uneasy here. I feel things that cannot be seen or heard. I feel death here." She stood abruptly. "Forgive me. I should not talk this way. This is beautiful place. Very rich. Very nice. You like it, no? Do not mind the silly talk of a frightened woman."

"Are you frightened, Lucia? What are you afraid of?"

"No, no, I am not afraid," she tittered nervously. "I am only a bored and restless wife. I see things where there is nothing. I fret for no reason." She wafted over and clasped my face in her smooth, graceful hands. "We are friends, Michelle, no? We talk again. I like you very much."

"I like you too, Lucia," I said sincerely. I tried to stand up, but she waved me back to the sofa.

"You get well, Michelle. You must be well for fiesta next Friday."

"Fiesta?"

"Yes, Frangipani Fiesta. You do not know about fiesta?"

"No. Tell me."

"Is big festival. Wonderful party here at hotel. Every year. Everyone on island come to Windy Reef. We eat and dance and sing and laugh. Everyone be happy. Forget troubles. You come, Michelle."

"Oh, I will, Lucia. David and I will both be there. After all, this is our honeymoon. It's time we had some fun!"

Strangely, for several days after my conversation with Lucia, I could think of little else but the novel I wanted to write. Somehow, Lucia had touched some vital nerve in my imagination, sparking my creative juices. I wanted to begin my novel now, a historical novel involving some tropical isle. Since David insisted I remain quiet for a few days after my accident, I spent Monday and Tuesday scribbling reams of awkward, scrawled notes with my bandaged hand.

By Wednesday morning, in spite of the lingering discomfort in my hand, I felt good inside, satisfied. My novel was taking shape—a nebulous beginning at least. But even as I visualized my main character, I somehow knew that he strongly resembled David—a six-footer with autumn coloring, a self-sufficient man with a firm, determined jaw, the shadow of a beard, and dancing mahogany eyes. I whirled around the room, my feet light and rhythmic, my heart all David's. Perhaps my fictionalized character would please him, delight him, tell him how very much I loved him.

My story would take place in the Caribbean—Solidad perhaps. And there would indeed be a mystery—a Spanish galleon wracked by pirate cannon fire, the vessel run aground on a coral reef. There would be a yellowed parchment map and a wild search for sunken treasure—gold bullion and chests of precious stones lost in the tides and sifting sands.

I was feeling wonderfully ridiculous as I slid back the patio door to the veranda and floated out, my spirits soaring, my adrenaline high. I ran my fingers along the top of the white-pillared railing, stopping finally where the patio jutted out over the Atlantic. I paused in my rambling thoughts. I absolutely had to find someone who knew the island, or someone who would explore with me. Jackie? Was she feeling well enough or free enough to wander around Solidad? Or Lucia? I considered her a special friend now, but I wasn't sure Esteban would want his wife snooping around the island. What about Ruth Glocke? She'd go if I told her we were looking for shells. But she wasn't exactly the perfect companion.

I leaned against the railing and trembled slightly as I watched the ocean slash against the cliffs beneath me. There was still so much of Solidad I hadn't seen. Shoal Beach and Cocoa Lake. Cocoa Falls on Mt. Peligro. Nothing could quell my excitement, the vivid images firing my imagination. Not even the ominous gray clouds that darkened the sky this morning. What if it rained? David and I would walk in the rain, run in it. A storm wouldn't darken our day.

I glanced down on the little stretch of beach where I had hiked on Saturday with Ruth Glocke. Javier, the weather-beaten old gardener in his crumpled tan fishing hat, hobbled along on his early morning walk. I looked again, startled. Someone was by his side—a figure as fragile and thin as Javier himself.

I craned my neck, following them with my eyes, but they were lost from view as they edged around the lava ridge. Surely Javier would remember the tides and turn back to the stone steps in time.

The minutes ticked away. Where had the old man and his companion gone? Should I warn Esteban Medina or call David from his computer project? Did I dare risk hiking along that dangerous shoal alone again?

I stared intently now, my eyes desperately searching the beach for Javier. I saw nothing except the waves plummeting Tamarind Bluff. The sun raced with the clouds, drifting in and out of the vaporous shadows, changing the hue of the rocks. Suddenly, my gaze focused on the darkening cliff where the fleeting sunlight carved out the menacing features of a skull. "Can it be? Cara de Muerte—the Face of Death!" I exclaimed incredulously.

As quickly as the sun moved behind a veil of mist, the spectral image was gone. The tide was rolling in now, washing over the beach, as threatening and tumultuous as the storm clouds gathering overhead. I stepped back from the balcony as lightning flashed and huge raindrops pelted me. The narrow stretch of beach was completely inundated now, but Javier and his companion were nowhere in sight.

CHAPTER FOURTEEN

I threw on my shawl and ran from the hotel, braving the torrential rain as I thrust through the sodden garden to Javier's cottage. Dooley Edington was just coming out the rough-hewn door, his raincoat collar raised around his ears. "Whoa, young lady," he bellowed, breaking my run. "Why are you out in this downpour?"

"Javier was—I mean, he—is he okay?" I blurted.

"Yes, of course, he's fine, Mrs. Ballard. I just gave him his medication. He's taking a nap now."

"But I just saw him on the beach. Then the tide came in. He never came back."

"That's impossible. I've been with Javier for the past hour."

"But I saw him," I insisted. The slanting rain streamed down my face and drenched my hair. The wet tendrils clung to my face and neck. "He was with someone—a frail-looking woman."

Dooley's pastry-brush mustache twitched slightly. A shadowy puffiness under his black, ballpoint eyes made him look unusually haggard. "Ah, Mrs. Ballard, now I know your imagination is working overtime. Javier is a loner. Surely you've noticed that. He would not walk on the beach with anyone." He planted his large hand on my shoulder and turned me around like a mere child. "You must have seen other hotel guests. Come, my dear. Let's get out of this deluge."

I jerked away from Edington's patronizing touch and slogged on alone back to the hotel, fighting a surge of loathing for the smug, intractable physician. Was it possible I had been mistaken about seeing Javier on the beach? David had accused me at times of having an over-active imagination. "But not this time," I said under my breath as I took the elevator up to the bridal suite. "It had to be Javier. I'd stake my life on it."

The rains abated by evening and the skies were clear on Thursday morning. On waking, my first thoughts were of Javier. I had to see for myself that he was okay. When David and I went downstairs to breakfast, I sent him on ahead while I went outside to look for the wizened, little old man. To my relief I found him puttering in the garden as usual in his baggy pants and worn beige sweater, that familiar glazed expression in his eyes. "Hello, Javier," I called out. "I was worried about you."

He lifted his tissue-thin hand to shield his eyes from the sun. The soil from the garden made dark half-moons under his nails. A flicker of a smile creased his wrinkled lips. "You are lovely lady, like lady in the portrait," he uttered in his raspy Colombian accent. Haltingly, he reached out one dirt-encrusted hand and touched my cheek. "You come to my cottage again for coffee."

"I'd love to, Javier, but I'm planning to spend the day exploring Solidad. Perhaps another day...?"

He nodded and turned back ploddingly to his flowers. I went on inside to the dining room, overwhelmed with a mixture of compassion and pity for the melancholy old gardener.

After a light breakfast, David and I returned to our honeymoon suite. As I picked up my writer's notebook and tucked it in my purse, I told him, "I'm going exploring around Solidad while you work at the computer—unless you'd like to go with me on my excursion?"

David's eyes twinkled slyly. "I've already made arrangements to go. Tell you what. We'll circle this island in style."

"Kikko style?"

"We'll start that way. It's better than walking 35 miles."

"Or pedal rented bicycles."

"Silas tells me he can get up a hotel tour to Cocoa Lake and a hike to Cocoa Falls next week. So today we'll head over some familiar territory to Frangipani Point."

"So we're getting ready for the Frangipani Festival tomorrow?"

David touched up his hair with a styling brush, took a glance at himself in the mirror, then said, "That's the best lookout point on the island."

"So says Kikko."

"Proudly, I might add." David picked up our camera case and slung it over his shoulder. "Let's not keep Kikko waiting."

"What else is on your agenda, David?" I asked as we rode the elevator down to the lobby.

"For you, lovely lady, the marketplace. It's souvenir time. Then Cobranza Bay, Solidad Lagoon. . .any scenic background you want for that historical romance novel of yours."

"Can we stop at the village?"

"We'll take it in on our way back. Kikko already promises some hot-pepper stew at his place."

"Great," I groaned.

The surrey was parked just outside the hotel door. Kikko leaned against the carriage, gingerly sucking an orange peel. Spotting us, he flashed a wide grin, all sparkling teeth and friendliness. He helped us on board, announcing, "Kikko take you long way to market."

I shot David a quizzical glance. He shrugged. "The long way is good for Kikko's business. Besides, we haven't been alone much since we've been on Solidad."

"Alone?" I challenged. "Kikko's with us."

Kikko whirled around and grinned. "You kiss. Me no look."

"See?" David laughed. "Kikko's just part of the family."

As we rode along on our familiar perch in the surrey, bouncing over the dusty roads of Solidad, I relaxed contentedly in David's arms. Even the earthy, fissured trail could not mar the jewel-like beauty of the island. She was cloaked in breathtaking colors, from her pastel-shaded coral reefs to the deep jade-green of the barely rippling sea. We caught the windborne scents of frangipani, hibiscus, and bougainvillea. The lush red-blossomed bushes obscured the tumbledown homes along the way. We had sea and sky at our fingertips—

wispy, roving clouds like spun cotton candy forming elusive, swirling images against a vault of periwinkle blue.

In the distance, tiny outcrops of black, sterile lava jutted through the waves, poking spiky heads above the submerged volcanic ridge. The waves hurled against the barren rocks, daring animal or man to venture there. At Alejandra Cove—a lonely stretch of pristine beach—David and I stopped to finish a roll of film. I took the final shot of Kikko, with David towering above him, their backs to the velvety plush hills of slumbering Mt. Peligro.

Kikko was reluctant to stop when we came to Solidad's smaller village with its handful of limestone block homes. Barefoot children stood shyly by the roadside as our surrey clattered by, showering them with dust. Tomorrow they would come with their parents to join all of Solidad for the festival at Windy Reef.

Just beyond the village, we passed a huge banana and coconut plantation—a sprawling maze of bushy vegetation. The dry, curled parchment leaves of the banana fronds stretched above the underbrush, their thick stems of bananas hanging upside down. The fanning, feathery leaves of the coconut palms towered over the banana plants.

A two-story, weatherworn plantation house sat tucked back beyond the roadway, remnant of a bygone generation of slavery and unbridled wealth. Only a profusion of poinsettias covered the latticework of the sagging porch, a colorful, ironic touch of glories past.

Close to Coral Beach, frothing waves of azure-blue and jade-green surged against each other like miniature whirlpools, dark and threatening—a watery Continental Divide between the volatile Atlantic and the crystal-clear waters of the Caribbean. All along the Caribbean side of the island lay sands of polished ivory. Tamarind trees and palms weighted with ripened coconuts lined the water's edge, their fronds dipping and waving lazily in the cooling breeze. David and I were entranced by the peaceful lure of the isle, the calm sea mirroring paradise and dreams for us as we nestled in each other's arms the rest of the way to Frangipani Point.

Kikko had been right. As we stood on the grassy tip of Frangipani, we looked down the golden hillside over all of

Solidad. I felt as if we owned the world, or at least a gorgeous slice of it. Just below us was the entrance to Cobranza Bay. Boats dotted the water in random patterns. Bare-chested seamen stood in their trading sloops, pulling in their fishing nets and sails. Rowboats, many of them laden with vegetables and wares, drifted near the docks, heading toward market. The sparkling bay hugged a wide swatch of white, untouched beach, the sand so clean and creamy I wanted to build castles and walk barefoot and feel the hot sands shift between my toes. For one fanciful moment I wanted to forget everything else and just live there forever with David.

When we finally left Frangipani Point, Kikko cut a path of his own, forcing Sweet Hibiscus down the steep, sandy incline. I grabbed David's arm with a death grip as the surrey tilted precariously, then slipped and skidded toward the beach. With frightened snorts, the mare plowed through the sand pebbles to the trampled weeds and scrub-high underbrush above the beach, plodding on to the quiet, blue lagoon. At last she wound her way around some Tamarind trees to the road that led back to the marketplace.

I was relieved when we reached town and Kikko pulled Sweet Hibiscus to a stop on the quay side of the dock. A trading sloop unloaded its exotic wares while shoppers bartered for the best price from the fishermen sorting their catch of conch, kingfish, and lobster. Wrinkling his nose at the stench of raw fish, David lifted me safely from the surrey. I wiped the dust and perspiration from my face with David's handkerchief, then took his hand and looked around.

The town of Solidad was a mixture of crowded pastel buildings with shuttered windows and galvanized roofs, simple cream-colored homes with orange and red rooftops, and an official-looking, coral rock structure with red awnings. Women with jet-black hair and snapping dark eyes scurried toward the open-air market, huge baskets of fruit perched on their heads. Across the street, wrinkled old women danced barefoot through giant trays of nutmeg, allspice, cocoa, and cloves, shuffling the spices so they could dry evenly in the sun.

Solidad's only policeman stood ramrod straight in the middle of the road, balanced on a crude, rough-hewn crate. He was spotless in his white jacket with its epaulets and shiny brass buttons. His striped black trousers were creased and his polished black shoes almost mirrored his wide sunglasses and puckered cheeks as he blew his whistle. His white-gloved hand shot into the air to stop the carts and bikes crossing our path. The officer tipped his captain's hat to David and me with the usual Creole charm and hospitality.

We crossed to the row of open-air booths where kilo scales dangled from makeshift burlap awnings while bulging sacks of dried beans and red peppers basked in the sun. The bins were heaping with red tomatoes, hills of onions, sliced water-melon, bruised bananas, fly-dotted mangoes, and pineapples with spiky stalks. Other booths displayed apples and grape-fruit, potatoes and cabbage heads, summer squash and bright-green limes. As quickly as one Creole husked the hulls, another tossed the hairy brown coconuts onto the counter.

A squat, buxom woman with sagging upper arms and short, crinkly black hair beckoned us into her booth. Straw hats and purses hung from the hooks above her; woven baskets, flowers, and placemats filled the table in front of her. "You like? You buy," she offered.

David scrutinized several baskets. "Michelle, I think I'd rather buy a carving or painting for Eva," he said.

The woman rubbed her broad, flat nose, then nodded vigorously. She swirled her wide, flowing blue skirt around her hips and stepped out of her booth. "No straw," she said. "Carvings." She crooked her finger and we followed her next door. "You see. You buy."

"Maybe they work on a commission," David chuckled. But the woman had chosen well. Seascapes, pictures of Cobranza Bay, a breathtaking painting of a lone schooner in the moonlight—all done by native artists. And exquisite carvings of dolphins and dancers and pirates and exotic birds. We went wild, buying gifts for my family and for Eva Thornton and souvenirs for ourselves.

Back at the surrey, Kikko brightened when he saw our packages. "You buy. You make Kikko happy."

"Ah," said David. "Kikko gets a cut too." We piled onto the surrey. "One more stop, Kikko. Your village and hot-pepper stew."

The village people were as curious about us as we were about them. They giggled, fascinated, as I took my pen and jotted a few descriptive phrases in my notebook. Their primitive homes hugged the roadway, but the children and animals ran freely. The family laundry was spread and drying on the surrounding rocks and bushes. Scarlet and yellow fuchsias sweetened the air.

Moses' larger home sat off from the rest under the sheltering fans of a travelers palm. Moses sat in the open doorway with poultices of wet leaves on his kneecaps. His neighbor, a bony, hollow-cheeked man with placid eyes, sat stooped on a box nearby while a gangly, grinning youth nervously trimmed his hair.

David and I walked over to the little porch while Kikko remained with the surrey. "Hello, Moses," I greeted. "How are you?"

He peered at me, his forehead ridged with deep-set wrinkles. His filmy eyes revealed unrelenting pain. Licking his cracked, leathery lips, he declared, "Thank God the breath is still in me."

"But your knees—is something wrong?"

His smile was as slow and deliberate as his speech. He rubbed his thighs and knees. "They be worn with many years."

"Doesn't Doc Dooley have medicine to help you?"

The old fisherman shook his head. "Not like herbs of Solidad. You see? Moses boil mango leaves. They make hurt go away. It is way of my people." He nodded at an empty oil drum beside him. "Sit." Then, noticing my notebook, he asked, "You write words?"

"Yes. About Solidad."

"Good words?"

"Yes." I wondered if I should tell him. How could I begin to explain to old Moses what a novel was, or what purpose it served? I gazed at his workworn hands that had fished for a lifetime, hands that skillfully maneuvered a fishing vessel. I sought to master something far more elusive. "I'm writing a story about Solidad," I said, realizing my answer was far from adequate.

David leaned casually against the door casing. "She wants to write about the buccaneers and pirates who used to roam your ocean and the sunken treasure that she thinks still lies hidden out there somewhere."

Moses followed David's gaze. "We still have treasures," he said seriously. "They be under Solidad."

"You mean in the ocean?" I asked excitedly.

"No. Under island."

David's interest sparked. "You mean, under the lava?"

The old man smiled tolerantly. "In the tunnels."

"There are tunnels under Solidad?" I cried.

Moses shrugged. "Tunnels? Caverns? No one know for sure. No one dare ride cliffs." He pointed toward the ocean. "Sr. Cobranza want me ride my fishing boat to ship—"

"A pirate ship?"

"Honey, Moses isn't that old," chided David. He crouched down beside the old fisherman. "What ship, Moses?"

Moses shrugged again. "I not go." His eyes followed the sea. "My fishing boat cannot ride angry waters. No man ride face of skull and live." He shook his head sadly. "My friends try. Long ago they take cocoa plants for Ricardo Cobranza. Go only at night."

"And?" I asked breathlessly.

"They die. Their boats lost."

I looked at David. His eyes were troubled. He straightened and squeezed my shoulder. "It's getting late. We'd better be going."

We said good-bye to Moses and his friends and continued our tour of the village, with Kikko lagging just behind us. Between smiles and handshakes and little children touching my skirt and patting my white skin, David and I tried to sort out the things Moses had said.

"David, why in the world would Cobranza risk the lives of the Creole fishermen in their frail boats? Especially at night! Look at the way the ocean batters the lava rocks. What chance would a flimsy fishing vessel have against such turbulence?"

David didn't answer. He had that quizzical expression that told me he was deep in thought.

"David, I'm talking to you."

He smiled down at me. "I know. I'm listening."

"Then answer me. Why did Cobranza want Moses to risk his life to sail out to some ship, some freighter? Why didn't the ship just anchor in Cobranza Bay?"

"Maybe the bay's too shallow for a large ship to dock."

"There's always Coral Beach or Frangipani Point—" I paused to smile at a woman casually nursing her baby as she gathered in her laundry. "Or why didn't Cobranza send his cocoa plants to Martinique or Grenada for shipping? Why did he insist they go at night?"

"There's only one reason I can think of."

"Tell me. Tell me!"

"If Cobranza was shipping something illegal, then he might risk lives and ships."

"What's so illegal about cocoa plants?"

"Their by-product. *Cocaine.*"

"Oh, David, you mean drugs—illicit drugs?"

"Why not? Rumor has it that Cobranza left Colombia after a political uprising. His wife was severely burned. He came here. Bought the island. Built his mansion. Think about it. His son had all the funds he needed to refurbish the old mansion, transform it into the luxurious Windy Reef Hotel. Where did the money come from? Cobranza had to make his living somehow on this isolated island."

"Then what Moses said about the caverns, the caves, hidden treasure—is it possible?"

David stopped abruptly, pivoted, and stared hard at Kikko. "You've been listening, haven't you?"

Kikko nodded. His Adam's apple bobbed in his throat.

"What about it? Are there caves under Solidad?"

"Me a boy," Kikko said defensively. "Me not know."

"You must be 16 or more, Kikko. Haven't you heard about Ricardo Cobranza? Didn't anyone ever mention Cobranza's ships?"

"Me not remember."

David was obviously exasperated. I patted his arm soothingly. "Don't frighten Kikko, darling."

"He's not frightened, Michelle, just guarded." David turned back to the boy. "Come on, Kikko, is it true? Caverns? Ships?"

Kikko's wistful eyes were suddenly piercing, glinting fire. He stared mournfully toward the ocean. "My grandfather— he die in fishing boat. Very dark. No stars. Never come back from freighter."

"Have you seen the caverns, Kikko?"

"No. No one see."

"But they're there. Somewhere?"

"On Tamarind Bluff."

"Are there maps, Kikko?" I broke in. He frowned. "You know, pictures of the island?" I spread my hands expansively.

"Maps?" He turned the word over in his mind, then shrugged. "Kikko no understand."

"Michelle, they wouldn't be apt to have maps of the island. Maybe blueprints of the hotel, or primitive sketches of Solidad, but probably nothing official."

"Where would we find them—blueprints, maps, whatever?"

"Who knows? I suppose Esteban Medina might have such papers stowed in the hotel safe. But right now—" He hesitated. "—I'm more interested in where Cobranza grew his cocoa plants, and where he might have made cocaine."

"We've been all over the island, David."

"Not quite, Michelle. We haven't been to Cocoa Lake or Mt. Peligro." As we walked on, David slipped his arm around my shoulder.

I glanced up at the stony set of his jaw. "You're worried."

"Yes," he said softly, so low that Kikko couldn't hear him. "If Cobranza was mixed up in drugs—cocaine—then why did the DEA choose this island for Steve and Jackie's hideaway?"

"Did Josh choose it? He was so sure it was perfectly safe."

"But Josh has never forgiven Steve for the death of his friend, Paul Mangano. It's a nasty thought, Michelle—God help me. But would Josh have sent Steve where the drug syndicate could find him?"

I started to tremble. "I want to go back to the hotel, David."

"I promised Kikko we'd go by his place."

Kikko was at our side immediately, grinning, standing at attention, ready to escort us to his little house. When we arrived at the modest dwelling moments later, Kikko's mother—a tiny, smiling, round-faced woman—greeted us with cups of steaming stew. Thanking her, I took a mouthful and felt the fire, like hot Tabasco sauce, burning my throat. I turned away, blowing against the pain.

David's dark eyes met mine and flashed with sympathy, but

his face remained sober. "Kikko, tell your mother the soup is exceptionally warm." He looked off toward the island cemetery behind Kikko's house. "Would it be all right if we walked up there? We'll drop the cups off on our way back."

"Thanks, David," I whispered as we stole behind the first knobby knoll. "I couldn't have taken another swallow for anything."

David glanced back. Kikko's home was far enough from view. He took my cup and emptied the contents on the ground behind some underbrush. "There, that should help cool your throat."

As the dark liquid soaked into the ground, I asked David, "Do you really think there's a cavern under Solidad?"

"I don't know about Solidad, but there'll be one in your novel."

"Be serious, David. Do you think there could be secret underground passages?"

He held open the cemetery's rusty iron gate for me. "Michelle, Michelle, why don't you just go to the Solidad courthouse and ask for their official records on the island?"

"Don't make fun of me, David. You know Solidad doesn't have a courthouse."

"And it probably doesn't have tunnels either."

"You've made your point, dear," I snapped and walked on ahead. Sometimes there was no reasoning with David. I turned my attention to the cemetery instead. To my surprise, the isolated graveyard was unkempt, the crypts nestled modestly among a profusion of exotic weeds and untended shrubbery. I studied the rustic markers with undisguised fascination—a handful of timeworn tombstones scarred by innumerable seasons of wind, rain, and sun. The quaint little cemetery possessed an eerie gothic quality that sent my imagination soaring. Old weatherbeaten crypts sat on top of the ground, piled high with smooth, pale stones. Several family crypts, actually long cement boxes, were decorated with crude carved crosses or tiny makeshift altars. Artificial wreaths hung forlornly on some. A broken vase with wilted flowers graced a child's headstone with bedraggled glory.

I walked solemnly among the crypts and markers, reading inscriptions that had not been obliterated by nature's buffeting.

The names were unfamiliar, strange on my lips. Nevertheless, I felt a sense of awe, knowing each had been someone's beloved father, mother, or child.

I followed a narrow, weedy path up a rocky incline to a large, finely carved stone that stood off from the others. The smooth granite marker was set apart by a stubby iron fence. David followed me over and we read the epitaph together: ALEJANDRA COBRANZA, AMOR DE MI CORAZON.

"I wonder what it means," David mused.

"Love of my heart," I said in a reverential hush. "Can you believe it, David? This is where she's buried. Cobranza's wife!"

A huge bouquet of freshly cut flowers—tulips, bougainvillea, wild orchids, and frangipani blossoms—stood at the foot of the marker, one blazing swatch of color on a mournful, muted landscape.

I reached automatically for David's hand, the only warm, pulsing touch of life in this deathly vale. I felt as if we were intruding on the past, trespassing into the forbidding realm of death itself.

I looked up at David, feeling tears sting in my eyes. "The portrait of Alejandra—it's so vibrantly alive, so beautiful. To think it ended for her here in this remote, forgotten graveyard."

"Someone didn't forget," said David, nodding toward the flowers.

"Yes—I wonder who put them here?"

"Someone who's still grieving."

"But David, her husband's dead and her son's in Europe." I stooped down and ran my fingers over Alejandra's name. "Alone in life, alone in death," I whispered.

David drew me back up beside him. "It's funny there's no marker for her husband," he said. "You'd think he'd get equal billing."

I nudged David scoldingly. "Really, how can you be so imperturbably practical at a time like this?"

"I just think it's strange that there's not a monument here for him as well. After all, he was the rich and powerful landowner—"

"You know what happened, David. Ricardo Cobranza dove from our balcony into the ocean." I shivered even as I said the words. "There was no body. He was never found."

David shook his head thoughtfully. "Just the same, you'd think someone would have erected a monument or carved his name in stone. Someone would have cared enough to see that Cobranza wasn't forgotten. Unless there was a good reason to forget . . ."

CHAPTER FIFTEEN

On Friday, Windy Reef turned into a buzz of activity, with a constant flow of traffic in and out of the hotel. Even in the usually sedate quiet of the dining room, there was an air of expectancy, a hustle and bustle among the waiters.

"Will you be at the fiesta tonight?" I asked our boyish, olive-eyed waiter as he handed us the menu.

He beamed, showing large, even teeth. "Yes, missus. Everyone go to fiesta. The dining room—no open. We eat with the stars. There be music, flowers, laughter. You like."

"Sounds romantic," said David after our waiter had gone. He reached for my hand and asked in his most seductive tone, "Would you care to attend the fiesta with me, Mrs. Ballard?"

Lightly I answered, "Why not? As long as Mr. Ballard approves."

David's eyes swept over me admiringly. With a veiled note of flirtation, he replied, "I can assure you, my darling, Mr. Ballard more than approves. In fact, he finds you absolutely ravishing."

"In that case, please inform him he has a date for the fiesta." I paused, eyeing David provocatively, thriving on our little game. "Is Mr. Ballard aware that the gala event will be held right under our bedroom window?"

He gave my hand a lingering kiss and said huskily, "How wonderfully convenient."

I lowered my voice to a whisper. "There's nothing that says we have to wait until tonight to start celebrating."

David put aside his menu and smiled invitingly. "Suddenly what I'm hungry for isn't on the menu."

After a hasty brunch and a leisurely hour in our private jacuzzi, David and I stepped out onto our veranda to watch the pool patio become transformed into an exotic flower garden. Waiters and bellboys in old work clothes polished the brass pool lights, swept the tennis courts, lined up banquet tables, and hung festive ribbons and streamers. A fresh gush of water gradually filled the pool.

David and I gazed down in wordless fascination as three Creoles dragged in the plump, stiff body of a wild pig and hung it on the rotating rotisserie. All day long, through our open sliding doors, we could hear the excited chatter of the Creoles as they prepared for the party. Caught up in their excitement, I laid out several outfits for the evening, changing my mind and my accessories three or four times until David finally said, "I like you best in the slinky gown."

"My silk sheath?"

He pulled me to him and kissed me gently. "Yes. It sets off the gray-green of your eyes and fits you like a—caress."

"That's what I'm afraid of," I smiled, easing out of his arms. "No more kisses, David. We have to meet Steve and Jackie in the lobby in a half hour, and you know how long it takes me to do my face."

"Your face is perfect already."

"My face is swimming in cleansing cream!"

He laughed. "Is that why I slid halfway across the room when I kissed you?"

I grabbed up a pillow and swung it playfully at him, but he caught it in midair and pushed it back at me. We struggled back and forth for several moments, then fell laughing onto the bed. As David kissed me tenderly, my heart started doing cartwheels.

We were a half hour late meeting Steve and Jackie in the lobby.

"Where were you?" Jackie exclaimed, coming to greet us. "The party's already begun."

Quietly I confided, "We were having our own little party."

"Oh really? Then maybe you should have skipped the fiesta."

"Oh no, never! I've heard too much about it. I've been looking forward to it all week."

We headed outside toward the pool, feeling the welcome brush of the trade winds against our faces. Jackie held little Stevie's hand while David walked on ahead with Steve. I heard David say, "Hey, Steve, you haven't got back to me yet with that report."

"Report?" Steve hedged.

"You know. Who owns the fishing net that Michelle got tangled in?"

"Silas was gone a couple of days," Steve answered evasively. "He's back now. We're on it, David. Trust me."

I linked arms with Jackie. "And where has the dashing, seductive, Argus-eyed Silas Winters been, pray tell?"

"Island hopping."

"What?"

"Grenada this time. Aruba the last time."

"Grenada?" I stopped in the middle of the walkway. Little Stevie pulled away from his mother and ran to David, who scooped him up and lifted him high onto his shoulders. "What was Silas doing in Grenada?" I asked.

"Michelle, how would I know? Silas Winters is a very private individual."

"I know. That's why he intrigues me."

Jackie laughed and pulled me over to the edge of the path while several other guests passed by. "Any hint of intrigue or mystery and old Hopewell College's Sherlock is right there following it up."

"And dragging you into it, right?"

Jackie sobered. "Lately, Michelle, I'm not certain which one of us is dragging the other along. But I think you're wrong about Silas. After all, when we first got here he told Steve he'd be gone two or three days each month." She paused, reflecting. "Besides, Esteban apparently sees nothing wrong with Silas' travels."

"But why a mini-vacation every month?"

"Who knows? If he's like Steve and me, it would keep him from going stir-crazy in Paradise."

"Well, nobody forced him to come here, did they? I thought he liked Solidad's easy, laid-back living."

"There's no doubt about that," Jackie agreed. "Actually, I think he applied for the position of concierge just to meet expenses. His real calling seems to be swimming, sailing, scuba diving, and—"

"And women, especially Nicole from the gift shop," I finished. "But I haven't figured that one out yet."

"What's that supposed to mean?"

"I keep telling David there's something more between Nicole and Silas than just romance. I can't put my finger on it—but I think he's using her."

Jackie uttered a skeptical chuckle, barely lifting one finely arched brow. "Using her? How? How, Sherlock?"

"She's a go-between, between the hotel guests and the islanders. I get the idea that Silas never misses a thing, and if he does, Nicole will keep him posted. She has a way with the people. Of course, she ought to. She's one of them."

"Not really, Michelle. Nicole came here to live shortly after Silas did."

"What?" I asked, startled. "I thought she was an islander, that Solidad was her home." I didn't admit that I had even fleetingly wondered if Ricardo Cobranza or old Juan Medina might have been her father.

Jackie shook her blonde, stylishly coiffed head confidently. "No. One thing I do know. Nicole came from Grenada."

"Well, you just burst my theory."

"It's more likely I blew your mystery, or put a flaw in your novel."

"That too," I conceded. "It's still a good thing that it's Nicole and not my kid sister Pam living here on Solidad. She'd be worse than Nicole."

"What are you saying, Michelle? Surely Pam wouldn't—"

I slipped into my most dramatic voice. "Pam would be totally hypnotized by Silas Winters' brawny good looks and his magnetic Machiavellian personality."

Jackie covered her mouth to stifle a laugh.

"Okay, you two," David called impatiently from a few yards

away. "If you want a seat at this fiesta, you'd better come along."

I wrinkled my nose at Jackie and whispered, "I guess I'll get used to that—someone telling me what to do." We giggled like a couple of schoolgirls and hurried on to join our husbands.

For the first time I consciously gazed around, taking in the milling, gaily-costumed crowd and the festive decorations. The Windy Reef staff had outdone themselves, creating an exciting, flamboyant atmosphere with Oriental lanterns, pastel lighting, and authentic native ornaments. The golden-brown Creole women looked striking with their long, graceful necks, quick smiles, and lively, flirty eyes. They were traditionally dressed from the tip of their multicolored turbans to the flat, scuffy slippers on their slender feet. Large brass earrings and ornate necklaces accented their madras outfits—bright silk scarfs and long wraparound skirts in vivid floral prints and wild plaids. The men strutted proudly in their long, white trousers and fanciest short-sleeve shirts made of sea-island cotton.

We made our way through the throng over to the front of the pool where, fortunately, we found a reserved section for hotel guests. We had hardly taken our seats when we heard a boisterous, complaining voice behind us. "Ruth, I'm not going to sit here all evening waiting for this thing to get under way."

"Hush, Orville."

"Hush me, will you?" he hissed. "I've paid my money, good money. A ritzy joint like this needs to be on time."

"Calm down," the woman urged. "You mustn't upset yourself."

"Upset? Who's getting upset!" he exploded.

"Take your medicine, Orville."

Finally I glanced around at the fat, toady-faced Orville Glocke, his sagging double chin bobbing as he talked. His nostrils flared on his immense, powerful nose, momentarily flattening the bulbous tip where someone's fist, perhaps his wife's, had once before forced him into silence. He flipped open the medicine bottle and popped a pill under his tongue. Unexpectedly, his snapping brown eyes met mine. Again, I felt that stabbing sense of pity. Even as his wide mouth creased to a half-hearted grin, his pouty lower lip hung low, creating a subtle sneer.

Embarrassed, I turned my gaze quickly to Ruth. Her face was rigid, expressionless. She stared straight ahead through her thick-rimmed glasses, her broad shoulders squared, as if to ward off the frowns of neighboring guests irritated by Orville's noisy tirade.

Somehow, though, I was certain Ruth had noticed me. Suddenly I heard myself calling, "Ruth—Mrs. Glocke, come and join us."

As David jabbed me, Jackie lamented, "Oh, Michelle, don't invite that old windbag and his grumpy wife over here."

It was too late. Ruth was already urging Orville's hulking frame out of his chair and toward us. He moved with the slow, feeble gait of a much older man.

"I'll get us some punch," David said, standing.

"Get some for the Glockes too," I whispered.

"Yeah—a whole jug of the rum stuff so he'll stop talking."

The Glockes took the empty seats beside me. Orville, smelling heavily of sweet cologne, dropped unceremoniously, his portly form filling the chair. Ruth sat stiffly, her large, bony hands folded on her lap. Her cotton frock hung well below her knees, almost touching her sturdy, laced shoes. "This is Mrs. Ballard, Orville," she said gratingly as he leaned toward me, "the young woman I told you about."

He reached across Ruth and gave me a weak, fishy handshake, sizing me up with beady eyes. "Evening," he said, his breathing labored. The top button of his gaudy sport shirt was open, his thick, stubby neck bulging at the collar. His sparse, gray-brown hair was well-greased and slicked down over his wide forehead, as if to forestall his advancing baldness. He leaned back in his seat and cleared his throat with a dry, hacking cough.

"I shouldn't have let him come out this evening," Ruth said out of the corner of her mouth. "Crowds are just too much for him."

I smiled. "I'm sure he'll have a good time, Mrs. Glocke."

"Maybe," she answered doubtfully. "But he has no patience at all. He's already worked himself into a sweat."

Orville glanced at me, his eyelids drooping slightly, and whined, "It's my heart. I have a bad heart."

"We should have stayed home in the Florida sunshine, not run off on some supposedly restful vacation."

Orville was fidgeting nervously now, rubbing his hand against his chest. "Ruth doesn't understand. She doesn't live with the threat of open-heart surgery every day of her life."

"Is that what you face?" I asked sympathetically.

"It's what he thinks he faces," Ruth snapped.

"And I'm a poor risk for a heart transplant," he fretted.

I noticed David working his way back to us, balancing a trayful of glasses. He nodded pleasantly when I introduced him to the Glockes. "Here, try this," said David, handing Orville a glass.

Orville scowled. "What's in it? I'm a teetotaler. Never drink. Never smoke."

"We don't either," David told him. "It's just fruit juice."

"You mean some of those strange, crazy fruits from around here?" He sipped cautiously, then sputtered and coughed. "Take it away. Take it." He thrust the glass back at David, sloshing the contents on David's new beige slacks.

"Oh, Orville, you clumsy fool!" cried Ruth.

Orville whipped out his handkerchief and awkwardly tried to dab at the darkening stain on David's trousers.

David drew back, obviously fighting for control. "That's okay, Mr. Glocke. I'll go change. But first, can I get you something else? Coffee? Water?"

"No, nothing." Orville glared at David. "I'm a heart patient, you know."

Ruth Glocke's jaw clenched taut; her eyes remained unflinching. David went off to change and was back minutes later. I sat waiting, staring silently into my fruit punch. We were all grateful when the sudden rhythmic beat of calypso music filled the air, drowning out the perpetual whine of Orville Glocke.

If the fiesta so far had had a rocky start, at least the entertainment was delightful: a fast-paced mixture of calypso and steel bands and Jamaican reggae. The musicians' instruments were as varied and colorful as their costumes—painted wood washtub drums, large kettle drums, maracas, saxophones, and painted saws. Several ebony-skinned natives played trombones, their sleek bodies bending back gracefully as they raised their instruments toward the starlit night. The sound was rich and full, flowing like a sweet, heady liquid, a mournful call streaming skyward.

A string of jet-black natives thumped on sawed-off oil drums, their long, loose-jointed fingers moving with a frenzy to produce the rhythmic, rat-a-tat beat. Their rippling chests glistened with perspiration; their faces gleamed with a beatific intensity. Increasingly caught up in their own lilting, pulsating cadence, their lean, muscular bodies presented a masterpiece of grace and tension—raw, pure music in motion. The audience loved it.

Within moments, the primitive beat got under our skin and swept up our emotions, turning us all into foot-stompers and amateur musicians. We picked up our knives and glasses or spoons and cups to tap out our own music, keeping time with the calypso bands.

I noticed a Creole youth handing out bamboo sticks. Soon, Steve, Jackie, the Medinas, and even little Stevie were echoing the sharp, throbbing beat with their bamboo instruments. Our laughter mingled with the pounding rhythm and eager voices singing the whimsical calypso lyrics.

The native dancers ascended on us then, their rich chocolate-brown skin accented by dazzling colors and ornate patterns. The women looked stunning in short skirts and bare midriffs, with bright turbans on their heads and red polish on their long nails. They danced in their bare feet, their long bead neck-laces swaying with their undulating bodies as they waved flaxen streamers in the air. The men wore wide-brimmed straw hats with a shaggy weave, long white trousers with shredded cuffs, and striped shirts with balloon sleeves that barely covered their lean, hairless chests. They moved with a sinuousness and fluidity that amazed and captivated all of us.

David, never taking his eyes from the dancers, leaned over and asked, "Think you could do that, hon?"

"Not without putting something out of joint."

When there was a brief lull in the festivities, I noticed little Stevie wiggle off his father's lap and work his way over to Orville Glocke. The blond four-year-old stared in fascination as Orville slipped another nitroglycerin tablet under his tongue.

"What's that?" Stevie asked.

"Sugar." Orville's dark eyes darted about with a surprisingly sly twinkle.

"Does your mommy let you eat sugar?" Stevie exclaimed, looking up at Ruth.

Orville seemed genuinely amused. "My mommy doesn't let me do much of anything."

"Why?" Stevie curiously tapped Orville's thick knee.

"He's sick," Ruth answered.

"Real sick?"

Orville rubbed his chest. "In here."

"Do you go to work like my daddy used to do?"

"When I'm well."

Stevie ran his miniature toy truck over Orville's kneecap. "Do you drive a truck like this?"

"He does not!" snapped Ruth. "He's an investment counselor."

Stevie puckered his lips, puzzled.

Glocke reached out with his smooth, hairless hand and gently rubbed his knuckle against Stevie's cheek. "That means I work for my cousin, son," he said, a frazzled, wistful note in his voice.

Ruth winced. "Actually, that means he's not able to work for himself because he's lazy!"

Even from where I sat beside Ruth, I could hear Orville's heavy wheezing and sense his fury with his wife. "I've tried," he rasped. "All my life I've tried. I can't help it if I've always come in a poor second." He was still looking at Stevie, touching Stevie's cheek, but I knew his words were for his wife. Again, I sensed the rejection, antagonism, and loneliness that divided the Glockes. Behind all that blatant braggadocio was an insecure man trapped in his own mediocrity, a man who had never learned to communicate with his wife. Or had he tried— only to be met by her judicious scorn?

"I think I'd better go to my room," Orville wheezed.

"I make that noise too," Stevie said, reaching up and patting Orville's barrel chest.

"Noise?"

I leaned over and explained, "He's asthmatic. He knows what it's like to have trouble breathing."

Orville's expression softened. Ruffling Stevie's curly hair, he mumbled, "You're okay, son. You're a good little boy."

Suddenly we heard a commotion a few tables away. Dooley Edington, waving a punch glass in the air, staggered past the musicians and dancers, bellowing, "Where're they hiding the good stuff—the whiskey and rum?" He shuffled over to our table and gripped the back of David's chair for support. Lowering his face close to mine, he huffed, "Did you try the punch, Mrs. Ballard?"

I drew back, repelled by the heavy odor of rum on his breath. "The punch is delicious, Dr. Edington," I said icily.

He reared back, raising his glass like a weapon. "Lady, it tastes like tepid water. No bite, no zest. The punch has no punch, Mrs. Ballard." He elbowed me clumsily. "Get it? The punch has no punch!"

David sprang to his feet and steered the tipsy physician away from our table. "Go sober up, Doc," he ordered. "Get some coffee and a good night's sleep."

The doctor reeled away, boisterously voicing his complaints to anyone who would listen.

"I don't know why they keep him here," I told David angrily. "He's no doctor. He's a menace and a boor!"

"I'm sure they'd replace him if they had any other takers for the job," mused David. He glanced around. "People are eating now. What do you say we head over to the refreshment table and help ourselves?"

"Sounds great to me." I looked over at Jackie. "Would you like me to bring you back a plate?"

"No, thanks. Steve's getting something for Stevie and me."

David and I made our way through the crowd over to the long, linen-draped serving table abounding with delicacies. Mountains of fresh tropical fruit spilled over their crystal bowls—great clusters of coconuts and bananas, pineapples, papaya, watermelon, and mangoes. The hotel chef was there to explain the exotic native dishes—curried goat stew, fried cornmeal with okra, boiled codfish with hot peppers. When I asked about the pungent aroma I detected, he pointed to the marinated goat, which he called "cabrito" and the wild hog cooked Creole-style over an open flame. I politely thanked him for the information and moved on down the table. My eyes were drawn to the huge platters of succulent pink lobsters, jumbo shrimps, and crabs.

David decided to start off lightly with some imported cheese and stuffed avocados. Then he tried some pepper-pot soup while I sampled the sea chowder. "Do you think this diet will ever replace a good old hamburger and fries?" he grinned.

I scanned the multitude of Creole dishes and mused teasingly, "You never know, sweetheart. I may develop a real taste for buttered conch or eggs mixed with sea urchins."

"Not if I can help it, my darling."

We had just returned to our table and sat down when we heard Dooley Edington's thick, strident voice again. "You all want to see some good swimming?" he challenged, his words slurred. "Watch an expert at work!" He lunged out of his chair and swayed across the patio to the edge of the pool. He teetered, made a low, sweeping bow, then toppled into the deep end and disappeared from view.

There was a gasp throughout the crowd, then a hushed silence. The pool lights cast eerie reflections on the water, but Dooley Edington did not break the surface. At last, Esteban Medina pushed his way through the throng and dove into the pool. Within seconds, they broke the surface together. Even from where we were sitting, I could see a smirk on Dooley's puffy face. He pushed Esteban's arms away, then swam with a powerful breaststroke across the full length of the pool. He hoisted himself out of the water, stood up, and straightened his wet, clinging sports attire, then waved jauntily to the crowd. A spontaneous burst of applause rose from the guests.

"An energetic swim for someone so inebriated," David noted in disgust. "I wonder what enjoyment he got out of spoiling the party?"

I patted David's hand. "Who knows? Some people may think he *made* the party."

I heard another voice, deep and commanding, coming from the pool area. Silas Winters stood beside the swimming pool, raising his hands to quiet the crowd. "Since everyone's attention has been focused on the pool, and since Esteban is already in the water, perhaps he will agree to demonstrate some of his masterful diving skills."

The crowd was on a roll now, clapping their hands, stamping

their feet, shouting Esteban's name, urging him on. Esteban stripped down to his swim trunks, discarding his wet sport clothes as he walked around to the diving platform.

We watched curiously as he mounted the ladder, strode boldly onto the springboard, and stood erect, arms at his sides. Then he took a springing step forward, propelled himself into a strong hurdle, and hung suspended in the air for an instant before gliding down effortlessly into the water. There was only the hint of a splash.

The crowd broke into cheers as Esteban went back to the high board for another dive, and another. He made forward dives and backward dives, somersaults and twists. Every dive was executed with precision and flair. The crowd went wild.

"He's good, really good," David whispered approvingly.

I nodded, recalling the fable of the ugly duckling who became a graceful swan. For the first time I saw what Lucia herself must have seen in Esteban Medina when she became his bride.

After the party as David and I were heading back to the hotel, I stopped Lucia and told her how much I had enjoyed her husband's performance. "Where did he ever learn to dive like that?" I asked.

"Oh, Esteban dive all his life. When he a little boy he learn to dive from high cliffs of Solidad. No one dive better than my Esteban."

I was about to ask her another question when I spotted someone hovering in the shadow of the bushes near the hotel entrance. As we passed by, I recognized Javier peering out at the exhilarated, slowly dispersing crowd. "Hello, Javier," I called out, but when I looked again, he was gone. I looked back at Lucia. "How sad that that gentle old gardener didn't join the party."

"Yes, poor Javier. He is always alone. He trust no one, except my Esteban."

"And Doc Edington, of course," I added.

Lucia scowled. "Is hard to be old and sick. Javier have no choice but to trust doctor."

In the lobby, David and I said good night to Lucia and stepped into the elevator. As we started up to our suite, I gazed through the ornamental gold filigree for a fleeting glimpse of Alejandra's portrait on the distant lobby wall. *You would have enjoyed the party we had at your home tonight,* I mused wistfully. *I wish you could have been here with us. I would love to have known you.*

When we reached our floor, David and I strolled arm in arm to our door, still savoring the enchantment of the evening. "Tired, darling?" he asked.

"Yes, but it's a good kind of tired."

"Not *too* tired, I hope."

"Never too tired for you, my dear husband."

"Ah, music to my ears!" David flipped his key in the air and reached for the doorknob. At his touch the door creaked open.

"Didn't you lock the door?" I gasped.

"Of course I locked the door." Gingerly he pushed it open and stepped in ahead of me. "Stay back, Michelle!"

"What is it? What's wrong?" I pushed in beside him and stared in horror at our honeymoon suite. Everything lay in disarray—books, clothing, and papers scattered everywhere. "Oh, Shakespeare!" I uttered in dismay. "We've been ransacked! It's Morro Bay happening all over again!"

CHAPTER
SIXTEEN

It was nearly 3 A.M. and I couldn't get to sleep. The chilling realization that a stranger had been in our hotel suite and had gone through our personal things left me feeling vulnerable, violated. Who could have done such a thing? And how? The lock hadn't been broken; someone had used a key!

David had rushed immediately to the Gauguin painting to see if the intruder had discovered our secret computer room. With relief, we saw that the picture hung evenly; the door panel remained sealed, the project safe. For the next two hours David methodically straightened the suite, returning everything to its rightful place. He worked in dogged silence, his chiseled features set with a sullen intensity. I tried to help, but I felt numb, unable to function, my mind fragmented with fear. Then, exhausted, we collapsed into bed. David turned his face to the wall and fell into a sound slumber, but I tossed restlessly for over an hour.

Finally, in exasperation, I rose, pulled on my silk robe, and walked out to the darkened veranda. The cool sea breeze felt marvelously refreshing. Already I could feel my mind clearing, my tension unraveling. I gazed down at the pool area that just hours ago had been alive with music and laughter. It was empty now, eerily silent, the hazy moonlight reflecting dimly on the pool's shimmering surface. Only the muted crash of the ocean waves broke the stillness. I shivered. A Cimmerian darkness had settled over the ghostly cliffs of Tamarind Bluff.

I leaned against the balcony railing, praying, relishing the solitude, sensing the Lord's comforting presence, feeling His refuge and strength, His unfailing love. I was no longer aware of time passing. Had I stood there an hour? A half hour?

I was about to turn and go inside when a flash of movement on the path below caught my eye. I peered down into the shadows, my breath catching in astonishment. In the dead of night a lone woman in a tattered wedding dress flitted across the patio, her long, flowing hair wafting with the wind. With the exuberance of a child she twirled, her petticoat flouncing, and reached for a streamer dangling from the brass pool light. She tore the ribbon free and clutched it to her bosom. Then, like a phantom from an elusive dream, she disappeared into the predawn darkness.

My mind was suddenly reeling as I stepped back inside. Who was the strange woman? Why was she out alone? Where had she gone? I knew as well as I knew my own name that I had to find out. Should I wake David? He would only scoff at my overactive imagination and tell me to mind my own business. I grabbed David's royal blue bathrobe from the four-poster and yanked it on over my own flimsy robe. Stealthily I tiptoed out of the suite and down the hallway to the spiral staircase. I dashed down the stairs to the lobby, took a fleeting glance at the haunting portrait of Alejandra, and slipped out the door, alone, into the night.

I made my way over the familiar path toward the pool, searching vainly for the woman. My disappointment mounted as I stopped by the lamp pole where she had broken off the streamer. I looked up. The torn ribbon fluttered in the breeze.

So! The woman was real, not just an apparition or an illusion. I glanced around. The mauve, star-flecked sky was already giving way to pale streams of light. Where moments ago there had been deep and seething shadows, now the first splintering rays of tropical sunlight were painting the landscape with raw, smoldering color.

I realized suddenly that I was standing on the hotel patio in David's bathrobe. I took a hurried step. My open-toed slipper struck something solid. Looking down, I noticed a shiny object on the concrete walkway. I bent to retrieve it. There, in the palm of my hand, lay a bejeweled, heart-shaped locket. There was something strangely familiar about it. Then it struck me. It was the same gold locket Alejandra had worn in her bridal portrait! David would never believe it!

As I darted toward the hotel entrance, I heard heavy footsteps behind me. I whirled around. Esteban Medina came striding up from the garden pathway. He raised a large hand in greeting and smiled, making his homely features almost palatable.

"You're an early bird, Mrs. Ballard," he said. "What has you out at the crack of dawn?"

Embarrassed, I wrapped my robe tightly around me. "I—I saw someone. A woman. She was all alone, dressed in a wedding gown—"

He chuckled good-naturedly. "Ah, yes, Dr. Edington told me you have a vivid imagination."

"I'm not imagining it, Mr. Medina. Look, this locket—I found it right here where she was standing. Don't you recognize it? It's the same as the locket in the portrait. It must have belonged to Alejandra Cobranza!"

Esteban smiled tolerantly as we began walking toward the hotel entrance together. "Oh, Mrs. Ballard, Sr. Cobranza made many counterfeit copies to protect the original priceless gem. After his death the imitation lockets were sold to the islanders."

"But it's so gorgeous. Couldn't this be the original?"

"Oh, no, absolutely not. It—it was buried with Alejandra."

"Then may I keep this one for a souvenir?"

"I'm afraid not," he said, casually taking it from me. "One of our guests must have dropped it at the fiesta last night. I'm sure she'll come back to claim it."

Medina held the lobby door open for me. "By the way, Mrs. Ballard, I have a message at the desk for your husband. I forgot to give it to him on Thursday—what with the excitement of getting ready for the Frangipani Festival yesterday."

"What message?"

"Your husband's business partner is arriving in Solidad today. Silas Winters and Moses are on their way to Martinique to pick—"

"Eva Thornton? Coming here?"

"No, that wasn't the name. Ken—Kendall, something like that."

"Kendrick?" I ventured.

"Yes. That was it. He is your husband's business associate, isn't he?" Medina's wide-set raven eyes studied me curiously. I swallowed uneasily, not wanting to lie.

"Perhaps your husband sent for Mr. Kendall?"

"Kendrick," I corrected. "Sent for him without confiding in me? Have you forgotten? My husband and I are on our honeymoon."

"I realize that—but does your husband?" Medina kept fingering the heart-shaped locket, its worn chain slipping between his fingers. "Wait one minute. I'll get the cable for you."

He strolled to his desk, rummaged in a drawer, then said, "Yes, here it is. This Kendrick fellow is due today—and bringing someone with him."

"And you said Silas Winters is on his way to pick them up?"

"Yes. They should be here by noon."

I turned to go. Medina's words stopped me. "Mrs. Ballard, I just wanted you to know how much my wife enjoys your company."

"Lucia? Yes, we've had some good visits. She's lovely."

"I know. I would do anything for my Lucia."

I gazed at the sturdy, rough-hewn face. *Anything?* I wondered. *Anything but leave Solidad.*

Moments later, as I walked alone down the east corridor, I glanced at the cable, my eyes riveting on the name, P. Merrill. Impossible! My kid sister Pam coming to Solidad with Joshua Kendrick? *Why!* As I rushed into the bridal suite to tell David, I found him up and dressed—with piles of clothes and suitcases all over the bed! "David, what are you doing?"

"Packing."

"But, David—"

He stopped and glanced at me, disapproval flashing in his eyes. "Where have you been in my bathrobe, Michelle?"

"Out—"

"I realize that, but where? I wake up and find you gone."

"I can explain."

"I'm sure you can." His tone was cool, edged with tension.

"David, why are you packing? Where are you going?"

"We are going home. Today."

"Leaving Solidad? Weren't you even going to ask me?"

"How, Michelle? You weren't here."

I knew my tears were coming. "David, why are we fighting?"

His gaze registered surprise. "Darling, I didn't know we were."

"But you've made the decision to—to run out on the Turmans."

"The Marshalls, you mean." David lifted a suitcase off the bed, then sat down. He patted the spot beside him. "Come here, Michelle," he said gently.

I briskly wiped away my tears. "Your timing's lousy."

"It's not what you think, Michelle. I'd love to make love to you, but right now I just want us to talk. Please."

I went reluctantly to him. He squeezed my hand as I sat down beside him. "I think the safest thing we can do for Jackie and Steve—and for ourselves—is to leave this island."

"But what will happen to them if we leave?"

David was thoughtful. "What I'm worried about is what will happen to them if we don't go. They were here for a week before we arrived. No problems. No threats on their lives. But the minute we arrived, bang! Too many coincidental happenings. Michelle, I think someone is using us to get to our friends."

"Who, David?"

He stared into space, his Vietnam battle scar pulsating slightly. "I don't know, but we've got to get off Solidad to get help. We'll catch the first flight out of Martinique. Today, if possible. As soon as we hit Miami, I'll telephone Joshua Kendrick."

"And if you can't reach him?" I asked cautiously, wondering how to tell him that Josh and Pam were arriving at Windy Reef at noon.

"I'll contact the DEA office in Miami. The government put the Turmans on this island. It's their responsibility to protect them."

"Can't we send a message to the DEA from here?"

"How, Michelle? We haven't made a move on Solidad

without someone knowing what we're doing. Whoever that someone is, I'm convinced he or she doesn't want us with the Tur—er, Marshalls." David gave me a twisted smile that mirrored his concern. "We've had enough invitations to leave."

"Wouldn't it be safer to take Jackie and Steve with us?"

David chewed on his lower lip. "That's even more risky. We didn't bring them here. We can't invite them to leave. Besides, Steve wouldn't budge. He trusts Kendrick implicitly."

At the mention of Joshua's name again, I groaned. "David, there's something I must tell you. I just don't know how to—"

A curious twinkle glinted in his eyes. "Really? I hope you're not carrying around the same kind of secret Jackie's sporting."

"What? You mean, me—pregnant?" In spite of the tension between us, I laughed out loud. "But wait a minute. I thought you wanted a family."

He drew me against him. "I do, Michelle. But not in the middle of my honeymoon and not on Solidad."

"I think it's worse than that, David," I told him, my words muffled against his chest.

He released me and tilted my face up to his. "Michelle, we didn't get another hate message, did we?"

I was alarmed by the fire in David's eyes. In his agitated state, how could I announce that Joshua and my kid sister Pam were arriving within hours? I unfolded the cable and handed it to him.

He read aloud: "J. Kendrick and P. Merrill from Ballard Computer Design arriving Saturday. Book rooms one week." He crumpled the cable and threw it in the basket. "What on earth is Kendrick thinking of—coming here with Pam?" David was on his feet now, pacing. "What's worse, Kendrick has taken the liberty of hiding behind my company's name! What next? Isn't anything sacred to that man?"

"Darling, do you think I'm jumping up and down to hear that my kid sister is coming to Solidad—on my honeymoon? Today, no less. I'm worried. What if Josh is involving her in something dangerous?"

"What I don't get," said David, "is how in the world Pam convinced Joshua to take her along in the first place. But one thing we can be certain of, he saw some gain in it."

David took long, anxious strides across the room and back, rubbing his head, scowling as if he had a tension headache. "Another thing. How did Esteban Medina get this cable? There are no phones on the island, no outside communication except the concierge's routine treks to Martinique. This couldn't have arrived today."

"It didn't," I admitted. "Esteban said he forgot to give it to us on Thursday."

"Thursday!" David exploded. "Medina had this cable for two days?"

"That's what he said. That's the day Silas brought the mail."

David paused in front of the open patio door and stared out at the Atlantic, his fury a match for the roiling ocean. "Esteban's a businessman, in management position. Organized. Efficient. I don't buy him forgetting to give us this message."

"Then what do you buy?"

"A deliberate delay." David turned around, offering a wan smile, his mood under control now. "So Kendrick is coming," he said, sounding almost mellow. "What time does he arrive?"

"In time for lunch."

"All right. He can get on it right away—do something about protecting Steve and Jackie. But I haven't changed my mind, Michelle. We are leaving Solidad! Come Monday, we'll be on Moses' fishing vessel, heading for Martinique."

"Then you're actually giving up the computer project?"

"Giving it back, Michelle. I've gone as far as I can. If Josh thinks it's safe for me to continue, then I can do it. Back home."

"Are we going to tell Jackie—that we're leaving?"

"If Josh feels that's best." David was back at the bedside, cupping my face in his hands. "I know that saying good-bye to Jackie won't be easy. But we have today and tomorrow. We'll spend as much time with them as we can."

"It ought to be a regular party," I said dryly, "what with Josh and my kid sister arriving."

Just before noon, David and I took a casual stroll through the hotel, keeping our eyes peeled for the surrey that would bring Pam and Josh to Windy Reef. Finally we sat down on a cushioned Mandarin love seat with a full view of the lobby door. The bamboo ceiling fans twirled lazily above us, giving a measure of relief from the unbearable heat of high noon.

When at last the surrey arrived, I jumped up eagerly, but David reached out a restraining hand. "We'll wait for them in here, Michelle. We'll let Joshua play his little game."

I sat back, but only for a moment. My sister Pam sashayed into the lobby in a low-cut sundress, her bare shoulders already crisp from the tropical sun. Joshua was right behind her, walking tall and confident, a spring in his steps, his briefcase in hand.

Pam uttered a squeal of delight and wrapped her arms around me, swinging me around in a dizzying whirl. "Oh, Michelle, I'm in love, I'm in love," she announced in her bubbly, effervescent voice.

David greeted Joshua with a reserved smile and brisk handshake.

"Would you believe? I'm in love!" Pam declared again.

I glared up at Josh.

He shrugged helplessly. "I'm sorry. It just happened."

"And your wife Nora? What about Nora? Obviously you two didn't get back together."

His eyes darkened momentarily. "Nora gave me her ultimatum. My job or my family."

"So just like that, you brought Pam to Solidad?"

"I didn't plan to, but she begged to come along—"

"And two days later, Josh called and said it was okay," Pam concluded. Her tone grew conspiratorial. "David, if you have your homework done, I'm supposed to take the secret documents to the—"

David leaned down hastily and silenced Pam with a brotherly kiss. "We'll talk in the room, Pam," he said under his breath.

Pam glanced around with anticipation. "Can we talk later, David? I have a date for lunch with that rugged, sexy, suntanned hunk of man!"

I followed her gaze and stared in utter dismay as Silas Winters charged through the lobby door in a swashbuckling strut, his muscles rippling as he brandished Pam's mountain of luggage. His dark, intense eyes, usually so shrewd and intimidating, met Pam's with irresistible charm. I could feel the magnetic spark between them.

"Oh, Michelle, isn't he totally awesome?" Pam gushed.

"Pamela Merrill, you don't know anything about him," I warned.

"Oh, but I do, Michelle. He's handsome, single, and 31. He's an only child, born in New York City—old Manhattan, to be exact. He's a college grad with a master's in political science." She paused breathlessly as Silas reached us. "And he spent a miserable four years in the Army, didn't you, Silas?"

With a cryptic nod, he set the suitcases down and told David, "I'll have the bellboy take these up to Miss Merrill's room." Then he looked down fondly at Pam and winked. "Meanwhile, my dear, shall we go to the dining room? The langouste is delightful." He glanced back at David. "Don't worry, Mr. Ballard. I'll keep an eye on the young lady for you. We'll see you tonight at dinner."

I slowly seethed inside as my innocent kid sister and the arrogant, wily Silas Winters strolled across the lobby hand in hand.

CHAPTER
SEVENTEEN

When Pam and Silas were out of sight, David turned to Joshua and said, "Would you like to come to our suite and freshen up a bit? We can talk—order room service for lunch, if you wish."

"Good idea," said Josh. "We do have business to discuss."

David was silent as he led us up to the suite. But once inside the room, he faced Josh squarely and declared, "We need to get something straight, Kendrick. Michelle and I are leaving Solidad."

Josh's face remained stoical, except for a muscle twitch along his temple. "That's it? There's no changing your mind?"

David's words erupted in a torrent of long-suppressed frustration. "Great Scott, man, do you realize what you've put us through already? And don't deny it. You've plotted and schemed and maneuvered us into an untenable situation, and we've gone along with the whole thing without protest or a whimper. I've even broken my back on that computer project of yours. But enough is enough."

"How is the project coming along?" asked Josh calmly.

David heaved a sigh. "Fine, just fine. I think I've got enough down that someone else can pick up the ball and run with it."

"It's not the project that has us worried," I told Josh.

"Then what?"

"It's all the strange things that have happened to us since we came here." I listed them for him—the hate note on my menu, the cocaine in the conch shell, my snorkeling mishap involving the fishing net, the vicious ransacking of our hotel suite.

"Someone wants us out of here," concluded David, "and I don't want to wait around to see what extreme measures he uses next time."

Josh walked over to our kitchenette and helped himself to a glass of water. "Is it always this humid here? Someone should install air conditioning. Those ceiling fans are—"

"Josh, have you heard anything we've said?" I cried.

He took a leisurely drink, then ambled over to the sofa and sat down. "David—Michelle, sit down. Let me explain a few things."

"Please do," said David as we took the love seat opposite Josh.

Josh sat forward with a confidential air. "I've been well aware of what's happening to you. Except for the cocaine and the ransacking. But you can be sure I'll check those out too. Would it ease your minds to know that we have two DEA undercover agents on the island watching every move you make? They won't let a thing happen to you or your friends, Jackie and Steve—the *Marshalls*."

"Why didn't you tell us? We've been so frightened, so—"

"Who are the agents?" David demanded.

"I'm not at liberty to say. That information in the wrong hands could put their lives in jeopardy."

"Are they men?...Women?...Strangers?...Friends?" I asked.

"I'm sorry, Michelle. For your safety and theirs, their identities will have to remain secret for now."

"But they must realize there's someone else on the island who knows why we're here," I argued. "Someone is responsible for the awful things that have happened—"

"We're working on it, Michelle. We know what we're doing—"

"It's still just too risky," said David, standing. "We're going home, Joshua—and taking Pam with us."

Josh stood too. "I'm sorry to hear that, considering . . ."

"Considering what?"

"That I have a new assignment for you. Something even more critical and confidential than the first project."

"What are you talking about?" David asked warily.

The two sat back down. "It's like this, David. You're aware of the increased warfare against the DEA—the drug syndicate's threats and violence, the kidnappings, the murders. Actually, we suspect that someone high up in the DEA is leaking information to the cocaine kingpins. That's why the project you're working on now is so vital. Only a few in positions of absolute trust will have access to the new data files. It should put our DEA turncoat out of business fast."

"But you just mentioned another project, Joshua," said David.

"Right, that I did. For the last couple of weeks our government has conducted high-priority meetings with a number of other nations on the drug issue."

"What does that have to do with us?" I asked.

"Just this. These nations have agreed to cooperate with us and compile all information available on drug dealers within their own borders. The data will be gathered, computerized, and distributed to all countries to aid in their battle against drug trafficking."

"Just tell us where we come into this," said David skeptically.

"I'm getting to that," said Josh. "David, I'm prepared to bring in an elite group of computer programming experts to help you set up a preliminary framework for this project. We're talking international ramifications here, David. If you help us come up with a foolproof system, you'll be serving your country and, in fact, the entire world in a way few people have."

"But why here?" challenged David. "Why on Solidad? Why can't I just work on the project in my office in Irvine?"

Josh shook his head. "You may not believe this after the hassling you've encountered here, but Solidad is one of the safest hideaways we could find. No one enters or leaves the island without our knowledge. There's no communication to the outside world that we've not privy to. Could we say the same about Southern California? Could we maintain this same 24-hour surveillance in Los Angeles with millions of people coming and going? Don't you see? We've got a hothouse environment here. We call all the shots."

"Not all of them," countered David. "Where were your

colleagues when this place was ransacked last night?"

Josh looked momentarily disconcerted. "I'll follow it up, David. Have you reported the break-in to anyone?"

"No, not yet. There were other...distractions," I replied, remembering the ghostly woman in the wedding dress with Alejandra's locket. How would Josh explain her?

"It wasn't a break-in," said David. "Someone had a key. In fact, it could have been Silas Winters or Esteban Medina. They both have master keys."

Josh's eyes narrowed. "What about the assistant concierge—your friend Steve Marshall? Doesn't he have a master key? Doesn't he live on this wing?"

"Steve? You suspect him?" I cried. "You've never trusted Steve, have you, Josh? Even after all you've done to protect him!"

"I'm paid to protect him. That doesn't mean I trust him."

"Steve and Jackie were with us the whole evening, Josh," I told him flatly. "Besides, if someone wanted to find something in our suite, why would he have been so obvious, pulling out drawers, throwing everything around?"

"Maybe he just wanted to scare us away. Nothing was missing."

"Let me get this straight," said Josh. "The intruder didn't discover the computer room?"

"No," replied David. "The project is safe...so far."

"But there's something else, Josh," I said. "David and I have heard rumors about the original owner of Solidad."

"Who? You mean this Cobranza fellow?"

"Yes. Ricardo Cobranza. We suspect that he was producing cocaine here on the island and shipping it somewhere."

"That was over 20 years ago," said Josh.

"Then you do know about Cobranza," I said accusingly.

Josh sighed audibly. "We know he was a rich drug baron who had a falling out with the powerful Colombian mob. He fled to Solidad with a price on his head and rebuilt his empire here. He and his wife died before the mob could track him down and finish him off."

I gasped. "Joshua, why in the world would you send Steve and Jackie here after his testimony against the Morro Bay cocaine ring?"

"Because, according to our sources, Solidad's been clean for 20 years. The mob has no ties here since Cobranza died."

"It's not clean enough for us, Kendrick—not after the scares we've had. Like I told you, Michelle and I are going home."

"Listen, David—I came to Solidad under the guise of your business partner. If you leave now, so must I. But first, would you just hear me out on this new project? Then I'll go along with whatever you two decide."

I looked at David. "It can't hurt to hear what he has to say."

David didn't look convinced. "If that's what you want, hon."

I slipped off the love seat and went to the phone. "I'll call down for some lunch. We might as well listen on full stomachs."

The three of us talked for long, tension-filled hours, until late-afternoon shadows stretched across the sitting room. I could sense that David was wavering. An undercurrent of excitement edged his voice as he and Josh batted ideas back and forth for the new project. But at the same time I could see the worry in his eyes for me. Finally he stood up and walked over by the louvered shutters. "All right, Joshua, I can see the feasibility here," he said. "I think I could come up with a workable system, but not here, not on Solidad. I won't risk Michelle's life for any project, however noble. You set this project up for me in Irvine or not at all."

"Sorry, David. I can't do that."

I went to David and embraced him. "Please, David, don't say no because of me. Don't let me hold you back."

He shook his head ponderously. "Michelle, Michelle. Right now I honestly don't know what's right...or what God expects of me."

"Neither do I, David. But I do know that once, in Vietnam, it was very important to you to serve your country. Is this so different? You'd be serving your country in another kind of war."

David gently kissed my forehead. "But don't you see, my darling? In Vietnam you weren't beside me on the battlefield."

"I would have been if I could have," I whispered.

David blinked back unaccustomed tears. He remained silent a minute, his eyes closed. Was he praying or just trying to keep from weeping? Finally he looked at me, his eyes glistening, and mouthed the words, *I love you.* Then he walked over to Josh and held out his hand. "Okay, buddy—I may regret it, but I guess I'm your man."

Surprisingly, the next two weeks passed by peacefully, uneventfully. Even though David was busier than ever on his new computer project, we found a few moments together for tennis and swimming, for romantic walks in the moonlight, and a schooner ride in the flaming sunset. On that special, rare evening, David and I nestled together—giddy, moonstruck lovers—while a swash of burnished orange, like fool's gold, cut a ragged, rippling path across Cobranza Bay. From the schooner, Tamarind Bluff was a towering silhouette of ebony black accented by a sprinkling of cheery beacon lights from Windy Reef Hotel.

With David working closely now with the DEA, there weren't nearly enough of those romantic interludes. Instead, I filled my days with leisurely walks on the beach with Jackie and Stevie, collecting shells with Ruth Glocke, and souvenir-hunting in the marketplace with Lucia Medina, whose appetite for tales of Hollywood was insatiable. I had hoped to give Pam the grand tour of Solidad, but Silas Winters was already showing her the island in grand style. The two were inseparable. When Pam wasn't with Silas, she was following Dooley Edington around, camped in his clinic, bombarding him with medical questions. Her nursing instincts thrived as she accompanied him to the villages and helped him treat the Creole children.

In the evenings, when David was locked in his computer room, I spent long hours on my historical novel, working in earnest now, writing out descriptions of the island and character sketches of the various people I'd met on Solidad. I put down everything I'd heard about Ricardo and Alejandra Cobranza. Joshua had called Cobranza a drug baron. Still, when I thought of Alejandra, the innocent young bride in the portrait, I could not imagine evil and corruption. Had she known of her husband's lawless rise to power? Had she approved, or had she simply been too trusting of the man she loved? The flawless, elusive Alejandra of the portrait was rapidly becoming the childlike heroine of my novel. Inevitably, the long-dead couple took on romantic, larger-than-life dimensions in my mind. I found myself daydreaming about them, wondering what their lives had been like, and what Solidad might have been like if they hadn't died. Would it have become a drug ghetto? Or would they have repented of their ways? I felt an irrational yearning to reach them, to find out if they had ever sought God's loving forgiveness.

And there was still so much about the island itself I longed to know. Several times I stopped Esteban Medina in the lobby or by the pool to inquire about some aspect of Solidad's history. He always answered simply, almost grudgingly at times. But his temper flared unexpectedly when I brought up the subject of Cobranza's cocaine involvement. "Who has told you these lies?" he demanded, his sudden wrath turning his misshapen features into a grotesque mask. "Sr. Cobranza was an honorable man! He was my father's closest friend!"

"I'm sorry, Mr. Medina. I didn't mean to offend you. I should have remembered. Your wife told me you were good friends with the Cobranzas' son. Carlos Cobranza, right? I can understand your wanting to protect his father's name." I paused. "Do you see Carlos often? When he visits the island, I mean?"

Esteban was suddenly gray, a piercing glint of sadness in his ebony eyes. "Carlos doesn't visit Solidad. He has not been here since he rebuilt his parents' mansion into Windy Reef Hotel and turned it over to my father to run. It's best that way. It is difficult to come home when your parents are gone, dead— when they have died so tragically. I know. It was hard for me—how much more for Carlos! But he pays me well to keep Windy Reef flourishing—"

"Then where has Carlos lived all these years?"

"In Europe—London, Madrid. But why all these questions?"

"I—I'm writing a book—a novel about the island." I held up my manila folder with SOLIDAD neatly printed in block letters.

Medina glared down at the folder. "May I see it?"

He caught me off guard. Wordlessly I handed it to him. He flipped through a page or two, then looked up, his tone suddenly icy. "I trust you will respect the Cobranzas' privacy—?"

"I hardly know enough about them to invade their privacy, Mr. Medina. But I was wondering if you have any maps of Solidad."

"Plan to do a little exploring, Mrs. Ballard?"

"I—I'm not sure. I've heard rumors about caverns on the island. Your wife said you'd be the one to ask about a map."

"I have no maps—or caverns. But if it's exploring you want, Silas will be taking a group to Cocoa Lake again on Tuesday."

"Then sign David and me up for the van. We'd love to go."

On Tuesday morning, we piled into the van for our ride to Cocoa Lake and Mt. Peligro. Silas, with Pam beside him, bounced his four-wheel-drive vehicle over a scenic route along the Atlantic side of the island. He cut his own dusty trail over the rocks and ruts and took the gravelly back roads like they were paved highways. Josh and the Glockes sat in the backseat. Doc, going along at Orville's request, sat slouched beside me, smelling of Old Spice, his rum bottle bulging in his hip pocket. He seemed strangely withered today, a hollow shell of a man. His eyes darted often to Pam, a peculiar wistfulness on his hangdog face.

"My sister enjoys working in the clinic with you," I offered.

He gave me an analytical squint, furrowing his ragged, uneven brows. "I enjoy her company. She—she reminds me of someone."

"Your wife?" I asked softly.

He brushed at his mustache. "So you know about Allison?"

"Steve Marshall mentioned her."

Edington stretched his lanky legs. "Your sister is a lot like Allison, with her laughing eyes and long, flowing hair—and her quick, direct manner." He sighed. "Allison was a nurse too—full of energy and life—" His voice choked, drifted. He stared out the open van window, taking the trail of dust in his face. "I'd do anything to be with her. Anything."

I was about to ask, "You mean, Pam?" But then I knew. Dooley Edington didn't care about life. He wanted to be with his long-dead Allison. Was that why he was drowning himself in the rum bottle, burying himself on Solidad—to forget?

From the backseat, Orville huffed, "Keep driving like this, Winters, and you'll get us all killed."

"Don't worry, Glocke. This van can handle these ruts."

"But my heart can't. Besides, you're smothering the Medinas' jeep behind us in a cloud of dust."

"So Esteban can take a bath at the lake," chuckled Silas. But, in spite of his bravado, Silas shifted gears, slowing noticeably.

We curved around Cabo San Carlos, caught a view of Shoal Beach, then came to the serene, crystal-clear Cocoa Lake at the base of Mt. Peligro. Silas looked back at David and me. "The lake flows into several waterways and lagoons along the Conch River—great scenery."

"Silas and I took a raft ride on the Conch River the other day, Michelle," announced Pam. "It's beautiful—and so romantic."

"And dangerous, too, I bet!"

"Of course, Michelle. What do you think Mt. Peligro means? The whole area spells danger. Don't you just love it?"

We piled out of the van and joined the Medinas by their jeep. Esteban seemed edgy, restless. He glanced at his watch. "If we're going to hike to Cocoa Falls, we'd better get started."

"I can't make the climb," Orville whimpered. "My heart—"

"Then sit in the jeep," his wife ordered. "The rest will do you good." She stomped over to Medina and snorted, "I'm going." Without another word, they started the arduous climb up Mt. Peligro, Ruth's footing surprisingly secure, her heavy frame moving with control.

"She makes it look easy," David said, taking my hand as we started up the trail, following Silas. Ten minutes later we stopped to catch our breath.

Joshua shaded his eyes, staring around intently at the lush, sweetly scented jungle maze. The sun rays caught momentarily on a shiny object and reflected back, almost blinding us. "I've got to figure out a way to get down there and explore without the others," Josh told David and me privately.

"With Ruth Glocke and Esteban along?" David shook his head.

"Then we'll get the others to go down the mountain ahead of us."

When we reached the base of the gigantic falls, we saw frothy water cascading over huge boulders, crashing down a rocky precipice, and finally converging into a pool where ferns and orchids abounded.

Ruth Glocke stared up in cold fascination at the violent force surging over the cliffs. "If only a body could harness that power!"

When Esteban suggested heading back, Josh asked casually, "Do you mind if the Ballards and I sit awhile and enjoy the scenery?"

"Suit yourself." Esteban gestured to the others to move on.

We waited until they were out of sight, then cut through the scrub, making our way down an obscure trail covered by vines and underbrush. Thirty minutes later we reached the shiny object we had spotted—an abandoned shack in a secluded thicket with an aluminum roof glistening in the sunlight. Several rusty oil drums and large glass jugs were scattered over the damp, gnarled foliage. Joshua stepped carefully around the deserted area, knocking off the lid of one steel drum, then picking up an empty chemical bottle. He examined the filters and siphons still attached to a crude metal press.

"Josh," I began, "don't tell me! Is this a—?"

"Cocaine refinery," finished David soberly.

Josh nodded. He kicked at a corroded barrel and watched it roll an inch or two. Lizards scurried from its path. Birds twittered overhead. "I'm sure if we searched farther, we'd find that Cobranza grew the cocoa plants here on the island too—the whole drug pipeline from cocoa leaf to pure cocaine."

"Then that old fisherman Moses knew what he was talking about," said David. "Cobranza really had the island at his fingertips. It's odd that he deliberately walked out on it, leaped to his death—"

"The love of a woman does strange things to a man," I said.

"That's true," Josh acknowledged, "but 20 years ago rival Colombian cocaine lords were closing in on Cobranza. We know that for a fact. Maybe he figured his time was up anyway."

"What about Cobranza's son? The Medinas? Were they involved?"

"We've had a spot surveillance on the son, Carlos Cobranza, over the years. He's clean. He apparently never knew what a scoundrel his father was. As for Juan and Esteban Medina, who knows?"

"What about the wealth Cobranza would have accrued?" asked David. "Sure, his son built the posh hotel, but where's the rest? Cobranza must have made millions. Did it all go out on freighters?"

"It's certain he didn't take it with him," mused Josh wryly. "Maybe he stowed it in Swiss banks or invested in gold bullion."

"Some of the wealth may still be here on the island—but where?" said David.

"What about the underground caverns of Tamarind Bluff?" I asked.

Josh whirled around and stared at me. "The what?"

"One of the Creoles mentioned caves, but that's all we know."

"Interesting," said Joshua. "My agents never told me that."

Two hours had passed before the three of us got back to the lake. Esteban was standing by the jeep alone. Everyone else had gone back to Windy Reef in the van with Silas. "I was worried," Esteban said, sounding agitated. "Where have you been?"

"We got off the trail," Josh admitted. "It took us awhile to work our way back. Sorry."

After our adventuresome trek around Cocoa Lake and Mt. Peligro on Tuesday, Wednesday seemed tame by comparison. I spent the morning on the sun deck working on my novel notes. Then, early in the afternoon, I strolled through the lobby, lingering by the portrait of Alejandra. Restless and bored, I decided to go out to the gardener's cottage and have that long-overdue cup of coffee with Javier.

As I cut across the lobby, I spotted Silas Winters by the elevator. When I reached him, he said, "Going up, Mrs. Ballard?"

"To heaven, not the sun deck," I answered impulsively.

He stepped back from the elevator before the door closed. "Come again?" I started to repeat my flippant answer, but Silas interrupted. "Never mind, you said heaven." His smile was mocking, sardonic. "It would be easier for me to get to the sun deck."

I smiled tolerantly. "Silas, I keep hoping you'll make it to the sun deck for our Bible studies. They're going well, you know."

"I didn't know. But Bible studies aren't exactly my style."

"Have you ever tried one? Why not join us on Sunday?"

"Thanks, but no thanks." He gave me a sly, cryptic glance. "You know—you and your sister aren't at all alike. Fortunately, she isn't as caught up in this God-business as you are."

I winced. He'd nailed me where it hurt. "We have the same footing," I countered, "although Pam's may have slipped a bit. But she'll get back to her spiritual roots and get her priorities straight."

"And you're hoping I won't be on her priority list?"

"Come on, Mr. Winters. Pam isn't serious. She's just—"

"But I am serious, Mrs. Ballard."

"I thought—I thought you and Nicole in the gift shop were—"

"Friends," he finished. "Just good friends." Ignoring the elevator, he strode off in an easy swagger toward the stairwell. To Pam's room perhaps. I watched him go, thinking, *Pam's right. Silas is handsome with his blond, wind-tossed hair and suntanned face. What's worse, she's already fallen prey to his sly, winsome ways!*

I felt uneasy, discomfited as I walked out the hotel door toward Javier's cottage. Was Silas Winters teasing me about his feelings for Pam? Did she really mean something to him? If so, what about Pam? Was she falling in love with a man so out of tune with God?

Just as I rounded the garden hedge and reached out to knock on Javier's door, I heard angry voices from inside—Esteban Medina and Dooley Edington arguing. "I don't know what your game is, Edington."

"Game, Mr. Medina? Surely you know I don't play games."

"You know what I mean, Edington. It seems to me you've been giving Javier too much medication."

"So now you're making diagnoses, my dear Esteban."

"I'm only trying to protect my father's friend."

"Yes, I'm sure that you are," Dooley shot back. "But what about your little secret, Esteban—your diving skills? Ever since I met you and Carlos in London, I've thought about those skills.

Why else would your father have inherited so much from the Cobranzas?"

"They were partners—"

"No, Esteban. Carlos Cobranza was very clear about that. Juan Medina was his father's trusted servant. Nothing more."

"You pretended to be friends with Carlos, Edington. But obviously you used him just like you use everyone else around you."

"Let's just say Carlos told me plenty. You've had everything you've ever wanted, Esteban. Poor boys don't usually fare as well as you did. Educated in Europe. All the money you ever needed."

"Get out," Esteban ordered hoarsely. "Get out!"

"Perhaps I should talk to your wife. Does she know?"

"Don't bring my wife into this, Edington. My Lucia knows nothing. You'll regret it if you say a word to Lucia or to my friend Carlos. Believe me, doctor, I could spill plenty about you!"

I slipped behind the hedge as the door opened. Their voices lowered, but I could still hear Dooley Edington say, "Listen, Esteban. You ought to be glad I'm taking care of Javier, giving him medicine. It keeps him docile, out of trouble. Otherwise, who knows what he might blab in his senile condition?"

"And I tell you, leave him alone, Edington," Esteban said hotly. "I've taken care of him all these years just like my father before me, and I'll watch over him until the day he dies!"

I ducked around the cottage and crossed through the garden back to the hotel. I'd heard enough to know I didn't want to be caught eavesdropping. In the lobby I ran into Lucia. She invited me for afternoon tea and a leisurely visit in the dining room. But even as we talked I wondered what mysterious secret Esteban was so desperately hiding from Lucia, his guileless wife.

I planned to ask David that very question, but when I returned to the suite, he was out—conferring with Josh, no doubt. My mind was immediately diverted by another disturbing question: Where were my novel notes? Surely I hadn't left them on the sun deck, yet they were nowhere in the bridal suite. I searched every nook and crevice, retracing my steps to the sun deck, the pool area, the garden, the lobby, the dining room. I grew increasingly frantic as I checked with Silas, Esteban, Steve, and Nicole. No one had seen my notes.

David thought I was making too much of their disappearance. "They'll turn up," he assured me, as if to say, Who would bother with my rudimentary scribblings? But I sensed that he was concerned too.

Every day for the rest of the week I kept a watchful eye out for my notes. But it seemed that the folder had simply vanished.

By Sunday morning the novel notes were no longer my first priority. David and I were busy preparing for our sun deck devotions. During the past two Sundays our tiny group had blossomed. Over a dozen hotel guests, including Jackie, Pam, the Medinas, and Orville Glocke had joined us as David led in Bible reading and prayer. We even sang some of the old-fashioned hymns, no doubt startling some of the surrounding worldly-wise sunbathers.

This Sunday, to our delight, our ranks swelled to 20. Steve came late and took a seat beside Jackie. She beamed. Even a few scattered sunbathers paused to listen as David read the Scriptures. We sat in a circle, Pam on my left, Orville Glocke on my right. As we sang "The Old Rugged Cross," I noticed Orville's strong tenor voice. He sang with amazing vitality, as if for one fleeting moment he grasped the truth of the gospel. For all of Orville's blustery, blundering manner, he briefly revealed surprising vulnerability.

Afterward, before we left the sun deck, I touched Orville's arm and said, "You have a fine voice, Mr. Glocke. Have you sung before?"

"No," he chuckled self-consciously. "In fact, I never made choir boy or altar boy. My cousin did," he added with a touch of undisguised envy, "but I couldn't even make it through confirmation class." His face grew wistful with a strange, unspoken yearning. He heaved a shuddering sigh, then turned and slowly shuffled away.

David and I were about to leave when Lucia stopped us and asked in a tentative voice, "How you know this Jesus as your friend? I no understand. I say prayers all my life. I follow traditions of my people. But you speak of person who love you as you are. How so?"

I clasped Lucia's hand. "He's the same Jesus you've known of, Lucia—Mary's innocent child, God's sinless Son. He took our punishment. He offers us His Spirit, so we never have to be lonely again."

"My Esteban and me—we talk with you again about your Jesus. Esteban say this is good for us to know. Maybe we talk— at dinner?"

"Why, yes, of course, Lucia. Shall we meet tonight at seven?"

Lucia's eyes brightened. "We come after Esteban feed Javier."

As David and I walked back to our suite arm in arm, we marveled over the turnout at our sun deck devotions. "Maybe Jackie will carry on the tradition after we've left Solidad," I said hopefully. "You know, David, we've met such a variety of people with so many different needs. I just wish there was some way to reach them all."

"Be patient, my darling. We've made a beginning. We've sown the seed. Now we must trust God for the results."

I tweaked David's cheek playfully. "Careful, sweetheart, you're slipping into your stained-glass voice. Church is over for now."

He clasped me at the waist and swung me around. "And now it's time to play, my darling! How about a dip in the pool?"

"Great! Brunch, a cozy nap, and a swim—in that order!"

David's brow arched provocatively. "I like that order."

Sunday afternoon was perfect for swimming, the sun warm and caressing instead of its usual scorching intensity. We found Pam already relaxing by the pool, stretched out on a lounge chair, getting a deep, golden tan to show off back home. David and I dove in the pool and played "cat and mouse" in the deep end, romping and chasing each other under the water like frisky, sportive children.

But our roguish fun was interrupted by a fretful bellboy balancing near the pool's edge, waving an envelope. "Awfully sorry, sir," he squeaked. "I was supposed to give you this a half hour ago."

David hoisted himself up out of the pool, toweled himself off, and took the envelope marked URGENT. He removed the note, read it, then looked at the bellboy and demanded,

"Where'd you get this?"

"Mr. Winters gave it to me," stammered the youth. "He said he found it on his desk addressed to you. He said to bring it right away, but a guest arrived with loads of luggage—a good tipper too, he was—and well, I—I forgot the envelope. Hope there's no problem, Mr. Ballard. Mr. Winters would have my job if—!"

"No, that's okay," said David distractedly. "You can go."

"What is it, David?" I asked, paddling over to the pool's side.

He stooped down and held out a letter on Windy Reef stationery. "It's from Esteban Medina," he whispered. "He insists I meet him in our hotel suite at two sharp. Says it's a matter of life or death."

"Oh, David, it must be after two already. You'd better hurry."

"I'm on my way—but what could be so important?"

I glanced automatically toward our second-story suite and blinked incredulously. "David, look, there's a man on our veranda!"

In the fateful moments it took to utter those words, the man pitched forward off our balcony, severing the railing, and plunged headfirst to the concrete below.

CHAPTER EIGHTEEN

A split second of sheer horror silenced us all. Then everyone sprang into action at once. Pam bounded out of her lounge chair, racing pell-mell toward the fallen victim. David pulled me from the pool. I yanked on my beach robe as we ran. The crowd was already gathering. Many shrank back in revulsion as they stared down at the bloody, broken body. The man lay facedown on the cement path, his neck and legs twisted grotesquely, one white shoe missing. Sprawled beside him was a blood-stained manila folder—my missing novel notes!

Pam knelt beside the victim, her fingers on his pulse. Joshua Kendrick hovered beside her. I didn't have to wait for Josh to mouth the name. I recognized the brawny shoulders, the large head, the thick crop of coal-black hair. *Esteban Medina!* I glanced helplessly across at Lucia—her ivory face drained, chalk-white. Silas Winters gripped her shoulders, holding her steady, refusing to let her go.

As Dooley Edington shoved through the crowd and reached Pam, she looked up at him and sadly shook her head. "Medina is dead."

Dooley dropped to his knees and bent over the stilled form. He turned Esteban's face slightly; the irregular features were barely distinguishable. Edington felt for a pulse, his strong manicured hand pressing on Esteban's temple, his throat. The doctor reeled back and glanced up toward the bridal suite. I followed his gaze to the empty balcony, the split railing.

Edington's voice was deep, husky. "Dear God, the man jumped!" His eyes focused on Lucia. She was trying to break free from Silas. "He's dead, Mrs. Medina," Edington confirmed. "I'm terribly sorry."

Lucia's scream split the air. Like a tigress, she clawed free from Silas' grip and threw herself on her husband's lifeless body. "Not my Esteban. Not my Esteban!" she wailed. She glared around at the stunned faces in the crowd, shaking her fist at us all. "Not my Esteban. He do not jump. This no accident. My Esteban, he swim, he dive. These cliffs," she shrieked, pointing blindly toward Tamarind Bluff, "—all his life he dive from them. He do not jump!"

Joshua put a firm hand on Dooley's shoulder and said, "Examine him thoroughly. I want a full report on this as soon as possible!" Then he strode quickly over to David and me and thrust my novel notes into David's hand. "David, get Michelle up to your room—now!"

David held out the note from Esteban. "Read this, Kendrick."

Josh scanned the letter, then ordered, "Just wait for me upstairs, outside your suite. I want to check the rooms first."

"But what about Lucia?" I asked.

"Take her with you."

I urged the enraged, disconsolate Lucia to her feet. Her clenched fist opened. Her cigarette lighter fell beside Esteban's body. She crumpled against me, cold and limp as I led her away.

Kikko stood just inside the lobby, his dark eyes wide with terror. "Kikko help Missus Ballard?" he asked.

"No, it's all right, Kikko. We can manage."

As we stepped into the elevator, Nicole shouted from the lobby desk, "Mrs. Ballard, have you seen Dr. Edington?"

"Out there." I nodded toward the pool.

"Thanks, Mrs. Ballard," replied Nicole. "Mrs. Glocke just called down. Mr. Glocke's in his room. He has severe chest pain."

"Send Kikko out for the doc, Nicole," I suggested breathlessly.

As David and I helped Lucia down the east wing corridor,

Steve Marshall stepped from his room and gave us a quizzical glance.

"Where have you been, man?" David asked. "There's been trouble."

Steve stared at Lucia's grief-stricken face. "What happened?"

"Esteban is dead," David answered. "He toppled from our balcony. Did you see anyone, Steve? Hear anyone?"

Steve frowned. "A few minutes ago I heard someone running. Heavy footsteps. But I didn't think much about it."

"One person?"

"How would I know? It could have been one, two. I don't know." He looked again sympathetically at Lucia. "I'm sorry, Mrs. Medina."

Lucia never heard him. She stood mechanically, her eyes fastened on the door to the bridal suite. "I do not go in there. I do not go in where it happened. Please, do not make me."

"Let her come in here with Jackie and me," said Steve. "We'll take care of her. Jackie will know how to comfort her."

"Thanks," I said as Lucia followed him wordlessly into his room.

Twenty minutes later Joshua joined us, breathless and tense. We crossed the corridor to the bridal suite. The door was unlocked. David and Josh entered first. When they were sure it was safe, they beckoned me inside. I followed them in silence out to the veranda. A knot of nausea was working its way up from the pit of my stomach. I didn't want to see the spot where Esteban had fallen, but I forced myself to look anyway. I couldn't help thinking that now two men had plunged from this balcony and died. Why had it happened? Why today, when Esteban had shown his first budding interest in finding God?

As we went back inside, Joshua leaned down and picked up a crumpled slip of computer paper beside the sliding glass door. He read it and handed it to us, his expression stony.

"I don't understand," I said. "This is from you, David, asking Esteban to meet you here at two sharp. Why did you send this note?"

"I didn't, Michelle. I never asked him to come, just as he probably never asked me to meet him here either."

"What are you saying, David?"

"It's a setup, Michelle," said Josh with a curt grimace. "Someone planted these notes to bring both David and Esteban to your suite at two o'clock. I think someone was waiting here for them."

"Are you saying . . . Esteban was murdered?"

Josh's voice quavered. "I'm saying I suspect someone had two victims in mind today—Esteban and David."

A wave of panic shot through my body, leaving me weak, trembling. I clasped David's arm for support. "Oh David, if your note hadn't been late, you—you might have been on the balcony too."

"The murderer probably intended to make it look like a struggle between the two men," Joshua surmised.

"But why didn't Esteban fight back?" I cried, near tears.

"He may have been drugged, or knocked unconscious," said Josh. "That's why I want Dr. Edington to do a full workup on the body."

We went to the living room and sat down. My legs were weak, my head spinning. I wondered if I would black out. I heard David ask, "What does all this mean, Kendrick? What aren't you telling us?"

"Our cover has been blown," Josh admitted flatly. "Someone obviously has access now to the computer room. They flaunted their knowledge in our faces by writing that note on your own computer."

"Then they may have tampered with the project," said David in alarm. He shot off the sofa and dashed to the bedroom. He was back minutes later. "Everything seems in order, the way I left it."

"But we can't be certain," said Josh. "Couldn't someone have made printouts, copies of classified data?"

"I don't think there was time. We weren't gone that long."

"All right, listen," said Josh. "Just before I came up here, I conferred with my agents. We're in agreement. The computer project and those connected with it are no longer safe at Windy Reef."

"I've thought that all along, Kendrick," said David curtly.

"All right, I admit it. Maybe we've overplayed our hand this time. But we haven't lost the battle."

"How can you say that?" I cried. "An innocent man is dead."

"We know no such thing. Medina may have been more involved than we think. Perhaps someone decided he had outlived his usefulness."

"How can you dismiss Esteban's death so lightly?" I challenged. "Nora was right! You are a cold, unfeeling man."

Joshua winced, the hurt evident in his eyes, but his voice remained hard-edged. "Regardless of what you think of me, Michelle, we're shutting down our operation on Solidad. We're removing the computer equipment and data files from the hotel to the dock. Tonight. From there everything will be shipped discreetly to Martinique and then on to a predetermined location."

"You have a boat ready and waiting?" I asked.

"Right. Moses and his fishing vessel have been on standby since you arrived, just in case of an emergency."

"You think of everything, don't you, Kendrick?" said David. "Are we all sailing out tonight?"

"As soon as it's dark, we'll load you, Michelle, and the computer project into Silas Winters' van. It's the most reliable vehicle on the island. We'll ship Pam and the Marshalls out later."

"Will Winters agree to our using the van?" asked David.

"Don't worry. I'll have Steve Marshall get the keys."

"But, Josh, there's no time to pack," I said.

"Take only what you need, Michelle. David and I will get busy now dismantling the equipment and packing the documents and data files in waterproof containers. Be ready to leave at dusk."

"Can't I say good-bye to anyone—Jackie, Lucia, Javier?"

"No, Michelle. I don't want you going out alone." Joshua left the suite for a few moments. He returned with sandwiches and a toolbox, gave me a quick nod, hit the hook behind the Gauguin painting, and disappeared into the computer room with David. Behind the door, I heard their voices, muffled and distraught, amid the clang-rattle of their crates and tools.

I cried as I took my clothes from the closet and folded them into neat stacks on the canopy bed. Cried for Lucia. For the dinner date we would never have. For a honeymoon that was ending. For Jackie and the good-bye we could not say. But mostly I cried for Esteban and chided myself for a missed opportunity. Word of his death had apparently spread, for a crowd was already gathering beneath our veranda—a death wail rising in a mournful dirge of Creole voices. Somewhere in the distance, near the cottage, was the rat-a-tat-tat hammering—the sound of nails being pounded into wood.

It was almost six when I locked the suitcases and carried them into the living room, lining them up in the corner. Moments later, Steve Marshall let himself in with a passkey. Pam was with him, the usual impish grin washed from her face. She looked drawn, tired as she collapsed in the nearest chair and stared at the suitcases.

"I need to see David and Joshua," Steve announced. When I hesitated, he added, "It's okay, Michelle. I know about the project. I'll just go back and talk with them."

Pam waited until Steve was out of sight, then said, "He told me you're leaving. Are those the suitcases I'm to take home for you?"

"All but the smallest two—we'll take those."

"I don't like it, Michelle. I don't like deceiving Silas, luring him away from the hotel tonight so you can steal his van."

I knew better than to argue. Pam was right this time. I didn't want us to lock iron wills. "What about—Esteban? The examination?"

"You mean, our makeshift autopsy?"

I nodded.

"Dr. Edington is thorough. He's confident that it was an accident. No burns on Esteban's lips or throat to indicate drugs, poisoning. Just. . .just a broken neck from the fall."

"Pam, Esteban didn't scuffle with himself. There were things out of place in the bedroom—shoe skids, a crumpled note. Esteban didn't just walk through the bridal suite and jump off the balcony."

"Sis, I've been around you too long—you and your nose for a mystery. Maybe that's why I'm wondering about the bump on Esteban's head. Dooley said it was from the fall, the impact. And you know doctors, they don't like a second opinion, especially from a nurse."

"So what are you trying to say, Pam?"

She was quiet, thoughtful. Then our eyes locked. "Esteban fell facedown, Michelle. But the bump I'm talking about was

across the back of his skull—as though he'd been hit, whacked
from behind with a blunt object."

"Didn't you point that out to Edington?"

"Yes. But he kept getting more agitated, taking swigs from
his old rum bottle. He's really upset about Esteban's death."

"Aren't we all?"

When Steve rejoined us, David and Josh were with him.
David slipped his arm around my waist. "Josh is going to watch
the suite while the rest of us go down to the cemetery."

I reared back. "They're burying Esteban already?"

"The climate, Michelle. The islanders have no way of
preserving the body until tomorrow." He gave a deep gut-sigh.
"According to Steve, Lucia wants me to say a few words."
David patted his New Testament. "It'll be very brief. We have
to race nightfall."

"Then David—the hammering I heard out by the cottage?"

He nodded. "The Creoles are building Esteban's casket."

Just before dusk, Kikko, Moses, and the other Creoles who
loved him carried Esteban's crudely built coffin down the
cobbled pathway from the hotel to the cemetery. Nicole and
Jackie walked supportively on either side of Lucia Medina,
slowly leading the procession of hotel guests and Creoles. The
crowd was as large as it had been at the festival, and as
brilliantly dressed. But their expressions were crushed,
distorted. David was brief, succinct, his voice deeply shaken
as he shared that a merciful God had been mindful of Esteban.
As the hushed crowd began to disperse, I noticed frail old
Javier leaning against Alejandra's tombstone, weeping uncontrollably.

Shortly after the funeral, Steve came to the bridal suite with
the luggage cart. "Plans have changed," he announced. "Josh
wants me to load all your luggage—make it look like you're
checking out."

As Steve and David pushed the cart down the corridor to
the elevator, Orville Glocke stepped from his room. "You're
leaving?"

"Honeymoons don't last forever," David said casually.

Orville popped a nitro pill into his mouth. "But it's late—
you can't leave Solidad tonight."

"No problem, Mr. Glocke," Steve told him. "They won't until morning—but they just want to be packed and ready to go, early."

When the elevator closed, David asked, "I thought you said the corridor was clear, that most of the guests were down at dinner."

Steve pushed the button. "They were—even the Glockes. Maybe he forgot his medicine or something."

"This is ridiculous, parading through the lobby," complained David. "You'd think this hotel would have another way down."

"They do, David," Steve answered. "Crazy, I know, but old man Cobranza had a back stairwell, like a secret passage—it's part of Edington's suite. As soon as the doc goes to dinner, Kendrick will start loading the boxes and waterproof containers out that way. It leads right to the carport."

"Why not take the suitcases that way too?" I whispered as we followed the luggage cart through the lobby.

"Josh wants people to know you're leaving Windy Reef. This is the most obvious way to announce your 'morning departure.' Josh is sending an open message to *someone*."

"Who?" I asked.

"We wish we knew."

I followed Josh's instructions: Stay in the lobby and strike up a conversation with one of the guests. I chose a sleepy old man with a hearing aid. *Give it 20 minutes,* Josh had said, *then head out the back of the lobby to the carport.*

I kept my eyes on my watch, then stood abruptly, leaving a sentence unfinished, and wound my way past the pool and tennis court toward Silas' van. I shivered with apprehension. Steve stepped from the shadows with the car keys. I jumped, startled.

"Take it easy, Michelle," he warned. "David and Josh have one more load to bring down. They'll be here any minute."

We leaned against the van. "Will you tell Jackie I'm sorry? Josh wouldn't let me tell her David and I are going home."

"I'll tell her later. She'll understand. Jackie's been worried about you. She'll be glad you're getting away safely."

I sensed the hollowness in his voice, the sense of frustration.

"Listen, Steve," I said quietly, "Josh promised to get you and Jackie off Solidad soon too."

"Off in time, I hope. But we'll still be running. Sometimes I feel like throwing this protection program over. Go home, take my chances. Or at least send Stevie and Jackie back to normal lives."

"Would they be normal—or happy—without you, Steve?" I reached out for his hand. "Thanks for everything. The conch shell. The snorkeling lesson. Rescuing me from the fishing net accident—"

"That wasn't an accident, Michelle. I thought you knew. We told David—"

From the dim garden lights, I could see Steve's troubled, deep-set eyes. "Not an accident?" I echoed.

"I'm sorry, Michelle. I assumed David told you. Silas Winters got right on it—a full investigation. One of the divers, possibly even Kikko, was paid well to toss that net your way. Silas is keeping his eyes on Kikko. Nothing so far." Steve shrugged sadly. "It's a way of life here. You make money any way you can. Kikko may have been paid just to look the other way. He probably didn't know what it was all about until we brought you up out of the water."

"And the guilty Creole diver?"

"Gone. Permanently. Whisked off Solidad the next morning."

"But why would some diver who doesn't even know me—?" I shuddered involuntarily.

"Our nebulous *someone* arranged it. Whoever it is, he or she wants to keep his own hands clean."

Steve and I waited by the van 5, 10, 15 minutes. "What's taking David and Josh so long, Steve? We're not keeping to Josh's time schedule."

Steve made a dry, chuckling sound in his throat. "Kind of cloak and dagger, isn't it? But there's still time. Moses won't take off without you."

"Really, Steve, would you mind going back and looking for them?"

"Will you be okay—alone?"

I pushed him toward the hotel. He went, reluctantly.

When he came back, he was balancing a heavy box of

equipment. He shoved it in the back of the van, then came around to the front of the wagon where I stood waiting. "Michelle, did you see someone coming this way?"

"No, no one. Why do you ask?"

"I thought I saw something moving in the shadows. Must be my overactive imagination." He went back and slammed the van door shut.

I followed on his heels. "Steve, where are David and Josh?"

"Who knows? They weren't in their rooms. Another change in plans, I guess. According to Doc Edington, David wants you to go on without him. To quote Doc, 'wherever it is you're going!' I guess they'll meet you at the dock."

"Then you drive, Steve," I urged.

Even in the shadows, Steve looked worried. "You go on, Michelle. I'll check on David and Kendrick."

"But, Steve—over these roads?"

"Just ride the coast. It's not exactly freeway, but there is a road." He squeezed my shoulder reassuringly. "Game plan: head out past Paradise Cove, skirt the village, and head on to Coral Beach. Moses will be leaving the fishing dock at Cobranza Bay shortly and sailing around to Coral Beach."

"But that's against the rules—no fishing boats there."

"That's right. If people are keeping the rules, you'll be okay. You can load the vessel without anyone noticing." Steve held the door open as I slid into the driver's seat and put the key in the ignition. Carefully I backed the van out of the carport.

I looked out the open window at Steve and told him, "Have David follow as soon as he can. I don't like traveling alone."

Steve nodded. "Hang in there, Michelle." He hesitated. "Jackie and I will be praying. I'll run interference for you in case Silas discovers his van missing. Now roll up the window and go!"

Steve's words weren't very comforting. I set out cautiously along the flower-lined driveway. Just as I reached the end of the winding, cobblestone drive, my headlights caught Silas and Pam strolling over the front lawn, arm in arm. Silas looked up, startled, then gestured wildly. "Stop!" he ordered.

I swerved left onto the dirt road, gunning the engine, and sped over the rocks and ruts, my hands knuckle-white on the steering wheel. In the rearview mirror I glimpsed Silas Winters sprinting back toward the hotel. My gaze darted back to the narrow, twisting road. The island cemetery loomed in the distance, its crumbling tombstones a ghoulish gray in the hazy moonlight. Without warning, my headlights framed a lone hiker as he sprang from the shadows into the middle of the road. He waved his hands wildly, flagging me down.

Panic-stricken, I floored the gas pedal, veering frantically to the left. Just in time the husky man leaped effortlessly from the path of the van, but not before I recognized Orville Glocke's puffy, outraged face. I hugged the wheel, staring blindly ahead. *Why is Glocke so far from the hotel?* I wondered. *How could he get this far on foot with his debilitating heart disease?* My hands were clammy, trembling. *He can't even walk short distances. Yet he sprinted with ease from the oncoming van.*

Storm clouds hovered over the ocean, muting the moon and stars. As I continued my perilous ride over the rutted dirt road, the sudden glare of headlights reflected in my mirror. I glanced back. A jeep with a lone driver was in hot pursuit. Terrified, I picked up speed, pressing along the zigzagging coastal route, praying that no other vehicle would be coming my way. The jeep closed in. I strained my eyes for a glimpse of the driver. Shadows cut across his face. Was it possible?— Silas Winters?

The village lay just ahead—a dozen kerosene lanterns flickering in the eerie darkness. Suddenly I heard a sound, something stirring behind me in the van. I realized with heart-stopping horror that I was not alone. A shadowy figure appeared from the cargo area and climbed into the passenger seat beside me. A woman's sturdy, powerful hands grabbed for the steering wheel. I glanced sideways, almost running off the road, and stared into the enraged face of Ruth Glocke. She grappled with me for control of the vehicle.

As the van roared on, rattling noisily over the rolling hills and gullies, my heel caught on the gas pedal. I wrestled frantically with Ruth. She slammed me against the door and grabbed the handle. The door flew open. I fell backward, half out of the van, still clutching the wheel as she lunged for me. The van weaved, veered to the left. I was thrown back inside. The door banged shut. Ruth's wig toppled off, tumbling to the floor. Sparse, fine gray strands of hair clung to her face. I stared straight into her icy gray eyes.

"You!" I managed breathlessly. "The stranger from my wedding!"

"Just an uninvited guest," she hissed, her venom chilling me. We continued our wild ride over the island's maze of dirt roads along the Atlantic coastline through the cloud-shrouded night. Then, unexpectedly, Ruth slapped the knob on the dashboard, knocking out the headlights, pitching us into blinding darkness.

There was a darting flash of light in the rearview mirror, drawing my eyes from the darkened road. The lone, pursuing jeep wound recklessly around the curves, gaining on us. An instant before it happened, Ruth Glocke screamed, "Turn, you little fool, turn!" She yanked my hands free. The steering wheel spun. I missed the sharp turn in the road. The van was totally out of control now, bouncing off the lava shoulder, through the spiky hedge, and careening like a stray missile over the steep cliffs of Alejandra Cove.

The vehicle was airborne, riding the wind down, down, until it broke the ocean's surface with a resounding whoosh. Like a flimsy bathtub toy, the van was swallowed by a voracious sea, its cogs and joints inundated by a quick, chilling rush.

I felt like a rag doll tossed helplessly against cushions and metal, pinned to my seat with the forward thrust, then propelled sharply into the dash as the van slammed against the shallow, rocky Atlantic floor.

Water poured through the splintered windshield. Dazed and disoriented, my limbs searing with pain, I fought against the surging force. The aquatic spray bubbled in my nose and mouth. I had a fleeting sensation of *deja vu*, as if I'd been here before, submerged in a cold, murky netherworld, gulping water uncontrollably, drowning. *Fight it, fight it*, a voice said. *Don't panic. Hold your breath!*

I thought of Ruth Glocke. Was she still with me in this battered, sunken van? I reached out, my fingers feeling the strange perimeters of my watery prison. Incredible! The vehicle was upside down. The cushioned seats were above me; I was sprawled on the padded ceiling. I felt inch by inch along the wall toward the door. If I could open it, perhaps Ruth and I could swim free. Yes, there it was—the window, and above, somewhere above, the door handle, upside down. *Okay, pull the other way, slippery, try again, nothing. Immovable! Jammed perhaps. Held fast by jagged coral rocks. All right, find the other door. Try again. Oh, Lord, please!*

I moved blindly, in slow motion through the miry maze of upturned cartons, sealed canisters, and debris. Then, reaching out through the wet, enveloping blackness, I felt the chilled, unmoving form of Ruth Glocke. I drew back instinctively, appalled. *Dead! The woman is dead! And, oh God, in minutes I'll be dead too! Oh, Father, have you brought me all this way to let it end like this?*

Fighting shock and panic, I maneuvered myself to the back of the van. Perhaps the rear cargo door had sprung in the crash. I pushed at it. Once, twice. It was locked tight as a drum. What now? My air was almost gone. The urge to breathe was overpowering. But I had learned from my snorkeling incident that the urge would pass if I just held on. How much time did I have? Another minute? Two?

Then I saw it—a dim, shimmering light outside the van window. My eyes searched the shadowy depths—and were rewarded! Someone was swimming just outside, moving near the window, beaming a flashlight my way, actually knocking now on the glass, gesturing to me! Thank God, help had come! Then I recognized the man—the cold, cunning face of Silas Winters. He seemed to be struggling with the door, his features taking on a blurred, surreal distortion as he pushed and pulled at the overturned vehicle.

Suddenly I understood what he was doing: *He's trying to finish me off for good, pushing the van into deeper water where no one will find me!* Frantically, I lunged upward, pushing against the padded interior with my legs. To my amazement, I breathed air! I gulped hungrily, too grateful to wonder at the illogic of it all. Imagine, air! As my mind stopped reeling, I realized I'd found an air pocket. I held perfectly still, wondering how long the small bubble of oxygen would last. And when would the tide come in? Would it wash me out to sea? For long, agonizing minutes I braced myself, my body numb now, keeping my face in the dwindling air pocket, sucking in precious breaths. The cold water lapped just beneath my chin.

Apparently Silas had gone. There was no movement outside the van. Only silence. Stillness. But would anyone else find me in time? *Lord, Lord, here am I. Save me!* I watched curiously as an odd assortment of items from my purse bobbed in the water around my face—a perfume bottle, lipstick, address book, sunglasses, comb. Suddenly I felt like Alice in Wonderland who had plummeted down the rabbit hole only to arrive in a topsy-turvy world where nothing made sense. The idea struck me funny, turned me giddy. I laughed aloud, then caught myself. *I'm on the edge of hysteria. Hold on. Stay in control. Don't panic. Help will come.*

Help? From where? Ruth Glocke tried to kill me. Orville planned to sabotage me. Someone in a jeep chased me. Even now Silas Winters stands on shore smirking over my plight!

Unexpectedly, the van shuddered in its rocky bed. *Heaven help me, Silas is back, pushing against the rear door!* The vehicle lurched forward, sinking deeper into its aqueous grave. My air pocket shrank drastically, bringing the water up over my mouth. Terror shot through me like an electric current.

I thought of David. My beloved. While I stepped from time into eternity, he would be returning home from his honeymoon, already a widower. I lifted my head for the last few gulps of air. My body was numb, frozen, beyond my control. I felt sleepy, dazed, delirious. Nothing fazed me now. Nothing mattered. Except that I would sink into the arms of Jesus and be carried Home.

CHAPTER NINETEEN

I awoke, not in heaven, but on shore, in Steve Turman's arms, wrapped in a blanket. The world was still spinning, fading in and out, in sharp focus one moment and blurred the next. I heard distant shouts breaking on the night air. Saw kerosene lanterns glowing in the dark like flitting fireflies. Steve looked down at me and managed a grin. "You're one gutsy lady, Michelle. How do you feel?"

"Awful!"

"You're alive. That's what counts." He carried me over the jutting coral reef toward the road. "You know, rescuing you from the briny deep is becoming a regular habit."

"Who?...How?" I began, but my throat burned with salt water.

Steve turned me so that I could see the Creole fishermen dragging the van belly-up onto the rocky shoal with their sturdy ropes. Several islanders gathered around me, reaching out, touching my hair, my bare arms, their high, shrill voices a cacophony of excitement. Out of the confusion I heard Silas Winters' deep, familiar voice, defending himself. "The older woman...too late...I went down twice...door wouldn't open...had to wait for the pressure to equalize itself inside and out..."

As Steve settled me into the front seat of the hotel jeep, I spotted Silas following behind, watching intently. Stiffening with fear, I opened my mouth to warn Steve, but I was too weak. I sank back into my cocoon of blankets and let sleep overtake me.

When I awoke again, it was daylight. I was in my own bed in the bridal suite. Pam sat beside me looking worried. Dr. Edington stood at the foot of the bed, fishing for something in his black satchel.

I tried to utter David's name but my throat was fiery and tight.

"Doctor, look. She's awake!" Pam reached out and embraced me. "Sis, I was so scared. I prayed so hard. You had to be all right!"

"David," I rasped. "Where's David?"

Pam and Dooley exchanged wary glances. "Bring your sister a glass of water, Pam," he told her. "I have some pills to calm her."

"I—I'm already calm," I managed irritably. "I just want David."

Pam patted my forehead like a fretful mother hen. "You just rest, Sis. Everything will be okay." Then she rushed from the room.

I felt too groggy to ask her *what* would be okay. Dr. Edington came over and sat beside me on the bed, his expression grave. He leaned over confidentially and whispered, "Listen carefully, Mrs. Ballard. I can say this only once. I am an agent with the Drug Enforcement Agency, working undercover with Joshua Kendrick."

I stared at him in astonishment. "You—?"

He chuckled mildly. "I know. You think of me as the boozing, grumpy old doctor." He pulled a rum bottle from his back pocket. "See this? It's part of my cover. Herb tea with just a teaspoon of rum. Frankly, I can't tolerate the taste of hard liquor."

"But why—why are you—telling me this now?"

He rubbed his jaw thoughtfully. "The whole plan—it's all gone haywire. Medina dead. The Glocke woman. Her husband missing."

"Where's David? Is he all right? Please, send him in."

Dr. Edington stood up and straightened his shoulders. "I'm

sorry, Mrs. Ballard. No one has seen your husband since last night."

"What? That's impossible! He was right here with Joshua."

"Kendrick is missing, too. My dear, that leaves me in charge."

I threw back the covers and swung my legs over the side of the bed. "I've got to find David." Weakness overwhelmed me. I sank back on my pillow, exhausted, weeping. "Please just leave me alone."

"Yes, you need your rest. But before I go, Mrs. Ballard, I must warn you not to trust Silas Winters. He may pretend to be your friend, but he means you harm—you and your friends, the Turmans."

"You—you know who they are—Jackie and Steve?"

"Who do you think arranged for them to come to Solidad?" He handed me two small, white pills. "Be sure to take your medication. And, until we find your husband and Kendrick, you and the Turmans will be taking your orders directly from me." He picked up his satchel. "There's one other thing, Mrs. Ballard. The van has been retrieved, but the entire computer project is missing. I'm sorry."

Dr. Edington left promptly, but I was too distraught even to say good-bye. Jackie and Steve arrived just as he was going. They both sat down, looking drawn and concerned. "Michelle, when I saw that submerged van," Steve blurted, his voice heavy with emotion, "I didn't think you had a prayer. But I prayed anyway. I promised God I'd trust Him with my own life if He'd just let you live."

"Oh, Steve!... Does that mean... a personal commitment?"

"I don't understand it all yet, but Jackie's going to help me."

Jackie hugged Steve endearingly. "He's just so glad he was there to rescue you, Michelle. And I'm so thankful, too!"

"How did you get to Alejandra Cove so quickly?" I asked Steve.

He smiled wanly. "When I saw Silas taking after you in the hotel jeep, I figured I'd better follow and check things out." His smile faded. "Trouble is, by the time I got back here to Windy Reef, David and Joshua were already missing. There's no trace of them."

Tears welled in my eyes. "What are we going to do now?"

"We talked to Silas Winters last night," said Jackie. "He's

organized a search party for David, Joshua, and Orville Glocke."

I drew in a sharp breath. "Glocke isn't missing—he's hiding. And we can't trust Silas either. After the Glockes' attempt on my life failed last night, Silas tried to kill me. He pushed the van deeper so no one would find it. Doc says Silas is our enemy."

"Really?" Steve looked incredulous. "Silas was already in the water when I arrived, but I figured he was just trying to help."

"Listen, Steve. Silas Winters frightens me. He's always there when things go wrong."

Steve glanced away, his dark eyes somber, shadowed.

"You will help me, Steve . . . Jackie?"

Their eyes met, then they looked at me. "How?" Jackie asked.

"I'm not going to wait for Dooley Edington's investigation. I'm going to conduct my own search for David. But I need your help."

Steve reached for Jackie's hand. "What about Pam helping us?"

"She's too enamored with Silas. Besides, I need someone who can get me into Esteban's office. Can you get me a passkey, Steve?"

Jackie's lovely face was taut. "We'll help you, Michelle."

Steve nodded, took a key from his pocket and handed it to me. "Be careful, Michelle," he said. Then he stood and helped Jackie to her feet. I noticed a slight bulge in Jackie's middle— the growing, unseen infant that pleased her so. I thought with a sudden pang, *Will I ever bear a child of my own—David's child?*

As soon as Steve and Jackie had gone, I tossed the pills Edington had given me into the wastebasket. Then, cautiously, I slipped out of bed and wobbled across the room to the suit-cases Steve had retrieved from the lobby. I rummaged through my smaller case for a blouse and slacks, then dressed hurriedly.

I was still trembling, my knees weak, as I rode the elevator down to the lobby and crossed to Esteban's office. The door was ajar. A solitary figure sat sobbing at Esteban's desk, desolate, abandoned, marooned in her loss. The sun cut through the open window casting ripples of light across her upswept auburn hair. Shadowy wisps of cigarette smoke curled up from her ashtray.

"Lucia?" I said softly. "May I come in?"

She lifted her tear-stained face mechanically and gazed at me. The usual luster, the stormy fire in her dark eyes was gone; only a gold cross sparkled against her delicate skin. "Michelle! Oh, Michelle, I know I should come to see you. But I—I—"

"It's okay, Lucia. You don't have to explain."

"But I so frightened for you and David. Please, sit down." She dabbed at her eyes as she pointed to a chair. "You are all right?"

I nodded. "As soon as I find David. And you?"

"I—I sort through Esteban's things." Her voice caught. "Silas Winters send word to Carlos Cobranza. Come. Take over Windy Reef."

"You're leaving then?"

"I go soon, before Carlos come. As soon as I pack." She moved her graceful, ringed hands over the marble-top desk. "I leave Esteban forever. Always before I threaten him. 'Esteban,' I say, 'I leave you to this island. I run to Paris, Bogota—' " Her tears kept flowing. "But I never really leave my Esteban. Never!"

"Esteban knew that, Lucia. He knew how much you loved him."

"Like you love your David? You do not leave till you find him?"

I swallowed hard. "No—never."

"We share—what you say—common grief. Esteban gone. David—"

I wanted to scream out, No, David's alive! But I couldn't hurt Lucia with my flimsy straw of hope. Mustard-seed faith inside me shouted, David is alive. David is alive! Absently I said, "Will you come someday to California, Lucia? And visit David and me?"

"Hollywood? Is no important now. But maybe. Someday."

I reached across the desk and touched her hand. "You won't forget what David talked about during devotions on the sun deck?"

"About God? About your Jesus?"

I nodded. "No matter what happens, Lucia, remember how

much God loves you." The words sent a new burst of hope through my own heart.

Lucia smiled. "My Esteban say he understand this Jesus—how He die in someone's place. But he say the cost too great. The guilt—"

"Do you understand what Esteban meant, Lucia?"

"No," she said sadly. "It was his own secret. He never tell me. He say he afraid I do not love him then. He say strange words. He say he bring needless grief to his friend." She clasped her hands. "Esteban sleep so bad. No peace until he hear David on the sun deck. Now his secret buried—buried with him on Tamarind Bluff."

I reached into my purse and took out my New Testament. "I want you to take this, Lucia, keep it—and promise me you'll read it."

She turned the book over in her hands. "You would give me your Bible after—after my Esteban take your novel? He was good man, Michelle. But afraid you take honor from Ricardo Cobranza."

I sat, stunned. "That's why he took my notes?"

"Yes. Esteban was—how you say?—ashamed. The Bible study make big print in Esteban's heart. He say he cannot face you at dinner. First, he make things right with you and David and God. He so happy when your husband send note to meet him in honeymoon suite and talk."

I shivered, afraid to tell Lucia that David never sent the note. The realization struck me, *Esteban was an innocent victim. He had no part in the other strange happenings on Solidad.*

"My Esteban fair man," continued Lucia. "Honorable. He only want to protect names of Ricardo Cobranza and his father, Juan Medina. You forgive my Esteban? He mean no wrong."

Suddenly we were both weeping. "I poor friend, Michelle. I not stay to find David. I go."

"Wait, Lucia. Maybe you can help me find him. I need the blueprints to the old mansion. Do you think Esteban knew where—?"

"Silas Winters—he already ask." Lucia stood and walked to Esteban's file cabinet, pulled open a drawer, and handed me a folder marked HOTEL BLUEPRINTS. It was empty.

"Silas has them?" I asked.

Her perfectly sculpted face clouded. "Perhaps Silas. I do not know. But how can map of hotel find David?"

"I'm not sure, but if there's the slightest chance..."

For the next two days there was still no clue to David's whereabouts. With growing urgency I sought the hotel blueprints, convinced they would reveal Solidad's underground caverns. I prayed and scoured my research notes on the island. Nothing. I spent hours with Kikko in his surrey tracking every trail of Solidad. At the fishing dock, the Creoles were guarded, tight-lipped, working their nets in gloomy silence. The villagers, caught up in their taboos and superstitions, saw me now as a victim touched by the *Cara de Muerte*.

Only Moses spoke freely, assuring me that everyone who left the island for the fishing zone that Sunday had also returned.

"Then David and his friend Joshua must still be here," I said.

Troubled eyes glistened in his wizened face. "Yes, somewhere."

"Where, Moses? Where? Kikko and I have searched the whole island from Tamarind Bluff to Cocoa Lake to Frangipani Point."

Moses coiled the hemp rope that secured his fishing schooner, then gazed up the hill toward Windy Reef Hotel. "The Face of Death, Missus Ballard," he said softly.

As I stared toward Windy Reef, Silas Winters' words came flashing back: *An ominous skull in the rock formation—a cave—a grotto washed out by the sea.* That's what Silas had said the day we arrived on Solidad. I remembered my own fleeting glimpse of the bluff when sun rays filtering through the storm clouds carved out the menacing features of a skull. I knew now that I had to get to the ocean side of Tamarind Bluff. But who could scale that sheer drop-off? There had to be another way, but I wouldn't find it without the blueprints.

I threw caution to the wind and went back to the hotel with the passkey Steve had given me. Then I stole to the west wing—to Silas Winters' room—and entered. The room was masculine, immaculate. I opened his desk drawers one by one, embarrassed to be intruding on his privacy. There were no blueprints. There wasn't even a clutter on the bathroom countertop—just shaving gear, a hairbrush, and Pam's New

Testament lying beside her snapshot. Scrawled across the picture were the words, *I love you, Silas.*

I started for the door. It opened abruptly. Pam stood there, staring at me in disbelief. "What are you doing here, Michelle?"

"I was about to ask you the same question."

"Don't bother. But just to stave off your curiosity, I was getting Silas' tennis racket. But you—you, Michelle!"

"I need the hotel blueprints," I stammered. "I must have them. I think Silas took them. He must know where David is."

A flash of doubt crossed Pam's countenance. She tossed her head defiantly. "You're looking in the wrong place, Michelle." She picked up the tennis racket and ran from the room.

I called after her, but she kept going.

Late that afternoon, I cornered old Javier in the garden. He was down on his knees, digging aimlessly in the soil, more muddled and uncommunicative than he had ever been. "Javier," I pleaded, "you must help me find my husband. There's no trace of him anywhere!"

He lifted his snow-white head and peered blankly at me. His shaggy brows drooped over glazed, melancholy eyes; his rimless bifocals slipped to the tip of his nose.

"You've lived on this island all your life, Javier. Surely you know if there's a hiding place in the old mansion."

He stood slowly, his scruffy fishing hat in hand, a pucker of a smile on his lips. "The days of glory—they are gone. The ships came," he whimpered incoherently. "We hide. They do not find us."

I shook my head in frustration. Whatever knowledge Javier possessed was lost in forgetfulness. "I don't have time to listen to this babble," I cried. "I must find David."

"Time?" he mumbled, pulling a shiny object from his pocket.

I stared dumbfounded at the gold pocket watch dangling from Javier's fingers. "Where did you get this?" I cried, grabbing it from him. I snapped it open and read the familiar inscription. "Javier, this watch is my wedding present to my husband!"

The old man stumbled back, stunned by my outburst. Then he retreated, shuffling toward his cottage. I followed. "Please, Javier, I'm sorry," I called. He fumbled with the doorknob and disappeared inside, slamming the door behind him. I knocked frantically. "Javier, I must talk to you. Please, take me to David."

Finally I tried the knob. The door creaked open. I peeked inside. Javier was gone. As I stepped into the cottage, a cold draft cut across the room. A strange, musty smell permeated the air. I glanced at the bookcase on the eastern wall. Something was askew. I crossed the room and picked up the photograph Javier had shown me on my first visit. Three men by the Tower of London. One was Esteban Medina, dead now. Another had to be Cobranza's son Carlos. But what about the other, blurred face, that strangely familiar profile? As I put the photo back in place, I stumbled against the bookcase. No wonder. It was pulled away slightly from the wall. I gave it a tentative push and felt a cold gust of dampness on my legs. Incredibly, the bookcase moved with a rumbling vibration, inching open to reveal a black chasm beyond. I stared aghast at the winding passageway that led down into an obscure abyss. I wondered, *Could this be Javier's secret pathway to the isolated stretch of beach by Tamarind Bluff?*

"Javier!" I called into the darkness. "Javier, where are you?" My words echoed back on the chill, damp air, resoundingly hollow. "I've got to get help," I said aloud, breaking the palpable stillness. My hands were like ice, my heart hammering as I raced back to the hotel for Jackie and Steve. Without argument, they came with me, dropping little Stevie by Lucia's suite on the way. As we hurried through the hotel lobby, we spotted Silas Winters and Dooley Edington in hot dispute at the registration desk. For their benefit, we slowed our pace, trying to look casual. Once outside, we broke into a run across the garden to Javier's cottage. I pushed boldly inside; Steve and Jackie followed. "See?" I said, hysteria edging my voice. "There! There's the secret entry to the caverns of Solidad!"

"I'm going in alone," said Steve, examining the tunnel entrance.

"No way, Steve. I'm going too. David needs me."

"We don't know what we're going to find, Michelle," said Steve.

"Javier for one," I said. "And David—I pray it will be David." Steve turned, flashlight in hand, and led the way down the musty, winding passageway that trailed under the east wing of the hotel toward the ocean. As we walked, the path widened and sloped downward. We encountered small chambers, narrow grottoes, and tunnels branching out on either side of us. Trickling underground streams of water still seeped through the cracks and fissures of the surrounding cliff walls. The atmosphere was heavy with a dank, fusty, mildewed scent mingling with indrafts of chill, moist salt air.

We followed the main tunnel along its meandering, serpentine path, feeling our way toward the distant, low roaring sound of the ocean. Far ahead on the twisting passage we caught a glimpse of the mammoth opening—the face of the skull—looking out on the raging, turbulent Atlantic, the jagged edge of the grotto framing it like torn tarpaper. Vines and moss grew unchecked on the outside rock formation. Winds from off the ocean whistled through the opening, sending eerie melodies bounding off the labyrinthian cavern walls.

Finally we rounded a curve and stepped into a huge, wave-cut cavern with glistening, sapphire-blue walls. The cave, clawed out by centuries of the ocean's fury, lay like a hidden fortress beneath Solidad. A well-used generator flooded the massive cave with light, its glow reflecting off the craggy rock formations with a magical softness. To our left was a natural lava-formed shelter—a primitive stone cottage sculpted in the sea-smooth boulders. Framed in the makeshift doorway was the ominous, hulking form of Orville Glocke, a sullen, waspish smile on his face, a rifle in his smooth, white, hairless hands. "So, we have uninvited guests!" he shouted. "Come in, come right along!" He waved the rifle at us, his eyes blazing with hatred as they settled on me. "You," he said savagely as we approached, "you killed my wife! All my efforts, my plans! This was my last chance to prove myself to Ruth. And you destroyed it all!"

Steve stepped in front of me. "Your wife caused the van to go out of control, Glocke. Not Michelle. The crash killed your wife!"

I pushed back my mounting terror. "Where's David, Mr. Glocke? Why have you and your wife been following us since our wedding?"

He flashed a churlish smile. "We were just doing our job,

following orders. But I'll get even with you, Mrs. Ballard."

"But why?" I cried again. "You don't even know us!"

He brandished his rifle. "No, but my cousin knows you."
He glanced at Steve and Jackie, a merciless gleam in his eyes.
"And my cousin knows the *Marshalls*." His laugh was high-
pitched, nasal. "But he knows them best as the *Turmans*."

Steve's suntanned jaw went rigid; his eyes glinted fire. He
squeezed the question from tight lips. "Who's your cousin,
Glocke?"

"Don't you know?" Glocke drawled. "Don't you remember
your boss, the cocaine kingpin of Morro Bay?"

Steve's face paled. "It can't be!"

"Look closely," said Glocke. "When we were kids they used
to say Clarence and me had eyes alike."

"Not Clarence Harvey!" Steve spat out the name.

"Yep," Orville boasted. "The same Clarence Harvey, owner
of Meadowgreen Airport and the mastermind cocaine lord of
Morro Bay."

I saw the resemblance at once—their squat, bullish bodies,
thin-lipped smiles, snapping black eyes, and deceptive folksy
images.

"Steve, it doesn't make sense," Jackie whispered at last.
"Clarence Harvey is in a high-security prison cell in California."

"But still running his West Coast operation from prison."

"How can he do that, Steve?" I asked.

"It happens."

"No more whispering," Orville bellowed. "You want your
husband, Mrs. Ballard? Come, all of you." He nudged us along
with the butt of his rifle through the curtained threshold, past
compact living quarters into another isolated cavern that
overlooked the grotto entrance. Javier, still dazed, wandered
around the room freely, at home in this strange setting. Then
I spotted David and Joshua secured to a stone bench near the
ledge, their hands tied behind them, their clothes rumpled,
a three-day stubble of beard shadowing their faces. David
looked tired, bruised, his right eyelid swollen.

"David, oh, David!" I broke free from Glocke's grip, flew
to David, and smothered him with kisses. "You're hurt," I said.

"We're better," David answered. "Old Javier washed our
wounds." He was smiling now, his eyes glistening. "If I knew

you were coming, I'd have showered and shaved." He kissed me soundly.

I nestled in the crook of his neck. "Oh, David, how I've searched for you." I tucked his gold watch in his shirt pocket.

"Oh, honey, I asked Javier to give that to you two days ago, hoping that you'd follow him back to me."

"He didn't give it to me. I took it from him in the garden."

"It's okay, Michelle, now that I know you're all right." He blew kisses in my hair, then pressed his chin on the top of my head.

"Javier, get some rope for the Turmans," Orville ordered. "Mrs. Ballard won't need to be tied—she won't leave her husband."

As Javier shuffled off, Orville stared at David and me. "Cozy," he said. "But an eye for an eye. Isn't that what you said on the sun deck, Mr. Ballard?" He rocked on his feet. "Michelle for Ruth—"

"Leave them alone," said Josh. "Give them some time together."

"Like they gave my wife and me?" Glocke glared at us, his dark eyes searing like a hot iron. "No, Mr. Kendrick, my job isn't finished yet. My cousin ordered me to Solidad for a purpose."

"You're a bit clumsy at it, aren't you, Glocke?" Josh's voice was harsh. "Your wife missed losing Michelle on the beach when the tide came in. And the net—did you throw the fishing net? You even foiled your own plot to kill David Ballard on the balcony."

Orville's eyes blazed.

Josh egged him on. "Clarence Harvey needs a better outside connection. Cocaine in conch shells. Notes on menus. Mere child's play in the world of drugs. You don't have your cousin's shrewdness, Mr. Glocke. Nor your wife's cunning and ambition."

Orville seethed, his double chin bloating like a lizard's. Yet he stood still, a gutless windbag. What was he waiting for?

"Can you complete your assignment without Ruth?" Josh baited.

At Ruth's name, Orville backed off across the room. He eased into a chair, his sullen eyes on us, his rifle aimed our way.

"Pathetic old fool," David whispered. "He really loved her."

"Great love," Josh said coldly, his eyes moving from the Turmans to David and me. "They were here to annihilate the four of you."

"And to steal the confidential computer documents." David nodded toward the waterproof containers stacked near the ledge.

"Who brought all those containers here, David?"

"The Glockes, I guess. Josh and I were knocked out for a time."

"It couldn't have been Ruth Glocke. She's dead."

Kendrick frowned. "The job's too much for one man alone. That must mean the Glockes have been working with someone else—"

"Nicole?" I suggested.

"Crafty enough, Michelle," Josh smiled, "but Nicole works for our agency out of Grenada. Still, I wonder if anyone's on duty on Solidad. Three whole days. My agents should have found us by now."

"Listen, Josh, Dooley Edington has been trying to find you. But I'm afraid Silas—" There was no time to confess my fears about Silas, the elusive concierge. From the distance came the pounding sound of running footsteps. Someone approaching along the narrow passageway. I caught the faint scent of Old Spice as Dooley Edington entered the chamber, a revolver in hand.

"Thank goodness, Dr. Edington!" I cried in relief.

"Quick, over here! Cut us loose, Edington," Josh demanded.

Dooley raised his high, shiny forehead quizzically as though his submerged self were rising with it. "Cut you loose, Kendrick? Why should I? You're right where I want you." He strolled over to Orville, his ball-bearing eyes cunning, malignant. "Well, Glocke, it looks like our honeymooners and their friends will be here for our bon voyage party—for our rendezvous with the freighter."

Beside us, Joshua twisted against the ropes on his wrists. His face was white with fury. "Why, Edington? Why?"

Dooley's lips curled. "For money. I did it for money."

Despair was etched on Josh's face. "I trusted you, Edington. A turncoat in my own ranks. You sold out your colleagues, your country—for money? Seven years with the agency, Edington—an impeccable reputation gone, dead."

"Life's unfair," Dooley's tone was strident. "A terrible joke."

"You've been leading a double life all this time?" charged Josh.

"For what it's worth, Kendrick, only the last two years. The first five with the DEA were impeccable. But no matter how many risks I took on the job, I couldn't die—couldn't join Allison." He fingered the trigger on his revolver. "No matter how I flirted with danger, I wasn't killed. I was still alive. Bored and broke. Then I remembered Solidad and concocted my plan to deceive the agency."

"Go on," Josh said hotly.

"Years ago, right after Allison's death, I roamed around Europe. That's when I met Carlos Cobranza and Esteban Medina. Carlos told me about Solidad and wanted me to visit the island. Juan Medina was running the hotel. The islanders told me rumors of wealth hidden on the island, about cocaine. When I joined the DEA, Solidad was clean. No problem. So it wasn't difficult to persuade the agency to set up their witness protection program and computer projects here."

"Turncoat, double agent," Josh said again.

Dooley's eyes narrowed. "*Triple* agent!" He thumped his barrel chest. "I'm the DEA's number one undercover agent. And, Josh, you suggested the role of the wry, harmless, tipsy island physician."

"But I didn't suggest being a callous, cold-blooded murderer— killing your colleagues and Esteban Medina!"

"Dr. Edington, *you* killed Esteban Medina?" I gasped.

A gnarled smile crossed Dooley's face. "Not directly. I was in the suite ready to administer an injection to stun him—and your husband too, if my note hadn't been tardy." He patted Orville's arm. "The Glockes struck the fatal blow and shoved him from the balcony."

"But why? Why did you want to kill David and Esteban?"

"Your husband's project was finished and we were ready to take it off his hands. Esteban was growing too suspicious. He knew about Javier. He was about to throw a wrench into a perfect setup."

"What are you talking about?" David demanded.

"I'm talking about the gold bullion hidden in this cavern. Only Javier knew its whereabouts. He brought it to me a little at a time. Javier trusted me, obeyed me. I couldn't let Medina spoil that."

"Why would Javier know about hidden gold?" I challenged.

Edington grinned ruthlessly. "Let Javier answer for himself. Javier, where are you? Come here, old man!"

After a moment, the frail gardener appeared from the darkness. "Javier, you fool," Edington said loathingly, "leading Mrs. Ballard to the caverns! Stupid oaf, if it weren't for the gold—!"

"Leave the poor old man alone," I cried out.

Edington's gaze was cynical, his laugh contemptuous. "Poor old man, Mrs. Ballard? Wrong! Let me introduce you to the long-dead multimillionaire of Solidad—Ricardo Javier Cobranza!"

CHAPTER
TWENTY

"You're lying, Dooley!" I exclaimed. "How dare you suggest—?"

"Go on, Javier," Edington ordered. "Tell them who you are!"

Javier gazed up through filmy eyes. "Sr. Cobranza welcomes you to Solidad, Mrs. Ballard. I have told my wife of your kindness."

"Then it's true? You are Ricardo Cobranza?" All motion and sound were caught in a freeze-frame of time as the preposterous reality hit home. My mind wrestled with the absurdities, the contradictions of it all. How could the once-wealthy, powerful drug baron, Ricardo Cobranza, find embodiment in the hapless, gentle, befuddled little man we knew as Javier? What bizarre chain of events thrust him into the anonymous, mundane life of a common gardener? "What happened, Dr. Edington? How did Cobranza fall from power? What about his fabled wealth?"

"It's a long, complicated story, Mrs. Ballard. Rest assured, Sr. Cobranza selected his own lot in life as a reclusive gardener."

"But you took advantage of him, didn't you? Betrayed him?"

"He never missed the money, Mrs. Ballard. He's worth millions."

"Then Esteban was right," I said, my voice a whisper. "You

were sedating Javier. But why did Esteban let you get away with it?"

"And risk blowing his own secret, risk having his wife know what happened on Solidad 20 years ago? Admit that his friend Carlos Cobranza has grieved needlessly for his parents all these years?"

I looked at David. "Wait, how can it be? If Ricardo Cobranza—Javier—never committed suicide, who jumped from the hotel balcony?"

"The young, skilled diver, Esteban Medina," announced Edington.

"But why? Why did Cobranza let a boy risk his life like that?"

"Why?" Edington chewed on the word, then answered, "Kendrick, you know why. The Colombian cocaine mob was closing in on the Cobranzas. He couldn't risk them finding him or his wealth."

Glocke nudged Edington. "Look, the men have the explosives."

"All right, good. We're on schedule." Edington motioned for Orville to join his two Creole henchmen at the cavern entrance.

"What are they doing?" Jackie's voice was edged with terror.

"They're setting up a detonation device, Mrs. Turman."

"For you, my friends," said Glocke smugly. "As soon as Edington and I leave the island with the gold bullion and the invaluable research data from Mr. Ballard's computer project, the entire cavern—and all of you in it—will be blown to bits."

"That means everyone—honeymooners, government witnesses, and you, Kendrick, loyal special DEA agent," said Dooley. He stepped carefully over to the ledge and scanned the horizon.

My eyes followed his gaze. I knew a large ship could never get in without being washed against the rocks. But a fishing vessel or a powerful motor launch might risk it—at low tide. Of course! This had been Ricardo Cobranza's passageway to illegal drug trafficking!

Parts of a rickety pier stretched out from the beach, its timeworn wood rotting in places. I wondered how many Creoles had loaded cocaine for Cobranza on waiting vessels. How many had made it in the dead of night to the waiting freighter? How many had died?

I nudged David and nodded toward the ocean where a freighter was silhouetted against the skyline. Darkness was not far off. Rain clouds hugged the horizon. The tide was rising. I realized then that Orville and Dooley Edington were racing against time and tide. "Why the sudden departure, Dr. Edington?" I asked, baiting him.

"Ah, Mrs. Ballard, it's necessary. That fool concierge has sent for my old friend, Carlos Cobranza."

"Your friend? Wait, that's it. You're the one—the blurred face in the snapshot—the three men by the Tower of London."

"I was afraid you'd recognize me, you with your keen curiosity."

Javier shuffled over to Edington, a wistful yearning on his face. "My son? Carlos, my son? He is coming for me?"

"What about Cobranza?" I asked. "Will you take him with you?"

Edington glared at Javier. "No. He is useless to me now."

"My island," rasped Javier. He tried to straighten his stooped shoulders, but he almost toppled. "You—you've taken my island!"

"And your gold, and your friend Esteban!" Edington fingered the detonator with a malicious playfulness, then shoved the old man away.

In the instant that Edington placed his ruthless hand on Javier, a ghostly apparition appeared from an obscure grotto near the ledge. The sheathed figure darted along the cavern wall. Was it possible? The still-lovely Alejandra Cobranza in her tattered wedding dress and bejeweled locket! She turned, wielding a knife, and sprang with a frenzy on the unsuspecting Edington. With a maniacal shriek, she raised the blade and slashed furiously at his back. As she attacked, I glimpsed the other side of her face—puckered skin ridged with purplish scars like melted wax, the ear nearly gone and the eyelid burned away, revealing a glassy sphere embedded in a mound of scarred flesh.

We all stared in stunned silence as Edington whirled around, grabbed the knife, and seized the crazed, wild-eyed woman. A Creole cohort came to Dooley's aid, handing him a cloth to bind his bleeding shoulder. "It's only a flesh wound," he panted. He glared at Alejandra, then back at us. "Now you have met the beautiful lady of the portrait! See what she has become? An insane old woman whose vestiges of beauty are lost in misshapen grotesqueness!"

"But she—she's buried in the island cemetery!" I blurted.

"No! Not buried. Dig up her grave and you'll find her casket weighed down with 99 pounds of sandbags. All part of Cobranza's plot—faking his wife's death and his own to foil the mob. But no more chatting. Time is running out." He turned to the Creoles standing near the explosives. "All set? Make sure everything's loaded on the schooner. Get our boys out of the cave, now!"

In the commotion that followed, I heard more footsteps pounding through the tunnel. Within seconds, Silas Winters, armed and alert, burst into the room with Kikko, Moses, and several other islanders. Seeing Silas, I sank against David in despair. The syndicate ringleader had come in time to join his men in their escape, to help carry the Cobranza millions and the sabotaged DEA projects to their rendezvous with the waiting freighter. With an air of absolute command, Silas raised his revolver and strode purposely toward us.

I buried my face against David's chest and sobbed, grieving for all of us who would perish at Silas' hand. Then, utter chaos reigned. I refused to look up, but I could hear the wild scuffle around me—Edington screaming out in pain, Javier calling for Alejandra, Glocke shouting angrily. Joshua's voice was forceful: "Grab Edington! Don't let him hit the detonator!"

Then, almost as soon as it had started, the uproar was over. A voice, not quite distinguishable, said, "I got out a two-way radio message, Kendrick. We can expect a helicopter in the morning."

"Then you knew about Dooley, the blasted traitor?" Josh asked.

The same strong, confident voice: "I suspected on Sunday. Dooley was supposed to guard the computer canisters in the raised van. He came back saying they had been stolen. I knew better."

"You didn't know about these underground caverns?"

"Only rumors. Edington must have beat me to the blueprints."

"Then how did you get here in time?" Joshua asked.

"I saw the Turmans and Michelle racing toward the cottage. When Dooley left, I followed him here, then went back for reinforcements."

I recognized the voice now, probably had all along—the wily Silas Winters himself! I stared up at David, baffled, relieved. His hands were loose now. He lifted me up and held me tight, as if he would never let me go. "It's okay, Michelle. Silas has set us free!"

The next day at noon, a government helicopter flew in low over Solidad and landed on the sun deck of Windy Reef Hotel, its rotating blades whirring noisily. David and I stood with Josh just inside the sheltering alcove. Jackie and Steve stood nearby, with little Stevie balanced on his daddy's shoulders, waving his arms at the pilot.

Silas Winters ran against the stirring wind, helped a man from the copter, then hurried him inside the glass door. The handsome, thirtyish Colombian in a stylish business suit acknowledged us politely, his eyes darting guardedly around the room. Then, his expression crumbling with emotion, he dashed across the room and wrapped his arms around Javier and Alejandra Cobranza. Their son, Carlos Cobranza, had come home.

I looked tearfully up at Joshua and whispered, "What will happen to the old couple? Will they be punished? Sent to prison?"

"They'll be turned over to the Colombian government."

"No mercy?" I asked.

"Perhaps because of their advanced age and deteriorating mental state, they'll be cared for in some medical facility."

"Or perhaps they'll be turned over to the care of their son," David suggested. "But whatever happens, Michelle, it can't be any worse than the prison they've made for themselves over the years."

As we waited for Silas to escort his prisoners to the waiting helicopter, David asked, "Can the computer project be salvaged?"

"We're not sure how much information was leaked to the

mob." Josh scowled as a handcuffed Orville Glocke passed us, his puffy face downcast, deflated. "Hard to believe that simple bumpkin has been Clarence Harvey's Florida drug connection for months," grumbled Josh. "Not to mention, Dooley Edington's point of contact here on Solidad."

As Silas urged Edington toward the copter, the crusty doctor glowered belligerently at us. Joshua looked away, disappointment written frankly on his face. "Dooley and I were friends," Josh said, "yet he sacrificed the lives of our colleagues and sabotaged the project from the beginning. It'll take us months to regain the confidence of other nations and to insure the safety of our agency and government witnesses. But we'll revamp and find a way."

Silas sauntered back to us. "We're ready to go, Kendrick."

I offered Silas my hand. "I'm sorry I didn't trust you—"

"No problem. It simply means I played my role well." He paused. "But not well enough for your sister Pam. I wanted her to fly out with me today. But I didn't make it on her priority list."

"I'm sorry, Silas." I hesitated. "Where will you go from here?"

"To Miami first with my prisoners. Then back to Grenada to file a report. Then, who knows? A new DEA assignment."

Josh came over beside Silas, offered a weary smile, and shook David's hand firmly. "Thanks, man, for everything."

"Give Nora our love when you see her, Josh," I said, giving him a quick hug.

"I will, Michelle. I haven't given up on that reconciliation." David slipped his arm around me. "We'll be praying, buddy."

Josh nodded toward Jackie and Steve. "The chopper will be back tomorrow for your friends, the Turmans. We're going to get them out of here to a little Swiss chalet near Lucerne."

"Isn't that where Jackie's parents are living?" I asked.

Josh winked and ignored my question. "Take care, you two." He took two long strides toward the copter, then looked back impishly. "Hey, David, Michelle, why don't you stay on Solidad for a few more days just to relax and recuperate. You'll have the place all to yourselves. I hear it's a great place for a honeymoon!"

As the great, fanning blades whirled like a magnificent dervish, whipping the wind around us, David crushed me against his chest. We watched as the whirlybird lifted powerfully into the cloudless blue skies of Solidad. Then, against the deafening roar overhead, David declared, "I love you, Michelle. Thank God we're together again."

"And I adore you, David. Today and forever."

Lost in our own tender reverie, we turned arm in arm and headed slowly down from the sundeck to Windy Reef's waiting honeymoon suite.